Published by Dedalus in 1984
9 St. Stephen's Terrace, London SW8 1DJ

ISBN 0 946626 05 7

Made and printed in Great Britain by
City Printing Works (Chester-le-Street) Ltd.,
Chester-le-Street, Co. Durham DH3 3NJ.

British Library Cataloguing in Publication Data

Lane, Eric
Oberammergau.
1. Oberammergau-passion play-History
I.Title II.Brenson, Ian
792.1 PN3235

ISBN 0 946626 05 7

The cover picture, and views of Oberammergau and Linderhof are
from photos taken by Raynor Jackson, and are reproduced by
courtesy of The German Tourist Board, Conduit Street, London W1.

The period prints of Oberammergau and the religious paintings are
from Mary Evans Picture Library, London.

The complete text in English of

THE OBERAMMERGAU PASSION PLAY

with an introduction by
Eric Lane & Ian Brenson

LIST OF CONTENTS

PREFACE

The first time I saw the village of Oberammergau I was amazed something so beautiful, I could even say perfect, existed without my knowing about it. My first impression is one I share with countless others. Set high up in the Bavarian mountains, surrounded by gentle undulating hills and lush rich vegetation, the village, with its painted houses, windowboxes and spotlessly clean and neat streets, seems almost too perfect to be true. The baroque profusion of wood carvings and religious objects in the shops adds, rather than subtracts from this feeling of perfection. The village having managed to combine the beauty of the Bavarian countryside, and the decorative traditions of wallpainting and woodcarving with commerce, without the latter taking over.

During the Passion Play season when every house resembles an Aladdin's cave, each item priced and available for sale, the commercial dimension is still kept in check and not allowed to get into the way of the religious, cultural event which has made the village world-famous. It is easy to look backwards and imagine times without the abundance of souvenirs and tourist shops as more the way things should be (although even during these bygone perfect times the visitor was doing likewise) but this would be to overlook how this small community has adapted with the times, while still remaining quintessentially the same. The fidelity to the past, to a way of life ruled by the family, hard work and devotion to the Church still remains the foundation on which Oberammergau is built.

In 1980 I was involved with The Passion Play as a tourist event, each week arriving with another group to spend two nights in the village before it was time to go. At the beginning of the season the visitors were to be deposited in the car-park, where little boys would magically appear to escort their guests and luggage to their homes. This part of the Oberammergau magic failed to work, and the coaches of the tour operators were to be seen winding their way through the narrow streets which had probably never seen coaches before, to deliver their charges to their lodgings. It was during this time that Oberammergau became a second home for me, and the women of the houses good friends. By the end of the season each street contained a home where I could appear to drink a beer and pass the time of day with the goodhumoured landladies. The friendliness and warmth of Oberammergau is unique in my

7

experience, and with the possible exception of China, I cannot think of anywhere where the inhabitants make such an effort to make the visitor feel at home. And now I still look for any excuse to make a detour to visit Mutti.Trissl and the other good ladies of the village. My intention of retiring from being a tour escort has been put back another year so that I can share in the events which will commemorate the 350th anniversary of the first play.

If you were given the task of arranging that 5,000 people arrived on the same day that 5,000 people left, (in a village whose population was 5,000,) stayed the next day to see the play and were lodged and fed without chaos and pandemonium breaking out you might decide that there are easier ways of making a living. It is the success of the village authorities in performing this task which contributes to the enjoyment of the Passion Play for thousands of people from all over the world. In 1980 the system of a ticket being connected to a voucher for accommodation and meals was employed, so if you received a ticket boarding was provided. There was no exception to this rule, although many people arrived in search of a spare ticket. Each morning there were long queues to buy whatever tickets the authorities had had returned to them, and many unsuccessful people had to turn to the black market where tickets went for as much as twice or even three times their face value.

Those who had booked in advance either stayed in a hotel or a private house and used meal tickets to eat at specified restaurants, while some ate in the houses where they stayed. The neighbouring villages and towns acted as an overspill for Oberammergau, with many people having to be bussed in for the play — a pity, as to stay in Oberammergau really adds to the joys of seeing the play.

As nine o'clock arrived every street resembled a procession as the temporary inhabitants of the village made their way, on foot, to the theatre, there being no problems of finding your way, you simply followed the person in front. After three hours it was time for lunch and shopping. $2^1/_2$ hours later the second part would start, and the play would continue till five o'clock. As the theatre doors opened to emit the playgoers, an excited babble of voices and a lively animation would fill the village streets, the play having triumphed yet again. Whether it was the excellence of the music, the sincerity of the acting, the spectacular settings or a higher personal dimension the play made its response with everyone. Or almost everyone, as one man, a self-styled theatre lecturer had the temerity to air his superior views on the play. The acting was amateurish —, he didn't manage to finish, as his superiority was pulled to pieces like his argument by his students. That's just the point he was told

8

countless times, it's naive, amateur if you like, home drama, and because of its amateurishness that it is such an overwhelming and moving experience. The lecturer, either through self-preservation or instantaneous conversion to the arguments he was listening to, ended up in total agreement. He had been misunderstood, he said humbly, as he tried to change the subject to his attempt to start a similar tradition in an English village.

Could a village in the English countryside put on a Passion Play and keep doing so for 350 years? I doubt it. The commitment to God, the honouring of a promise and the building of a tradition which dominates the lives of the inhabitants would not transplant easily to either England or the second half of the twentieth century. We are all too sophisticated, cynical, and our way of life too transitory for this to be possible. The nearest we can get to this is a visit to Oberammergau, where we marvel at how well a medieval art form adapts itself to the needs of a 20th century audience.

The play is continuously being revised for each performance, with a constant battle taking place between innovation and tradition; modern entertainment and medieval folk festival; commerce and culture. Burgomaster Lang in his speech at the opening of the new theatre said: ". . who can blame us if we now give our Play the stamp of our own great epoch, so far as we may do so in consonance with the tradition handed down to us? But, however much we may be inclined to meet the wishes of the public, we do not desire to be betrayed by popular applause into opening the door wide to innovation. We wish to hold fast by the ideals which are at the foundation of The Passion Play. May the day never come when Oberammergau will break with its traditions! May the old spirit, the spirit of our fathers, inspire us in this new house!" He said this in 1899, and today with a new theatre having taken the place of the one which he inaugurated his words still ring true

This book has been written to help the cause of the Oberammergau Passion Play as a medieval work of art, which the guiding hands of Ottmar Weiss and Alois Daisenberger brought to perfection in the 19th century, by providing the best available text in English of the play, and avoiding the changes which damage the play as a literary text. This translation establishes the text of the Oberammergau Passion Play as a classic of European Literature, and one worthy of the widest audience. In the battle between tradition and innovation we have sided firmly with tradition.

The Oberammergau Passion Play, 1850

PART I

CHRONOLOGY OF EVENTS

9th C.	Founding of the Oberammergau by the Guelph duke, Ethiko
10th C.	First medieval play: the Quem Quaeretis
11th/12th C.	Development of medieval drama
1200	Performance of first Passion Play in Siena
1330	Founding of the Benedictine monastery of Ettal
1517	Beginning of the Reformation
1545	Counter-Reformation
1555	Peace of Augsburg (tolerance of Lutheranism)
1618 - 1648	Thirty Years War
1632 - 1633	Deaths in Oberammergau due to the plague
July 1633	The Oberammergau vow
1634	First performance of the Oberammergau Passion Play
1644 - 1674	Further performances of the Passion Play
1662	Earliest surviving text of the play
1680	First performance of the play at the beginning of a decade
1680 - 1760	Uninterrupted decennial performances
1736 - 1742	Building of the present Oberammergau village church of St. Peter and St. Paul.
1750	New version of the play by Pater Rosner
1770	Passion Play banned by Munich authorities
1780	Revised version by Pater Knipfelberger
1780 - 1800	Performances of the Knipfelberger text
1801	Further performances as the 1800 season was interrupted by Napoleonic wars

15

1803	Dissolution of monastery at Ettal
1810	Ottmar Weiss completes new version of the play. Performances not permitted by authorities
1811	Permission granted for special season
1811 - 1815	New Passion Play score by Rochus Dedler
1815	Weiss revises his text for that season
1817	Fire in schoolhouse destroys Dedler's score
1820	Dedler's new score
1820 - 1910	Further Passion Play seasons
1870 - 1871	Franco-Prussion War interrupts season: further plays in 1871
1899	First theatre completed
1914 - 1918	World War I
1920	No performance: aftermath of war
1922	Special season to compensate for 1920
1930	New theatre opened in time for the season
1934	Tercentenary Performance of the Oberammergau Passion Play.
1939 - 1945	World War II
1940	No performance
1949	Founding of the German Federal Republic
1950 - 1970	Further cycles of the Passion Play
1950	Dedler's musical score revised by Professor Eugene Papst
1980	Deletion of the "anti-semitic" scenes for 1980 - 84 seasons
1984	350th anniversary performance

Passion Play – Jesus' arrival in Jerusalem

THE DEVELOPMENT OF MEDIEVAL DRAMA

Medieval drama grew up out of the church's own ritual. From the very beginning Christian worship was full of drama. The Mass itself can be seen as a dramatic commemoration of a critical moment in Christ's life, which is heightened as it developed in conception from a symbolic act to an actual repetition of the initial sacrifice. In an age where there was no theatre, the church service provided dramatic entertainment, with the clergy acting out the biblical stories, in mime and chant, bringing the faith alive for their mainly illiterate audience. The symbolism of the medieval service was always full of dramatic potential, witnessed in the Palm Sunday procession of the Sacrament, the Night Office of the last three days of Holy Week, the washing of the feet on Maundy Thursday, the creeping to the cross on Good Friday. The Passion of Christ was read in different tones to represent the narrator, the Jews and the Christians, whereas the leading figures of the choir would represent the Three Kings during the Feast of Epiphany. The Holy Ghost's coming would be portrayed by a host of pigeons being released in the church.

One reason for the drama of the medieval church was the belief that by nurturing man's craving for spectacle and entertainment the gap left by the suppression of secular drama would be filled. From the moment that the Roman Empire was converted to Christianity in the second century AD, the church fought against the theatre, seeing in the pagan tragedies and comedies the work of the devil. The Roman populace so loved its farce and spectacles in all their lavishness, that the church had to tolerate them, and even offered up to the world Christian tragedies in the Greek manner. Classical theatre which had started in Greece as part of religious festival and was part of the worship of Bacchus, lost its sober religious character in Rome, where licentious spectacle and bawdy comedy were prefered to the high-minded drama of the Greeks which was confined to the drawing rooms of the educated rich.

The marauding German tribes which destroyed the Roman Empire had no interest in theatre, and with the church's influence extending itself throughout the Western world drama died. The church succeeded in suppressing the heathen theatre with all its profanities, but could not root out the dramatic instincts of the people. In the village games and folk festivals pagan drama lived on with all the attendant excesses of the pagan past. Even the clergy had their own Feast of Fools, regardless of the displeasure it encountered from the clerical hierarchy. And it was to satisfy this need that the church created its own drama and mysteries to entertain and edify the people.

It was through music and mime that liturgical drama developed. From the very beginning the choir would divide in two and chant responses to the other half. This antiphonal singing is just a short step away from dialogue. By the end of the 6th century the choral portions of the Mass had been compiled in the Antiphonarium, a compilation credited to Gregory the Great. For two hundred years these works served as the basis of the church service. In the ninth century with greater stability and increased trade and travel in the **western world, society began to emerge from the Dark Ages.** The church which dominated society reflected this change by building splendid churches, with vestments and ornaments becoming finer and processions grander. Just as the church succumbed to the desire for elaboration so did its liturgy. The traditional Antiphonarium was now inadequate for this new age and so it was supplemented by melodies at the beginning and the end, and even in the middle of the Gregorian texts. It was the words which were written for these melodies, called tropes, which produce the first liturgical drama. An Easter trope about the three Marys, called the Quem Quaeretis, which was presented in the church in a dumb show became expanded until the congregation was watching the first play of the Middle Ages. What they would have seen during the Easter Office was three priests representing the three Marys, slowly advancing up the church to where a grave had been prepared. An angel sitting by the side of the grave asks them whom they seek, and the women reply Jesus of Nazareth the Crucified. The dialogue and action follow the Gospel story until finally a priest appears, impersonating the Saviour and announces his resurrection. This is the signal for the choir to join with a joyous Alleluia, and the play end with the singing of the Te Deum.

The Quem Quaeretis play existed by the middle of the 10th century, and is mentioned in the Concordia Regularis drawn up by Ethelwold, the bishop of Winchester, between 959 and 979. There are lots of manuscripts, from the 10th to the 12th centuries, where versions of the play are to be found, the play's form getting increasingly more elaborate, with non-biblical characters and episodes being added on. There is a predominance of French and German versions of Quem Quaeretis, which may indicate the play's origin was somewhere in the Frankish area of Northern Europe. Wandering clerics obviously circulated the new motives and amplifications from church to church round Europe and manuscripts in nearly every country of what was then the Holy Roman Empire of the Franks exist. This play became attached to the Easter sepulchre — the burial or placing the cross in the sepulchre — a ritual which enjoyed great popularity during the Middle Ages. Until the Reformation most churches, especially in continental Europe, would have a sepulchre, and this would serve as the setting for the play. The Quem Quaeretis remained imperfectly detached from the church service out of which it sprang. The actors were priests, nuns and choirboys, with the dialogue chanted and not spoken as if it was still an antiphon, and the Te Deum which ended the performance made it seem like an integral part of Matins. In later versions of the text the congregation would sing the hymn "Christ is Risen", making the play even more a part of the Easter service.

Side by side with the Quem Quaeretis developed another Easter play, the Peregrini. This later, and lesser work, attached itself to the processio ad fontes in the Easter week service, and was performed at Vespers. The play has the Last Supper as its kernel and ends with the Marys meeting the risen Christ. Both the Easter plays are dramas about the Resurrection which do not stretch back into the events of The Passion. There is very little in liturgical drama about The Passion. In some texts the Marys sang laments about Christ's Passion and these can be seen as the starting point of the Passion Play. In the Benedictbeuren manuscript there is a short text which serves as a sort of prologue to the Quem Quaeretis, with the action stretching from the Last Supper to the burial of Christ, mainly portrayed in dumb show with a little accompanying dialogue taken from the Bible. It is when drama starts to be portrayed outside of church, that the Passion Play develops side by side with the Resurrection plays.

Just as the Easter trope developed into a play so did the Christmas one, with the drama of the Three Kings and Shepherds, which was usually centred round the Christmas crib . (The introduction of the Christmas crib into the churches is attributed to St Francis of Assisi in 1223). Three kings enter by the great choir door singing and showing their gifts. When they see the star they follow it to the High Altar where they offer up their gifts, before a boy representing an angel announces to them the nativity and they retire singing to the sacristy.

The other Christmas play the Prophetae marks a more important development in church drama, as it comes from a sermon and not a chant and is on an epic scale, requiring a large number of performers. Believed to come from a 6th century pseudo-Augustinian text, it was used as a lesson for part of the Christmas office. The preacher would call on the Jews to bear witness out of the mouth of their own prophets to Christ, and a vast array of prophets would appear to bear witness. The play was probably chanted to begin with, but later versions are in dialogue form.

These plays were called Mystery plays. There were other plays on the life of the saints, the Miracle plays, which were written in this period for the intervals in the church services and for other Feasts. Plays on the life of St Nicholas were especially popular.

By the middle of the 13th century the evolution of these plays as liturgical texts had been completed. In the next hundred years their character underwent great changes as they were moved from the church choir to the church grounds until they found a home in the market places and guild halls. The greater elaboration and need for greater space in which to be performed coupled with their popularity led to the secularization of the plays. Once out of the church and the control of the clergy the plays could be developed as entertainment, with non-biblical scenes and characters being added. Comic relief supplied by the devil, Judas or Herod would bring guffaws of laughter and enjoyment, with the early life of the unrepentant Mary Magdalene becoming the excuse for scenes of debauchery. The plays in the 14th century were primarily spectacles which created mirth, wonder and delight in their audience. Latin gave way to the vernacular and so the dialogue became intelligible to all and the plays, popularity increased still further. Another result of Latin being replaced by the vernacular is that from being universal the drama of the Middle Ages became increasingly national, with each country developing its own literary tradition free from the bondage of a universal language and culture.

The plays lent themselves to accretion and amplification and whole cycles of plays developed. These expanding cycles, which took on the whole of human experience from the Fall to the Resurrection, with their vast cast lists presented difficulties of time as well as space. Two days were often given over to a performance, or the cycle divided into parts and played in successive years. As the plays were performed outside, the weather made it necessary to detach them from their feast days, and the cycles were transferred to the new Feast of Corpus Christi, introduced by papal bull in 1311, on the first Thursday after Trinity Sunday.

The plays were attached to the great procession of the host through the streets. Later the procession became a mere preliminary parade for the actors. The action of the play was like a procession with the actors' carts or pageants moving from one station to another, until the audience had seen the whole drama.

It was the guilds who provided the actors, the pageants and the costumes for the plays. The various guilds in a city were allotted the production of a particular Mystery or specific scenes; for instance in Chester, the guild of Slater & Wrights presented the birth of Christ, the Painters and Glaziers the Shepherds' play, while the Vintners performed the visit of the Three Kings. The rivalry of the guilds stimulated the actors and the wealth of the guilds was freely spent on the plays, with the merchant guilds, rich from their commerce with the East, providing lavish fittings and costly accessories. The venues for the plays were at first assigned by the authorities but later the players were allowed to perform their Mysteries opposite the house of those who were prepared to pay for the privilege. Guildsmen would keep order at the various stations of the play, with the audience forbidden to wear arms on the days of the play. The pageants on which the plays were performed, were like moveable carts, with a lower part enclosed by curtains which served as a dressing room, while the upper stage to which the players ascended through trap doors, was open at its front and sometimes on the sides as well and was where the action of the play took place.

A third form of religious drama which developed after the Mysteries was the Morality play. These were plays full of allegory and very abstract in nature, with characters such as Everyman there to teach a moral. This was the first of the dramas to decline with the Reformation in the 16th century, as they lent themselves too easily to debates between the old religion and the new. In England they were forbidden by Royal Proclamation in 1549. The Mystery and Morality plays survived until the end of the century in England. With the end of papal power there was no incentive to attend them for the indulgences which had been attached to the principal plays. The Renaissance was producing secular drama more fitting to a secular age, and religious drama died a natural death in this country, with the last performance of the Chester cycle about 1594, and the Coventry Miracle play in 1591. Theatre houses and William Shakespeare replaced the market places and the pageants, the amateur gave way to the professional, Protestant England having no place for the art of the Middle Ages.

The first recorded Passion Play was in Italy, in Siena about 1200. By 1244 the plays of the Passion and the Resurrection had been played side by side in Padua, and were later merged into one, the Passion Play absorbing the Quem Quaeretis. By the end of the 13th centrury it had developed into a cycle; beginning with an Old Testament prologue and ending with a finale in which the action extended from the Ascension to the Second Coming of Christ in the Last Judgement. It juxtaposed the Nativity with the Passion. At in 1298 and 1303 this vast framework was put together and performed. This was the great age of the Passion Play throughout Europe. In France La Passion de Semur with 9,500 lines, (the action beginning with the Creation and ending with the Ascension and needing two days to perform,) was put on with great success. The even longer Mystère de la Passion of Arnoul Greban which takes four days to perform and was written in 1450 is the most tragic and famed of French Passion Plays. Most German towns had had their Passion Play until the Reformation came. The plays survived in the **German States which remained Catholic, especially in the towns and villages of Bavaria.**

The dramatic tradition of Oberammergau can be traced back to the 10th century, to Hrotsvitha, the abbess of Gandesheim, who wrote plays for the edification of her nuns, some of which are still extant in manuscript form. These were later translated into the vernacular and gained a wide popularity during the Middle Ages. We do not know when the first Mystery play was being performed in Oberammergau, although regular performances of Christ's Passion were taking place in the 14th century under the supervision of the collegiate church of Rottenbuch, some 12 miles distant. After the founding of the Benedictine House of Ettal in 1330 it is probable that it **took over the supervision of the play, being only two miles away from the village.**

During the 1630's Germany was embroiled in the Thirty Years War and a virulent epidemic swept through the lowlands in the Winter of 1632 and 1633. As it spread to the Bavarian highlands the authorities of Oberammergau imposed a protective cordon of sentinels round the village to stop people entering and bringing with them the plague. So successful was this cordon that only Oberammergau remained untouched by the plague. An Oberammergau man, Kaspar Schisler, who had been working in Eschenlohe during the harvest, managed under the cover of darkness to avoid the sentinels and return to his home. He had made the journey to take part in the Kirchweih Fest, the commemoration of the founding of the village church, a celebration which began in the Middle Ages and that ranked with Christmas and Easter as the highlight of the year. The day after he was dead from the plague. By October 28th and the feast of St Simon and St Jude, less than two weeks after the Kirchweih Fest, 84 people had died of the plague. (The population of Oberammergau was less than one thousand in 1632.)

Not even the harsh Winter climate of Upper Bavaria and the extra precautions of the villagers could stop the plague now that it had taken root. Whole families disappeared, including some of the commercially most important in the village. Names which are destined to become famous in connection with the Passion Play are prominent in the Plague List — Khriegel, Perchtolt, Promberger, Glogl, Steinbacher, Faistenmantel, Zwink and Ruez. With the warmer Spring weather the deaths caused by the plague must have mounted. We do not know how many victims it took, as the church registers are incomplete for 1633, with comparatively few deaths recorded, as the parish priest Primus Christeiner, and his successor Marcellus Fatiga, both died of the plague.

Surrounded by pestilence, war and famine and without even a parish priest to record the names of those who died, there seemed little hope of salvation for this Bavarian village. The town council (called the council of Six and Twelve) continued to meet during the plague. As they could see no earthly solution to their problems they turned to God for help, and what they had resolved was solemnized in the village church one July morning, in front of all those villagers who were physically able to attend. They vowed that if they would be spared from plague, they would enact the Passion of the Redeemer evey tenth year with the utmost skill and devotion of which they were capable.

Such a vow was commonplace during the Middle Ages, where records survive of Mystery Plays being put on to ward off the Pest, such as the one performed in Chalon-sur-Sâone on the life of St Sebastian in 1497. Even during the 17th century, in the towns and hamlets of Bavaria such vows were far from unusual, the plague of 1632 producing a whole crop of them. In Kohlgrub, another village in the Ammerthal, a church was built in 1633 in honour of St Rochus, their patron saint, who had been asked to intercede on their behalf and free them from the plague. What is unique about the Oberammergau vow is that three hundred and fifty years later it is still being honoured.

Passion Play – Jesus chases the merchants from the Temple

The plague abated that Summer and the villagers were able to prepare for the first performance of a Passion Play in 1634. The text was largely drawn from two Augsburg plays: a 15th century version by the founder of St Ulrich and St Afra, and a 16th century play by Sebastian Wild, the Augsburg tailor and Meister-Singer. Several thousand lines of the Oberammergau text were copied word for word from these plays. There were also borrowings from the 16th century Weilheim Passion Play, written by the town's parish priest, Johann Abl, and performed in Weilheim in 1600 and 1615. The Oberammergau play when it was first put on was very much a medieval work, with scenes of great poignancy and tragedy interspersed with moments of farce and burlesque.

The first performance took place during the Whitsun of 1634 in front of the altar of the village church. The play was repeated in 1644 and 1654. The text was revised in 1662 for the next performance, and it is this text which is the oldest surviving version of the play. By 1674 the play's fame made it necessary for it to be performed in the greater space of the churchyard. It was then decided to move the play's performance to the beginning of the decade, and it was performed without interruption at ten yearly intervals from 1680 to 1760. By 1750 it was felt a new version of the text was required, and a Viennese Benedictine monk at the monastery of Ettal, was commissioned to undertake the task. Pater Rosner did little more than transpose the text into Alexandrine verse, and introduce a lot of homilies, which were put in the mouth of abstact figures such as Death, Sin and Avarice. This made the text more in keeping with the baroque taste of the age.

The 18th century was the great age of the baroque in Austria and Southern Germany and little escaped the effects of this movement. Medieval churches were given baroque facades and ornamentation, while music, painting and poetry were full of baroque fantasies and excesses. At this time most of the Bavarian towns had their own Passion Play, and the baroque excesses, and overfondness for comic relief provided by the devils, fiends and Judas, attracted the disapproving attention of the authorities in Munich. There was too much which was profane and unworthy for the Elector's Board of Book Censors in these plays in this, the Age of Enlightenment, and so they were banned. The Enlightenment was opposed to all kinds of pilgrimages, processions and religious plays, believing that reason and not religion held the way forward. The popularity of the Passion Play, it was also argued, interfered with commerce and industry, disrupting the working week. There were interdictions in 1763, 1770, 1781, 1789 and 1801. The ban was lifted in 1763 for communities who had been performing their play since time immemorial, and special licences were granted for Schongau, Weilheim, Tolz and Wolfratshausen. In 1770 there were no exceptions made, not even for Oberammergau. The church warden wrote on the door of a vestry shrine: "1770 the Passion Play was abolished." The deputation which was sent to Munich failed to get them to change their minds, despite the considerable expense incurred by the village and the large number of visitors expected from outside the State of Bavaria.

In order to change the authorities' mind, a revised version of the Rosner text was undertaken by another Ettal monk, the Tyrolese Pater Magnus Knipfelberger. The allegorical figures were removed from the general action, a chorus taking their place. There was less overt moralizing and the play submitted to the censors was more refined and controlled than the Rosner text. The flamboyance and excess of the baroque was still much in evidence despite the changes. The community of Oberammergau appealed successfully against the edict, with the Elector giving his permission for the play to be put on during the Summer of 1780. The Knipfelberger text was performed again in 1790 and 1800.

The Napoleonic wars interrupted the Passion Play season of 1800 after only 5 performances. Because of this, permission was given for a further 4 performances in 1801. The success of Napoleon's troops led to Bavaria being briefly under French control, and the suppression of the religious houses of Ettal and Rottenbuch. But by 1810 it was possible to begin thinking about putting on the play again. To the consternation of the village the special privilege of Oberammergau was declared null and void, and its Passion Play, like the plays of other communities, was banned. A deputation led by Georg Lang to Munich failed to change the authorities' mind. They enlisted the help of Georg Sambuga, a former royal tutor, and petitioned the Elector directly. Max Joseph gave his personal consent. The Passion Play season was termed a "People's Festival", and as such was outside the scope of the official ban.

For this "People's Festival" a new text was prepared by Ottmar Weiss. Born the son of poor Bayersoien peasants he was educated in the monastery of Ettal, where he served at Mass. He continued his education in Munich and Ingolstadt, and returned to Ettal as a Doctor of Philosophy. He was ordained a priest in 1795, and was then sent to Eschenlohe, where he began his ministry. The dissolution of the monasteries in 1803 led to Weiss leaving his parishioners and returning to Ettal as a government pensioner. A man of great energy he set up a school at Oberau. He was later chosen to administer the confiscated property of the monastery of Ettal for its new owners. Weiss proved himself an able administrator, a good teacher and a gifted writer.

In his version Weiss returned to the simplicity of the early Gothic text, following closely the biblical narrative. He retained the Tableaux Vivants and the Guardian Spirits from the Rosner version but rid it of the baroque flamboyance. The Alexandrine verses were replaced by a sober prose style. Ottmar Weiss managed to create a harmonious whole, suitable for the beginning of the 19th century, from the texts of his predecessors. The work had balance, clarity and dramatic force. After seeing his text put on in 1811, Weiss revised it for the 1815 performance.

As Weiss had made such considerable changes to the text it was necessary to commission a new score. This task fell upon Rochus Dedler, who had written the melodies for the Tableaux Vivants verses for the 1811 version. He rewrote the whole score, with only two songs remaining from the previous one. Rochus Dedler was the only one of the play's shapers to have been born in Oberammergau. An innkeeper's son, Dedler's musical ability led to him being educated in the collegiate school of Rottenbuch and then in a Munich seminary. He would have probably become a priest at Rottenbuch if it weren't for its suppression. The life of the city was little to his taste, and despite the success of his opera Regulus in Munich, he returned to his native village to become the schoolmaster. Unhappily married with little money and poor health Dedler's only solace was his music. He wrote the music for the 1811 and 1815 productions, and because of the fire in 1817 which burnt down the schoolhouse, where his score was kept, he had to rewrite the score for the 1820 production. That year he also conducted his music and performed the bass solos. The effort was too much for him and he became ill, dying of consumption in 1822 at the age of 44. His last musical task was to compose the Mass for the ordination of Alois Daisenberger.

Daisenberger was educated at Oberau in Weiss' school, before going on to the Lyceum in Munich, and the university at Landshut. After his ordination he became the parish priest at Oberammergau. It is fitting that the task of revising the text of Ottmar Weiss should have been entrusted to his former pupil. Daisenberger basically followed his former teacher's text, making very few changes. What he did do, however, was to reconstruct the lines to make them more poetic and easier to sing. The Weiss-Daisenberger text continues to be revised, but still remains the basic text of the Passion Play.

There have been several attempts at revision of the Play throughout its long history. When the Oberammergau Passion Play became famous, the government of Upper Bavaria decided a new text and score were needed. The music and text prepared in Munich in 1888 for the community of Oberammergau met fierce local resistance and had to be dropped. During the Hitler period there was talk of a new version which would proclaim the truths of National Socialism, but happily this did not come about, and Oberammergau was spared from becoming a second Bayreuth for the Nazis. The rather tedious playlet, "The Pest", was written by Leo Weismantel, commissioned in this period was put on as a introductory piece in 1934. It tells the story of the plague and the vow, but adds nothing to the main body of the text.

Since 1820 the Passion Play has been performed at ten-yearly intervals, with the exception of 1871, 1922, the jubilee performance of 1934 and the present 1984 performance. There was no performance in 1920 because of the economic and social turmoil caused by the First World War, explaining the 1922 season. Owing to World War Two there was no performance in 1940. The Franco-Prussian War led to the suspension of the Passion Play season in 1870 after only five performances, with some of the players having to go off to join their regiments, including Joseph Mayr, who was playing Christ for the first time. The German victory and the return of peace was celebrated by special permission to perform the play in 1871.

It was in 1820 that the world outside Bavaria started to take a real interest in Oberammergau and its Passion Play, largely due to the efforts of Baron Vautier, who proved an able publicist for the village and its play. This is the year in which the first sizeable English contingent witnessed the play, and the first English account of it was written by Gray McQueen, a journalist. The 1830 performance led to Baron de Rosin publishing his essay, "A Passion Play performed in the 19th century", the first account in French of the play. The impressions of Ludwig Steub, Guido Gorrea in 1840 and Edward Devrient in 1850 firmly established the play's fame in Europe. The Bavarian royal family took to patronizing the play, with Oberammergau becoming especially popular with Ludwig II, Wagner's patron, who fell in love with the area. He had a simple farm rebuilt as a model of Versailles at Linderhof, and a fairytale castle at Neuschwanstein, both in the vicinity of his favourite village. The most generous of his gifts to the village was the massive crucifixion group at Osterbichl.

In 1871, an incognito Prince of Wales, later King Edward VII of England, brought his young bride to see the Passion Play at Oberammergau.

The journey to Oberammergau was far from easy at this time (the railway was extended to Weilheim in 1870, Murnau in 1880, and Garmisch in 1890) and only the most intrepid and committed made the journey. When they arrived they would watch in great discomfort a play which began at 8 a.m. and finished at 6 p.m., with a $1\frac{1}{2}$ hour interval. The railway and the new theatre built in 1899 made Oberammergau more accessible and more comfortable for the visitor. By the end of the 19th century it became a tourist event, with European travellers including it as part of their grand tour. It became almost obligatory for the traveller to write his own account of the Passion Play. Lady Burton's comments are typical: "Everyone is natural, there is no striving after effect, no one strives to shine, he does it as if he lived for that and nothing else. Thus it is a perfect whole and this is the secret of the 700 people all doing a natural act of devotion at one and the same time, falling into perfect harmony."

The charm of Oberammergau seemed to work on everyone, and produced a deluge of books in England and America, including several novels inspired by the play. By 1880 guide books were being produced and the first English translation of the play was made. By 1900 the community of Oberammergau was commissioning official translations of the play, as a copious literature developed on it. Even writers as notable as Jerome K. Jerome felt the need to apologize for writing on Oberammergau in the wake of so many.

Since the First World War the literary interest in Oberammergau has decreased, although every season produces a book or two, while its popularity as a religious, cultural tourist event has achieved new heights. Four performances a week from May to September are sold out far in advance, the play's success seemingly now eternal.

The Rochus Dedler music had been tightened up by Professor Papst for the 1950 season, and this is the score which is used today. The text goes on being revised with major deletions taking place for the 1980 performance. A lot of the scenes between Judas and the Pharisees were omitted, as they were considered to be antisemitic. While one can admire the thinking behind their omission, their deletion makes the text unreadable and stilted, and it is to be hoped that they will be reinserted for the 1990 performance, when the full text will once again be performed in its entirety. The Weiss-Daisenberger text remains the most fitting monument to Oberammergau and its vow, and to the Passion Play as a religious celebration and a work of art.

The Last Supper (from a painting by Leonardo de Vinci)

Jesus offered by Pilate to the people (from a painting by Antonio Ciseri)

THE TEXT OF THE
OBERAMMERGAU PASSION PLAY

THE PASSION PLAY

FIRST PART

From the entrance of Christ into Jerusalem until the moment of His being taken prisoner on the Mount of Olives.

ACT I. REPRESENTATION

PROLOGUE.   Bend low, bend low in holy love,
God's curse hath bowed an humbled race.
Peace unto you! From Heaven above,
Where righteous wrath in justice reigns,
Yet pales before the touch of grace, —
So saith the Lord, "Eternal pains
Of Death from the Sinner I release.
I will forgive — he shall have peace!"
Thus came His Son to free the world. Oh, praise
To Thee we raise,
And thanks, Eternal One.
Thus came His Son!

TABLEAU: *The Expulsion from Paradise*

THE EXPULSION

This first picture serves as an introduction. Adam and Eve after their temptation are driven from the Garden of Eden.

PROLOGUE.   Man is doomed from Eden's plains to wander,
In darkest sin his soul to live; on death to ponder.
The path to the Tree of Life to him denied,
By the flaming sword defied,
Yet from the heights where hung the Crucified —
Sifts through the gloom a morning glow!
Yonder the Tree of the Cross from whither softly blow
Pæans of peace to all the world below.

CHORUS.   God All-Merciful, Thou Pardoner supernal!
Of them who scorned Thy word at every breath,
Exalting the Sinner to the way eternal,
Thou gavest Thy Son in death!

37

TABLEAU *The Adoration of the Cross*

THE ADORATION

The second picture represents the Adoration of the Cross, with little children dressed as Cherubim.

PROLOGUE   Hearken, Lord, unto Thy people bending,
Even as little children who come before Thee;
To the great Sacrifice their footsteps wending,
In reverent awe, Thy people all adore Thee.

CHORUS   Follow now the Saviour's way,
Along the roughened thorn-path leading —
Bearing for us in the fray,
Suffering, and for us bleeding!

ACTION

THE ENTRY INTO JERUSALEM

Christ enters Jerusalem amidst loud rejoicing from the throng, and drives the money-lenders from the Temple.

FIRST SCENE

Men, Women, and Children; then Christ and the Apostles, followed by a crowd – advancing from the background.

CHORUS   Hail, Son of David, we raise songs to Thee!
Hail, Thy Fathers's throne belongs to Thee!
To Thee belongs!
In God's holy name You come a light
To give —
In God's Holy Name You grant us right to live —
To Thee, O Son of David, we raise songs.

CHORUS A.   Hosanna! God in Heaven hear us!
Bestow unto the Son of David grace.

CHORUS B.   Hosanna! Enthroned above, yet ever near us,
Grant us eternally to see Thy face!

CHORUS.   Hail to Thee! Hail to Thee!

C.A.   Blessed be to Him who gives once more Unto the people and their kingdom trembling;

38

C.B.   Bless ye the Son, exalt Him, and adore The Son on high, the Lord our God resembling!

CHORUS.   Hail to Thee! Hail to Thee!

C.A.   Hosanna to the Son, our own — Hearken, ye winds, and sound the song abroad!

C.B.   Hosanna! there upon His Father's throne, He will deliver the Message of the Lord!

CHORUS.   Hail to Thee! Hail to Thee!

SECOND SCENE

Christ, the Apostles, and People; Priests, Pharisees, and Money-changers within the portico of the Temple.

CHRIST.   What see I here? Thus would you dishonour the abode of My Father. Is this God's House? or is it naught to you but a market-place? How can the Strangers who come from out the land of the heathen perform their devotions here in such a throng of usurers? And you who are priests and guardians of the sanctuary! — you see this abomination and yet you endure it! Woe unto you! He who fathoms the heart well knows why you yourselves sanction such outrage.

MONEY CHANGERS.   Who, forsooth, is this?

THE PEOPLE.   It is the great Prophet from Nazareth in Galilee.

CHRIST.   *(approaching the dealers).* Away from here, Servants of Mammon! I bid you go! Take what is yours, and leave this holy place!

RABBI.   See the fire in His eye; I cannot endure Him.

EPHRAIM.   Come, let us depart, that His wrath may not completely undo us. *(Departing in awe; the others hesitate.)*

JOSUE.   Why do you interfere with these people?

EZEKIEL.   This place has been specially set aside for the sacrifice.

SADOK.   How can you forbid what the High Council allows?

BOOZ.   Shall we no longer be permitted to make sacrifice here?

39

CHRIST. Outside the Temple there are many places for your business. My house, so saith the Lord, shall be called the House of Prayer for all ! But you have made it a den of thieves. *(Overturning the Tables.)* Away with all this!

RABBI. It cannot be. You dare not do thus!

KOAN *(a Trader)*. My gold, ah, my gold!

DATHAN *(a Trader)*. My doves! *(The doves fly away.)*

ABIRON *(a Trader)*. Who will restore this loss to me?

CHRIST. *(striking out with a lash)*. Hence! It is my will that this profanéd Temple be once more restored to the worship of the Father! *(The Traders withdraw, some in fear, others menacingly.)*

SADOK. Tell us, by what authority do you so command?

AMON. Through what miraculous sign are you able to show the power you have to do this?

CHRIST. You ask for a miracle? Verily, one shall be given you. Destroy this Temple here, and in three days will I have it again rebuilt.

RABBI. What boasting, what insolent speech!

AMON. Six and forty years was this Temple in the building, and you would do it in three days!

CHILDREN. Hosanna! Hail to the Son of David!

PEOPLE. Glory be to Him who comes in the name of the Lord!

RABINTH. Hear you what these people cry?

DARIABAS. Forbid them!

CHRIST. I say unto you: If these were silent, then would the very stones cry out.

CHILDREN. Hosanna to the Son of David!

PHARISEES. Be silent, you foolish ones!

CHRIST. Have you not read: Out of the mouths of babes and sucklings you have made ready your praise? That which is hidden from the proud is revealed unto the little children. And the scriptures must be fulfilled: The stone which the workmen rejected has become the corner-stone. The Kingdom of God shall be taken from you, and it shall be given unto those people who will bring forth fruit. But that stone — whosoever falls upon it shall be bruised, and on whomsoever it falls, he shall be crushed to pieces. Come, my Disciples! I have done what the Father has commanded of me. I have vindicated the honour of His house. The gloom remains gloom; but in many hearts will it soon be day. Let us within the Temple, and there pray to our Father in Heaven. *(They go.)*

PEOPLE.   Praise be to the Anointed One! Hosanna!

PRIESTS.   Be silent, you contemptible beings!

PHARISEES.   You will all be ruined along with Him!

PEOPLE.   Blesséd be the Kingdom of David, which shall again shine forth!

THIRD SCENE

Priests and People

NATHANAEL.   Whoso continue true to our Fathers Abraham, Isaac, and Jacob, let them remain with us! Upon all others fall the curse of Moses!

RABBI.   He is a misleader! an enemy of Moses — an enemy to the Holy Law!

PEOPLE.   Why then did you not lay hold on Him? Is He not a Prophet? *(Some of the multitude follow Christ.)*

PTOLEMAUS.   Away with the Prophet!

RABBI.   He is a teacher of false doctrine!

SADOK.   A heretic —. an enemy of Moses!

JOSAPHAT.   An enemy to the tradition of our Fathers! A deceiver!

PEOPLE *(again).*   Why did you not seize Him?

NATHANAEL.   Oh, you blind people! Would you indeed follow this new One, would you forsake Moses, the Prophets, and your Priests? Do you not fear that the curse hurled by the Law against this faithless creature will crush you? Would you willingly cease to be Jehovah's Chosen People?

PEOPLE.   Indeed, no! That is far from our minds!

NATHANAEL.   Who guards the purity of the Teacher? Is it not

41

the holy Sanhedrin of the People of Israel? Which would you heed — us or Him who has proclaimed Himself the Prophet of a new faith?

PEOPLE.   We will hearken unto you, we will follow you!

SADOK.   The God of our Fathers will bless you for this.

NATHANAEL.   Now then! This Man, so full of deceit and of error, hastens to His ruin!

PEOPLE.   Yes, we will stand by you! We are the followers of Moses!

FOURTH SCENE

The Traders, with their chief, Dathan, enter, weeping and moaning.

TRADERS.   This insult must not remain unpunished. Come, let us hasten retribution. Vengeance, vengeance!

DATHAN.   He shall pay dearly for His brazen manner!

BOOZ.   Gold, oil, salt, doves — He must pay us for the loss of all! Where is He? He shall know our wrath!

JOSUE.   He is there within the Temple!

PRIESTS.   He has gone away!

TRADERS.   We will after Him.

NATHANAEL.   Hold, friends! The followers of yonder Man and His Disciples are yet too many. Your meeting with them now might cause a disastrous struggle which would be stopped by the sword of the Roman. Trust to us. He shall not escape punishment!

PRIESTS.   With us, for us — that is your salvation.

SADOK.   His downfall approaches.

ALL.   Our triumph is near.

NATHANAEL.   We go now to inform the High Council of this day's happenings.

TRADERS.   We will go with you; we would have satisfaction.

NATHANAEL.   Nay, in an hour's time come to the outer court of the High Priest's house. In the meanwhile I will bring your grievance before the Council and will plead eloquently in your favour. At the right moment you shall be called. *(The priests go.)*

TRADERS AND PEOPLE *(moving off stage).* We have Moses! Down with all others! We are faithful to the death unto the Law of Moses! Praise be to our Fathers and to our Fathers' God!

END OF ACT

ACT II. REPRESENTATION

The Plot of the High Council

PROLOGUE. Greetings be unto you all, who in love are
> gathered here,
> Gathered round the Saviour mourning, you who come from
> far and near,
> Fain to follow on the thorn-path, fain to suffer in His doom,
> Through the trial and the torture, from the cross unto the
> tomb.

> Oh, ye people now assembled, followers from sea to sea,
> Prompted by the love of brothers, bound as one in unity,
> One in faith and one in feeling, one in love for Him who died,
> Him who bore the cross and suffered, Christ who is the
> Crucified!

> Who in pity for the Sinners, chose Himself the world to save,
> Leaving life unto the living, for the life beyond the grave —
> Toward Him turn your countenances, toward Him turn your
> hearts in praise,
> Turn you hearts in deep thanksgiving, and your
> countenances raise!

> For behold, the Cup of Sorrow overflows the beaker's brim,
> While the bitter force of envy holds the bitter dregs for Him.
> Avaricious ones conspire, breathing hate with every breath,
> Hate that only breeds destruction, avarice that knows but
> death!

> Even as when Joseph's brothers all the bonds of blood
> defied,
> Prompted by the thoughts of murder to the verge of
> fratricide.

43

Even now, the priestly Council, met to stem the Prophet's sway
Spurs itself, by false deception, to put Death within His way.

PROLOGUE *(Recit.).* Intent on the blasphemous deed, they depart.
The mouth hath proclaimed what was hid in the heart!
The sting of their consciences hastens their blunder,
The masks from their faces are now rent asunder!

CHORUS. Away! Let us go to reap vengeance, they cry,
Our work we must do; He must die, He must die!

TABLEAU: *The Sons of the Patriarch Jacob plot as to how their younger brother Joseph is to be put out of the way. Gen. 37: 18. Joseph symbolizes the humiliation and exaltation of Christ: like Jesus, he is the beloved son of his father, and so his brother would quickly despatch him; hated by then, insulted, his very coat taken from him, he is sold to the stranger for a single piece of silver.*

PROLOGUE. O God! we would enter the sanctified temple of prayer;
Of that which occurred in the Past we are all made aware.
Even as Jacob's cruel sons did conspire,
So, in blind ire,
O God, will be heard the murderous cry:
He must die! He must die!

SOLO *(Tenor).* Behold the dreamer,
False teacher, blasphemer,
Our King!
Away with this vision,
This Man of derision!
Come, fling
What we hate to the depths of yon pool,
And there let Him rule!

SOLO *(Bass).* Thus, thirst
The brood accurst!
He is against our people — Let Him die!
They cry.
The honour of our faith is in danger
Of this stranger.

44

For the world is filled with those who pray
To follow Him; who travel not our way!

DUET.　Come, let us hasten to slay Him!
Let us capture and flay Him!
No one from Death can stay Him!
　　Come, come!
Away! to our purpose stand fast.
Away! for His glory is past.
Away! for the die is cast.
　　Come, come!

CHORUS.　O God, destroy this wanton band,
Which seeks to bind Thy righteous hand;
Which comes, with jibe and jeer, to kill,
To murder, to oppose Thy will!

Let them feel Thy holy wonder —
Flash of lightning, roar of thunder —
Of Thy power let them know —
In thy might, oh, bend them low!

For He came not to destroy,
God the Father, Thou above
His the mission to bring joy
To the Sinner, Grace and Love!

We before Thy throne incline,
In humility are Thine,
Bless Thy passion, Thy design,
God, the Father, the Divine!

ACTION

The High Council decides to take the Christ captive.

FIRST SCENE

The Assembly of the High Council

CAIAPHAS.　Venerable Brothers, Fathers, and Teachers of the people! An extraordinary occurrence is the immediate object of this present meeting. Learn of it from the mouth of our worthy brother.

NATHANAEL.　Have I your permission, wise Fathers, to speak?

45

ALL.   Yes, worthy priest.

NATHANAEL.   Wonder not then that you are convoked at so late an hour for deliberation. You know what we to our shame have witnessed to-day with our very eyes. You have seen the triumphal way of the Galilean through the streets of the Holy City! You have heard the Hosannas of the infatuated people! You have perceived how the haughty One arrogated unto Himself the dignity of the High Priest, and dared, as Master, to rule in the Temple of Jehovah! What could more unerringly hasten the upheaval of all State and ecclesiastical order? Yet, one step further, and the sacred laws of Moses will be supplanted by the innovations of this false Teacher. The dogmas of our Fathers will be despised, the fasts and purifications done away with, the Sabbath profaned, the Priests of God divested of their charges, the holy sacrifices ended. Such is the situation.

ALL.   True, very true, painfully true!

CAIAPHAS.   Yes, and still more! Soon this Man, encouraged by His success, will proclaim Himself King of Israel. Then will schism and rioting flood the land, then will the Romans come with troops and desolate the land and people. Woe unto the children of Israel! Woe unto the Holy City! Woe unto the Temple of Jehovah! Woe, indeed, if some force is not set against this evil while yet there is time! This is urgent, for the vindication rests with us. We must this very day frame some strong course of action, and what is resolved upon must be executed regardless of all else. Will you, O Fathers, by the raising of your hands, signify your agreement with me?

ALL.   Yes, yes, we do, we will. An end must be put to this Imposter!

CAIAPHAS.   Express your opinion freely as to what were best to be done!

RABBI.   If I may be allowed to speak frankly, then I must confess that we ourselves are somewhat to blame for what has come to pass. Against this danger which has slowly gathered, we have put too mild, too gentle remedies. How have our arguments stopped Him; what does it matter whether, by our questioning, we have at times embarrassed Him? What avail that we have pointed out inconsistencies in His teaching, and His every violation of the Law? What even has been the effect of the anathemas hurled by us upon all who acknowledged Him as the Messiah? Our trouble has been useless. They turn their backs upon us, and they follow Him. If we would have peace, them must we do what should indeed have been done a long time ago. We must secure His person, must cast Him into prison; that is the way to make Him harmless!

ALL.   Yes, we are perfectly agreed!

THIRD PRIEST.   Once He is in prison, the credulous people will no longer be held by the force of His manner and the magic of His speech. When there is no longer any miracle for them to gape at, then will He soon be forgotten.

FOURTH PRIEST.   In the depths of His dungeon let His light shine; there let Him proclaim Himself Messiah to the dungeon walls.

FIRST PHARISEE.   Quite long enough has He misled the people, and stigmatized as pretence the rare virtues of the holy order of the Pharisees.

SECOND PHARISEE.   Then will the enthusiasm of his adherents cool when He, who promised them freedom, Himself lies in fetters.

ANNAS.   Now indeed, venerable Priests and Teachers, a ray of comfort, of hope, enters my heart once more, for I note your unanimous determination. Ah, what inexpressible sorrow has weighed upon my soul because of the rapidity with which the false teachings of this Galilean have spread! Had I forsooth attained old age, only to behold with mine own eyes the destruction of the Holy Law? Yet I will not despair. The God of our Fathers still lives, and is with us. If you, my Friends, are thus emboldened to interpose, if you stand together tried and true, and follow unswervingly a definite aim, then indeed is deliverance near. Take courage, and save Israel! Immortal glory will be yours as a reward.

ALL.   We are of one intent! Our Fathers' faith shall not perish!

PRIESTS.   Israel must be delivered!

CAIAPHAS.   All praise to your unanimous decision, worthy Brothers! But now give me aid with your wise consel, how it were best to secure this Seducer under our authority.

RABINTH.   To take Him now, at the time of the feast, might be fraught with danger. In the streets and within the Temple — everywhere He goes, He is surrounded by a multitude of inspired adherents — He could easily bring about a riot.

EZEKIEL.   And yet, it must be done immediately; it suffers no delay. Suppose He did provoke an uproar, then we might take Him on the spot, as we have determined shall be done.

OTHER PRIESTS. No delay! No respite!

JOSUE. At present, nevertheless, we dare not seize Him by open means; our work must be done secretly and cunningly. We must in some way discover where He usually spends the night; there suddenly and without excitement might He be taken and carried off in perfect safety.

NATHANAEL. Should it please the High Council to offer a considerable reward for the purpose, no doubt someone could be found to track the fox to His lair.

CAIAPHAS. If you sanction it, holy Fathers, I will, in the name of this, our august body, send forth the command that anyone knowing His nightly haunts should declare the same to us, and also that to that informer is assured a fitting recompense.

ALL. We are quite agreed.

NATHANAEL. No doubt some man among those so grievously insulted by the Galilean, when He drove them from the Temple with a scourge, could inform us. Once these men were firm believers in the Law, and now they thirst for vengeance against this One who has made such an unheard-of assault upon their privileges.

ANNAS. Where may the Traders be reached?

NATHANAEL. They are already here in the vestibule. I promised them to champion their rights before the holy Sanhedrin, and they await the issue.

CAIAPHAS. Worthy Priest, tell them that the High Council is disposed to listen to their grievance. Bring them hither.

NATHANAEL. This will delight them, and profit us! *(Goes.)*

SECOND SCENE

CAIAPHAS. The God of our Fathers has not yet withdrawn His hand from us. Still does Moses watch over us. If we succeed in draw-ing to us the flower of manhood among the people, then need we have no further fear. Friends and Brothers, let us take courage — our Father, from out the bosom of Abraham, watches over us.

PRIESTS. God bless our High Priest! *(The Traders are led in.)*

THIRD SCENE

NATHANAEL. High Priest and chosen Teachers of the People, these men, deserving of our blessing, appear before this Assembly in order to lodge complaint against the infamous Jesus of Nazareth, who has to-day insulted them beyond reason in their Temple and has wrought them harm.

DATHAN. We beseech the High Council to obtain satisfaction for us. The High Council should favour our lawful demands.

PRIESTS AND PHARISEES. You shall have justice done you, we promise that.

BOOZ. Is it not granted us by the High Council to place on sale in the portico all things necessary for the Feast?

SADOK. In truth, we do allow that. Woe unto anyone who disturbs you in that right!

BOOZ. But the Galilean has driven us out with a scourge!

ABIRON. And He has overturned the money tables!

DATHAN. And He has emptied my dove-cots!

TRADERS. We demand recompense!

CAIAPHAS. The Law grants you satisfaction. Meanwhile, your loss shall be restored to you from the Temple treasury. But in return, that the Transgressor Himself may be punished in proper measure, we need your help. What can we do to Him so long as He is not in our power?

ESRON. You know, He goes daily to the Temple; there He could be easily caught and carried away.

CAIAPHAS. That would not do. He always has around Him a passionate crowd which might begin a dangerous riot. It must be done silently.

BOOZ. The night time is best.

CAIAPHAS. If you could but reconnoitre, and ferret out where He hides under cover of darkness, then, without any disturbance, He would soon be in our hands. Afterwards, not only would the pleasure of seeing Him punished be yours, but also you would have share in a considerable reward.

NATHANAEL. So! And furthermore, you will be rendering a

great service to the Law of Moses, if you aid therein.

TRADERS.   We shall not fail.

EPHRAIM.   Nor shall we spare ourselves trouble.

DATHAN.   I know one of His Disciples. Through him I may learn something, especially if I offer him a suitable reward.

CAIAPHAS.   If you find such a one, make him every necessary promise in our name. Only, waste no time, for we must reach our goal before the Feast.

ANNAS.   And be sure to observe strict silence.

TRADERS.   We swear it!

CAIAPHAS.   But, my men, if you would satisfy your thirst for revenge entirely, then take good care that you kindle in others the same holy ardour which burns in you.

EPHRAIM.   Since to-day's disaster, we have made use of every moment; already we have brought to our side many of our friends and relatives.

RABBI.   We will not rest until everyone is against Him.

ANNAS.   In return, you will gain the rare thanks of the High Council.

CAIAPHAS.   Publicly shall you than be honoured before the people, even as you have just been openly insulted by this arrogant Man.

KOAN.   We dedicate our lives to the Law of Moses and to the holy Sanhedrin.

CAIAPHAS.   The God of Abraham be with you!

TRADERS.   Long live Moses, long live the High Priest and the Sanhedrin. *(They go.)*

KOAN.   To-day, maybe, the Galilean has played His role for the last time! *(Goes.)*

FOURTH SCENE

CAIAPHAS.   As though by sweet slumbers strengthened, I live again. With such men as those, we can accomplish everything. Now we shall see who conquers: He with His followers to whom,,without

50

cessation, He preaches Love, a Love which embraces sinner and publican alike, even the heathen — or we, with this multitude of His enemies, filled with a desire for vengeance, whom we are sending forth against Him. There can be no doubt on which side the victory will be.

ANNAS.   The God of our Father grant us victory! Such joy in my old age will make me young again!

CAIAPHAS.   Let us adjourn and confidently await success. Praise be to the Fathers!

ALL.   Praise be to the God of Abraham, Isaac, and Jacob!

END OF ACT

ACT III. REPRESENTATION

The Parting at Bethany

PROLOGUE.   He who glances in the future with a penetrating
   eye,
 He who has the gift prophetic feels a violent storm is
   nigh —
 Which with menace is approaching, which obtains about His
   head —
 A menace which approaches and which gathers and will
   spread.

 There He tarries in a circle of His people who believe;
 He has said the word of parting, He has made the heart to
   grieve.
 Ah! a word which wounds to utter and a word which brings
   no rest —
 Only sorrow to the Mother, only pain within her breast.

 See the mother of Tobias, how she wept with every sigh,
 As she saw her son departing, as the grievous time
   drew nigh -
 How her sorrow and her grieving broke the floodgates
   of her tears,
 When she saw her son departing as fulfilment of her fears.

51

Even so, thus weeps the Mother of the Son of God who
    goes —
Thus she gazes at her Loved One, knowing all the grief
    He knows —
Through His love He seeks atonement, for the world
    ordained to die,
To destroy the sin of Sinners, even though they crucify.

TABLEAU: *Young Tobias takes leave of his home. Tob. 4 : 1. The
picture suggests the departure of Christ from His Mother, as
He leaves for Jerusalem.*

SOLO.   Friends! what bitter pain is this,
    Torturing a Mother's bliss?
    Hearken to the Lord's command —
    Yonder Raphael by the hand
    Leads Tobias from the land.

    Woe! Alas, a thousand woes!
    Thus she calls to him who goes —
    Come thou, tarry not for long,
    Comfort thou, and right the wrong —
    But return, and make me strong!

    Ah, Tobias, ah, my son!
    Come to me, beloved one!
    For my arms are opened wide —
    Fain to hold thee by my side —
    Thus to make me satisfied!

CHORUS.   Mournful she, and comfortless.
    Neither joy nor happiness —
    Till one moment, doubly blest,
    Finds her son held to her breast!

SOLO.   A Bride there was, you know the song —
    Of her lamenting loud and long.
    'T was Solomon in all his glory,
    Told in lofty words the story!

    Greater the pain in Mary's heart,
    Which pierces like a cruel dart;
    And yet submission is a rod
    Aiding her to walk with God.

TABLEAU: *The beloved bride bewails the loss of her bridegroom. S. of S. 5 : 1. In a wonderfully beautiful flower-garden, we see the Bride of the Sublime Song; she stands in a rose arbour, surrounded by her trusted women clad in white and adorned with blossoms. An allusion is here made to the Church as a maidenly bride; or to Mary's grief over the departure of her Son, her one great joy. For the lament, c.f. Canticles.*

SOLO.   Whither, whither has He departed?
For I, alas, am broken-hearted!
Beloved One, my soul is yearning!
Beloved One, my tears are burning!

Whither, whither art Thou hiding?
Speak, oh, speak, one word confiding!
Dost Thou tarry — Dost Thou wait —
Have I lost Thee — am I late?

My heavy eyes are searching still —
From path to path, from hill to hill —
Beloved, in the early morn,
I think of Thee — and Hope is born!

CHORUS.   Belovéd, ah, Belovéd, woe is me —
The pain I feel for Thee!

Friends, be ye comforted, and learn
Thy Belovéd will return!

Behold the Bridegroom on His way —
Tarry thou, and for Him stay —
No longer any cloud shall dim
The joy to thee of meeting Him!

Oh, come, my eyes are opened wide!
Oh, rest, Belovéd, by my side!
No longer any cloud shall be,
To dim the joy of meeting Thee!

ACTION

Christ is anointed by Mary Magdalene in Bethany, where Judas complains. He then takes leave of His Mother and of His friends.

FIRST SCENE

Christ and the Twelve Disciples

CHRIST.   Know you, my dear Disciples, that the Passover is in two days' time. Therefore, let us now make a last visit to our friends in Bethany, and then go to Jerusalem; there, in these days to come, all will be fulfilled which has been written by the Prophets of the Son of Man.

PHILIP.   Has the day then truly arrived when you will again restore the Kingdom to Israel?

CHRIST.   Then shall the Son of Man be handed over to the Gentiles, and He shall be ridiculed and spat upon, and they will crucify Him. But on the third day He will rise again.

JOHN.   Master, what dark and terrible meaning for us in your words! How shall we understand you? Make it clear to us!

CHRIST.   The hour has come when the Son of Man will be glorified! Verily, verily, I say unto you: If the grain of wheat does not fall to the ground and die, then it remains alone; but if it dies, then it brings forth abundant fruit. Now the judgment goes forth over the earth: The Prince of this world will be cast out. And I, if I be raised, will draw all men unto me.

THADDEUS.   What does He mean by such speech?

SIMON.   Why does He liken Himself to a grain of wheat?

ANDREW.   Lord, you mention shame and victory in one breath, and yet I know not how to reconcile these in my thoughts.

CHRIST.   What to you now is dark as night will soon be as clear as day. Thus have I said unto you, so that whatever happens you may not lose courage. Believe and hope! For when the turmoil is over, then shall you see and understand.

THOMAS.   I cannot grasp what it is you say of suffering and death. Have we not then learned aright of the Prophets, that the Messiah shall live eternally?

54

PETER.   What can your enemies do to you? A word from you would crush them all.

CHRIST.   Thomas! reverence the decree of God, which you cannot fathom. For a short while still is the Light with you. Walk so long as you have the light, lest darkness overtake you.

DISCIPLES.   Lord! Remain with us! Without you we will be as sheep without a shepherd.

SECOND SCENE

The same. Simon, then Lazarus, Martha, Mary Magdalene

SIMON.   Best of Teachers, greetings unto you! Oh, what joy! how you bless my house with your presence. *(To the Disciples.)* Be there welcome unto you all, friends.

CHRIST.   Simon, for the last time do I lay claim upon your hospitality — I, with my Disciples here.

SIMON.   Speak not so, my Master. Many times shall Bethany still afford you resting place for brief repose.

CHRIST.   *(Lazarus approaching).* Behold our friend Lazarus.

LAZARUS.   Oh, Conqueror of Death! Benefactor of Life! Master! I see you again, and I hear again the voice which called me from the grave! *(Concealing his face on the breast of Christ.)*

MARY MAGDALENE.   Rabbi!

MARTHA.   Greetings to you!

CHRIST.   God's blessing rest upon you.

MARY MAGDALENE.   Will you have from me a token of love and gratitude?

CHRIST.   Yea, do what you purpose doing.

SIMON.   Enter, Master, beneath my roof; let you and yours be refreshed. *(They all go in.)*

THIRD SCENE

The Guest-room in Simon's House

CHRIST.   Peace be unto this house!

DISCIPLES.   And to all who dwell therein!

SIMON.   Master, everything is ready. Be seated at the table, and bid your followers to do likewise.

CHRIST.   Let us then, my dear Disciples, with thanks enjoy the gifts which our Father in Heaven grants us through Simon, His servant. *(After they are all seated.)* O Jerusalem! Would that to you my coming were as dear as it is to these, my friends! But, alas, you are stricken with blindness!

LAZARUS.   Beloved Master! Dangers there await you. In expectation, the Pharisees abide your coming to the Great Feast. Eagerly they watch for your destruction.

SIMON.   Remain here with us where you are safe.

PETER.   Here indeed it were best to be beneath the portals of this house, served by true love — here until the storm which will arise has spent itself.

CHRIST.   Get thee behind me, Satan! You have no thought for that which is of God, but only for that which is of Man. Should the Reaper be permitted to rest in the shadow while the ripe harvest beckons Him? The Son of Man came not unto this world that He might be served, but that He might serve and give His life as ransom for the many.

JUDAS.   But, Master, what would become of us if you should lose your life?

APOSTLES. Alas! All our hopes would then be ruined!

CHRIST.   Calm yourselves! I have the power to give up my life, and I have the power to bring it back again. This has the Father granted me.

MARY MAGDALENE *(comes and pours ointment upon the head of Christ).*   Rabbi.

CHRIST. Maria!

THOMAS.   What delicious odour!

BARTHOLOMEW.   That is costly — it is rare spikenard oil.

THADDEUS.   Such honour has never before fallen to our Master.

JUDAS.   To what purpose such wastefulness? One could better employ the gold it cost.

THOMAS. Thus it almost seems to me. *(Mary Magdalene kneels and anoints the feet of Christ.)*

CHRIST. What is it that you whisper — one to the other? Why do you censure what is done out of grateful love alone?

JUDAS. Thus to use such precious, such costly ointment! What prodigality!

CHRIST. Friend Judas! Look on me! Is it waste on me, your Master?

JUDAS. But I know you care not for such useless extravagance. One might have sold the ointment, and the poor could have profited thereby.

CHRIST. Judas, your hand upon your heart! Is it only compassion for the poor which moves you so?

JUDAS. At least three hundred pieces could have been got for it. A loss indeed to the poor — and to us!

CHRIST. The poor have you always with you, but me have you not always. She has done good work; let her be! For inasmuch as she has poured this oil upon my body, so has she in advance prepared me for my burial. Verily, verily, I say unto you: Wheresoever the Gospel is preached throughout the world, there also will the memory of what she has done be preserved. Let us rise. *(To Simon, after they have risen.)* Thank you, kind friend, for your entertainment. The Father will reward you.

SIMON. Say naught of thanks, Master. I am aware what I owe to you.

CHRIST. The time has come to depart from here. Farewell, inmates of this hospitable house! My Disciples, follow me!

PETER. Master, where you will, — only not unto Jerusalem!

CHRIST. I go whither my Father calls me. Peter, if it so please you to remain here, then remain!

PETER. My Lord and Master, where you stay, there will I stay also, and where you go, there also will I go.

CHRIST. Then come! *(They go.)*

FOURTH SCENE

CHRIST *(to Mary Magdalene and Martha.)* Stay, dearly beloved! Once more, farewell! Peaceful Bethany! Never again shall I tarry in thy restful vale.

SIMON.   Then, Master, will you, in truth, leave here forever?

MARY MAGDALENE.   Oh, I have forebodings of most terrible things. Friend of my soul! My heart, alas, my heart, I cannot let you go! *(Falls at the feet of Christ.)*

CHRIST.   Arise, Mary! The night approaches and the winds of winter are raging near. Still, be of good hope! In the early morn, in the Garden of Spring, you shall see me again!

LAZARUS.   My Friend! My Benefactor!

MARTHA.   Joy of my heart! My strength! Alas you go to return no more?

CHRIST.   Our Father wills it, dear one! Wherever I am, I will carry you always in my heart, and wheresoever you are, my blessing be upon you. Farewell! *(As He turns to go, Mary, the Mother, comes with her companions.)*

FIFTH SCENE

MARY.   Jesus, dear Son, with yearning have I and my friends hastened after you, to see you once more, ere you go, alas, from hence!

CHRIST.   Mother, I am on my way to Jerusalem.

MARY.   To Jerusalem! 'T is there, in the Temple of Jehovah, I once carried you in my arms to offer you unto the Lord.

CHRIST.   Mother! The hour has come when I shall offer myself, even as our Father has ordained. I am ready to fulfil that which the Father exacts of me.

MARY.   Alas! I have a fear of what the sacrifice will be!

MARY MAGDALENE.   O dearest Mother, how ardently we have wished to keep our beloved Master here with us!

SIMON.   But He is resolved!

CHRIST.   My hour has come.

ALL THE DISCIPLES.   Beseech the Father to absolve you.

58

ALL THE WOMEN.   He will as ever hearken unto you.

CHRIST.   My soul is indeed cast down. Yet what is it I should say: Father! save me from this hour? Was it not for this very hour I came into the world?

MARY.   Simon, Simon, you worthy old man, now will it come to pass — that which you once prophesied to me: "A sword shall pierce thy heart!"

CHRIST.   Mother! the Father's will has ever to you been held in sacredness.

MARY.   Even now is it so. I am a hand-maiden of the Lord. What He imposes upon me, that in patience will I bear. But one thing I beseech you, Son!

CHRIST.   What do you crave, my Mother?

MARY.   That I may go with you into the midst of your suffering, yea, even unto death!

JOHN.   What love!

CHRIST.   Mother! Indeed you will suffer with me, you will bleed with me in my death agony, but then you will rejoice with me in my victory. Therefore, take comfort!

MARY.   Ah, God, give me strength that my heart may not break!

THE HOLY WOMEN.   Mother of mothers, we weep for you!

MARY.   My Son, with you I go to Jerusalem.

THE WOMEN. Mother, we go with you!

CHRIST.   Later, you may unto the city; but now remain with our friends in Bethany. *(To Simon, Martha, etc.)* Unto you, trusted souls, I commend my Mother, together with these, her companions.

MARY MAGDALENE.   After you, there is no one dearer to us than your Mother.

LAZARUS.   If only you, Master, could remain!

CHRIST.   Comfort you one another! In two days you may proceed together on your way, so as to reach Jerusalem for the great Feast.

MARY.   As you will, my Son.

WOMEN. Alas! how sadly the hours will pass with you far off!

CHRIST. Mother, Mother! For all the tender love and care you have shown me these three and thirty years of my life, receive the thanks of your Son! The Father calls me. Farewell, best of Mothers!

MARY. My Son, where shall I see you again?

CHRIST. Yonder, beloved Mother, where the Scriptures shall be fulfilled: He was led as a Lamb to the sacrifice, and He opened not His mouth.

MARY. Jesus! Your Mother — alas! O God! — my Son —

WOMEN (hastening to Mary, the Mother, to support her). Oh, dearly belovéd Mother!

DISCIPLES. (departing). We cannot bear it. How will it end?

ALL. What great affliction threatens us?

CHRIST. Give not up in the first struggle! Have faith in me! (Goes).

LAZARUS, THE WOMEN (looking after Christ). Oh, our dear Teacher!

SIMON. Benefactor of my house! (To Mary.) Mother, come with me and deign to enter.

MARY MAGDALENE. One consolation there is, even in the midst of our trial.

MARTHA. How fortunate to have our Master's Mother with us!

LAZARUS (to the women)). You also, belovéd ones, come with us! We will share together our sorrow and our tears. (They go into the house.)

END OF ACT

ACT IV. REPRESENTATION

The Last Journey to Jerusalem

PROLOGUE.   People of God! Thy Saviour is near thee.
Behold!
He has come, He has come as the Prophets foretold!
Hearken His voice, and follow His leading,
Grace has He brought to thee, and Life — for thy sins
interceding!
Yet blind is the faith of Jerusalem, deaf is the land —
She will turn from the hope of Salvation, and thrust back
His hand!
And soon will the Saviour no longer give heed to her
call,
On the day of Jerusalem's fall!

Vashti in scorn the royal feast disdained,
The king in anger spurned her from his side —
Vashti in scorn complained,
The king turned from her to a nobler bride.

Thus will the Synagogue be in time forsaken!
Thus will God's Kingdom from the Synagogue be
taken!
To other righteous Nations that in fruitfulness have
thriven,
God's Kingdom will be given!

(Recit.).   Jerusalem, awake! Thy slumbers cease!
Awake, Jerusalem, while there is peace!
The hour of woe is coming as you wait,
Unhappy one, behold your fate —
Soon it will be too late!
Awake!

CHORUS.   Jerusalem, Jerusalem,
Behold thy Father's face!
Jerusalem, Jerusalem,
Let not hate replace
The touch of grace,

61

Lest, unhappy one, some day
The Lord of Hosts from thee should turn away!

TABLEAU: *King Ahasuerus casts Vashti from him and exalts Esther.*
Esther 1 - 2. Queen Vashti, the proud, symbolizes Jerusalem and
Judaism, while Esther typifies Christianity. As Vashti is dis-
carded by the king, even so is Christ rejected by the Jews.

PROLOGUE *(Recit.).*   Behold, of Vashti's fate we tell!
Such fate the Synagogue befell!
"Away, proud woman, from my throne—
Unworthy one, I thee disown!"

Thus spake Ahasuerus in his ire:
"Come, Esther, to my side,
Through life abide
As Queen unto thy sire."

"The time of grace has passed—
Away," saith the Lord, "I cast
From me the faithless, and unto me I bring—
Even as Esther came unto the King—
A better people in their faith supernal,
To whom my love will be eternal!"

CHORUS.   Jerusalem, Jerusalem!
Ye sinners, unto God give heed!
The leaven of your sins replace
By opening your heart to grace —
That is your greatest need!
Jerusalem, give heed!

ACTION

Christ goes with His Disciples toward the city of Jerusalem, is
sorely grieved at the signs of sin, and sends before Him two
of His Disciples to make ready the Paschal Lamb. Judas con-
ceives the idea of betraying his Master.

FIRST SCENE

Christ and the Twelve on their Way toward Jerusalem

JOHN. Master, look yonder, what a glorious view toward Jerusalem!

MATTHEW. And the majestic Temple — what a noble pile!

CHRIST. Jerusalem, Jerusalem! Oh that thou couldst but know even now in thy day what were best for thy peace! But it is hidden from thine eyes. *(Weeps.)*

PETER. Master, why do you grieve so sorely?

CHRIST. My Peter! The fate of this unfortunate city hurts me to the heart!

JOHN. Lord, tell us what that fate will be.

CHRIST. The day shall come when the enemy will undermine her walls, and close her in, spreading alarm on all sides. She and her children will be dashed to pieces, and there shall not be left one stone upon another.

ANDREW. Why such a sad fate for this city?

CHRIST. Because she hath not known the time of her visitation. Alas! The murderer of the Prophets will even kill the Messiah Himself.

ALL. What a horrible deed!

JAMES THE ELDER. God forbid that the Holy City should bring upon herself such a curse!

JOHN. Belovéd Master, for the sake of the Holy City and of the Temple of Jehovah, I beg of you to go not thither. Let there be no occasion for the evildoers to perpetrate their deed.

PETER. Or go forward, Master, and reveal yourself to them in all your excellence, so that the good may rejoice and the wicked tremble.

ALL. Yes, do so!

PHILIP. Strike down your enemies!

ALL. And establish the Kingdom of God among men!

CHRIST. My children, what you desire shall come to pass in time. But my ways have been ordained by my Father — for so saith the Lord: My thoughts are not your thoughts, and your ways are not my ways. Peter!

PETER. What would you, Master?

CHRIST. It is now the first day of the Unleavened Bread, a day on which the Law exacts that the paschal meal be kept. Both you and John proceed ahead of us and make ready the Paschal Lamb, that we may eat of it at the evening hour.

PETER AND JOHN. How, Master, would you have us do this?

CHRIST. When you come unto the city, you will meet a man carrying a pitcher of water. Go with this one unto his house, and say unto the head therein: Our Master would know of you: Where is the room in which I with my Disciples may partake of the Passover? He will show you a guestchamber, made ready for our coming: there set forth the meal.

PETER. Your blessing, Master. *(Both John and Peter kneel.)*

CHRIST. God's blessing be with you both. *(The two Apostles go.)*

SECOND SCENE

CHRIST. You who remain, come with me for the last time to the House of my Fathers! To-day, thither will you go with me, but to-morrow—

JUDAS. Yet, Master, if you are really to leave us, at least grant us some assurance of our future maintenance. See *(pointing to a purse)*, this cannot suffice much longer.

CHRIST. Judas, be not more anxious than is needful!

JUDAS. The value of yon wasted oil — how much better if the money lay herein *(holding up the purse)*. Three hundred denare! what days we could have lived upon it without want or care!

CHRIST. Till now you have wanted for naught, and, believe me, you at no time in the future will be in need.

JUDAS. Still, Master, when you are no longer amongst us, then will our good friends draw back, and—

CHRIST. Friend Judas! See to it that the Tempter does not overtake you!

THE OTHER DISCIPLES. Judas! Trouble not the Master so.

JUDAS. Who would have thought of this, if I did not trouble?

Am I not appointed by the Master as keeper of the purse?

CHRIST.   Verily you are, but I fear—

JUDAS.   I also fear that it will soon be empty — and that empty it will remain.

CHRIST.   Judas! Forget not my warning! Now let us proceed onward! I desire to be in my Father's House. *(He leaves with all of His Disciples, save Judas, who remains behind.)*

THIRD SCENE

JUDAS *(alone).*   Shall I follow Him further? I am of little mind to do so. The Master's way is unaccountable to me. His wonderful works gave us hope that He would restore the Kingdom of Israel, but He does not seize the opportunities which offer themselves, and now indeed He speaks repeatedly of separation from us, and of death, consoling us feebly with mysterious words about a future too dim, too far away. I am tired of waiting, of hoping. With Him, I well can see there is naught in view but this continued poverty and lowliness. Life shall drag along, and instead of sharing in His glorious Kingdom, we shall be persecuted, and with Him thrown into prison. I will withdraw. Fortunately, I have always been prudent and cautious, and now and then have laid aside from the purse a trifle in case of necessity. How useful at this moment would be the three hundred pieces that heedless woman wasted as an empty mark of esteem. If the company breaks up, as it seems to me it will, then would I have had three hundred denare in my hands — which would have served me a long while! But as it is, I have to consider the problem where and how I may find a livelihood. *(Remains standing in reflection.)*

FOURTH SCENE

Judas. The Trader Dathan

DATHAN *(Entering).*   Ha, Judas! The time is favourable, he is alone! He appears to be in deep perplexity. I must exert every means to win him over to our cause. Friend Judas!

JUDAS.   Who calls?

DATHAN.   A friend. Has some sad happening befallen you? You are so deep in thought.

JUDAS. Who are you?

DATHAN. Your friend, your brother.

JUDAS. My brother, my friend? You?

DATHAN. At least, I wish so to become. How is it with the Master? I, too, would like to be of His company.

JUDAS. You? . . . His company?

DATHAN. Have you then truly forsaken Him? Are things so unwell with Him? Tell me, so I may act accordingly.

JUDAS. If you could be silent, I might tell you . . .

DATHAN. Assuredly I can, friend Judas.

JUDAS. Then things are no longer well with Him. He Himself confesses that His last hour has come. I shall leave Him, for He will yet bring us all to ruin. I am Treasurer — see here how it stands with us!

DATHAN. Friend, then I remain as I am.

FIFTH SCENE

Dathan's companions steal hither.

JUDAS. Who are these? I will not speak further.

KORE. Remain, friend. You will have no cause to regret it.

JUDAS. Why have you come here?

KORE. We would return to Jerusalem, and if it so please you, will keep you company.

JUDAS. Probably you also would follow the Master?

ABIRON. Has He gone to Jerusalem?

JUDAS. For the last time, so He says.

RABBI. For the last time? Will He then never again leave Judæa?

ABIRON. Where in Jerusalem does He abide at night?

JUDAS *(suspiciously)*. Why do you ask so eagerly? Would you become His followers?

TRADERS. Why not, if the prospects be good?

JUDAS. I see naught of the brilliant prospects.

DATHAN. Explain, Judas — what do you mean by what you said a short while ago — that He would bring you all to ruin?

JUDAS. He always says to us: Be not anxious for the morrow. But if perchance aught should happen to Him to-day or to-morrow, we should all be destitute. Is it thus a Master cares for His own?

ABIRON. Under such circumstances the outlook is truly a sorry one.

JUDAS. Moreover, only to-day He allowed the most absurd waste, committed by a silly woman in His honour; and when I disapproved of it, I encountered reproachful glances and reproachful words.

DATHAN. And yet you still can be on friendly terms with Him?

BOOZ. Will you remain with Him any longer?

DATHAN. Friend, you should look after your own future. It is about time.

JUDAS. I am thinking of that — but where to find immediately a good living — that is the difficulty!

DATHAN. There you have not far to seek. The best of opportunities offers itself.

JUDAS. Where? How?

EPHRAIM. Have you heard naught of the High Council's proclamation?

JUDAS. About what?

EPHRAIM. Never again in your lifetime will you meet with such an excellent chance to make your fortune.

JUDAS. Tell me what proclamation?

DATHAN. Whosoever reveals the nightly haunt of Jesus of Nazareth shall be granted a considerable reward.

KORE. Mark you! — a considerable reward!

JUDAS. A reward!

EPHRAIM.   Who better than you could earn it so easily?

DATHAN *(aside).*   We are nearing the goal.

ABIRON.   Brother, do not trifle with your fortune!

JUDAS.   Indeed, a rare opportunity — shall I let it slip me?

DATHAN.   Bethink you further: the reward is not all. The High Council will in addition look after you. Who knows what may yet be in store for you as a result of this?

KORE.   Speak, friend!

TRADERS.   Give us your hand upon it.

JUDAS.   Well, so be it!

DATHAN.   Come, Judas, we will lead you forthwith to the High Council.

JUDAS.   Nay, for the present, I must after the Master. First of all, let me reconnoitre, so as to be on the safe side.

DATHAN.   In the meanwhile we will go to the High Council and announce your intent. But when and where shall we meet again?

JUDAS.   Three hours hence, you will find me in the street of the Temple.

DATHAN.   Brother, your word!

JUDAS.   My word of honour. *(The Traders go.)*

SIXTH SCENE

JUDAS *(alone).*The word is given — I will not regret it. Shall I forsooth avoid the good fortune at my very hand? Would I not be foolish to let such a pretty little sum escape me, when I can earn it with no trouble? My fortune is made! It cannot fail. I will do what I promised, but let me be paid in advance. Then, if the Priests succeed in imprisoning Him, if all is indeed at an end with Him, my own prospects are assured, and, moreover, I shall have acquired fame throughout Judæa as the one who did most to save the Law of Moses, and thus further praise and recompense will be given me. But should the Master triumph instead — then I will throw myself repentant at His feet! Surely He is good; never have I seen Him drive away a contrite being. He will take me unto Himself again, and I may even claim for myself the credit of having brought about the outcome. No, I will not entirely cut myself aloof, or pull down the bridges behind me — for I would return if I cannot go forward. Judas, you are a prudent man! But now I fear to meet the Master, for His searching look will be hard to stand, and my comrades will see by my expression that I fear, that I am a — No! I am not, I will not be a traitor! Then, what is it I am doing but notify these Jews where the Master is to be found? Yet that is not betrayal; a traitor's work requires more. Away with these crotchets! Courage, Judas, your future welfare depends upon yourself! *(He goes.)*

SEVENTH SCENE

A City Lane. Baruch. Immediately afterwards, Peter and John. Then Mark.

BARUCH *(proceeds with a water-jug to the well)*. My! but this day is a busy one. Work is not scarce this Passover. To judge by the crowds of pilgrims, it cannot be otherwise. My master must expect many guests, for he bustles about the house continually. *(Draws water.)*.

JOHN. *(coming on with Peter from the opposite side of the stage)*. See, here is someone at the well!

BARUCH *(still drawing water)*. There must be something of moment this Passover, for the Priests of the High Council go hither and thither. *(Turns with the jug towards his house.)*.

PETER. This must be he. He carries a water-jug which the Master bade us take as a sign.

BARUCH *(at the door of his house and turning around)*. What would you, friends? Be you welcome!

JOHN. We would speak with your master.

BARUCH. Perhaps you come to keep the Passover with us?

PETER. Yea, our Master bade us make this request of your master.

BARUCH. Come with me! For it will please my master to receive you in his house. Look, there he is himself. *(Mark enters.)*. Behold, master, I bring guests.

MARK. Welcome, Strangers! In what way may I serve you?

PETER.   Our Master bade us say to you: My time is near. Where is the room, that I may partake of the Paschal Lamb — I with my Disciples? With you will we keep this Passover.

MARK.   Oh the happiness! Now do I recognise you — the followers of the Worker of Miracles who restored my sight to me! How have I deserved that, among all houses in Jerusalem, He should choose mine in which to partake of the Holy Meal! How is it I am so fortunate? Indeed blessed is this house which He honours with His presence! Come, dear friends, I will immediately show you the guestchamber.

PETER AND JOHN.   Good man, we follow you.

END OF ACT

ACT V. REPRESENTATION

The Lord's Supper

PROLOGUE.   Before the Friend of Heaven above
　　　　Unto his Passion goes —
He turns unto the call of love,
Nor Death can haste the fall of love,
His sacrament the all of love—
　　　　The earthly pilgrim knows.

The sacrificial meal He takes,
　　　　Forever and a day!
Behold, this is a sign He makes;
'T is Life from bread and wine He makes;
And Life from Death divine He makes;
　　　　Nor Love shall pass away!

He came to them in desert wide—
　　　　To ancient Israel!
With manna them He satisfied,
With Canaan's grapes them gratified—
Thus did the Lord beatified—
　　　　And all to them seemed well.

But now in blood and body trace
　　　　A mystery, a sign!

70

'T is Christ who came to save the race,
Whose spirit in the change took place,
Who works through sacrament His grace-
Our Saviour, Christ Divine!

SOLO *(Recit.)* The hour is nigh
When He shall die-
The Prophets thus did prophesy!
The truth was told
To them of old-
And now the awful truth behold!

"The ancient race
I will efface,
Their offering shall now give place,
For lo! in them—
And woe! in them—
No better love will grow in them!

"I consecrate,
I dedicate
Unto myself a Son's estate!"
The Lord thus spake—
"I now forsake
The old — and this new Symbol make,
Of which the whole Earth will partake!"

TABLEAU: *The Lord gives manna unto the people. 2 Mos. (Exodus) 16 : 31. The manna is the symbol of the holiest of altar sacraments. As God gave aid unto the Israelites in their irksome course through the wilderness, so Jesus with His holy love aids the Christians through the wilderness of this life.*

The mystery in the wilderness of sin
Is measure of the spirit here within,
The Covenant which Christ at His Last Supper did begin.

TABLEAU: *The bunch of grapes from Canaan. 4 Mos. (Numbers) 13 : 23. The same as in the foregoing picture – a beautiful allegory of the bread and wine of the new Covenant.*

The Lord is good! The Lord is wise!
The Lord His people satisfies!

The Lord is good,
For this new food
He brings to us in wondrous wise.

Oh, death has swept the wilderness!
To Israel food was comfortless,
Nor filled the wand'rers in their grief!
But see the holy bread we break;
If we in humbleness partake,
'T will bring our souls relief!

The Lord is good! The Lord is kind!
The Israelites He bore in mind!
And brought the fruit of wine to them,
And brought from Canaan's vine to them!

But all the fair fruit of the field
Can naught but to the body yield;
    The soil instilled it so!
Yet this new Covenant begun,
Shall be the blood of God's own Son;
    The Lord has willed it so!

The Lord is good! The Lord is just!
He gives the wine and breaks the crust,
As pledge of Life beyond the dust;
And flesh and blood is in its place,
And Salem's hall is warm with grace!

ACTION

*Christ with His Disciples partakes of the last Passover, and establishes
the New Covenant to His memory.*

FIRST SCENE

The Guest-chamber. Christ and the Twelve, standing at the Table

CHRIST.   Most anxiously have I longed to take this Passover
meal with you ere I suffered. For I say unto you: Henceforth I will
no longer eat therof, until all be fulfilled in the Kingdom of God.
Father! I thank Thee for this potion of the vine. *(Drinks, and passes
the cup to His Disciples.)* Take this, and divide it among yourselves,

for I say unto you: Henceforth will I no longer partake of the fruit of the vine until the Kingdom of God shall be.

THE APOSTLES. Ah, Master, is this then the last Passover?

CHRIST. A potion I will drink with you in the Kingdom of God the Father; as it is written: From the stream of happiness will you make them drink.

PETER. Master, when this Kingdom comes, how will our positions be meted out to us?

JAMES THE ELDER. Who will have precedence among us?

THOMAS. Will each one of us, perchance, be granted the lordship of a separate land?

BARTHOLOMEW. That would be much the best way; for then no dispute would arise among us.

CHRIST. Thus long have I been with you, and still you are most concerned in earthly matters. Verily, for you, who have with me borne my trials and temptation, I assure the Kingdom which my Father has made ready for me; that therein you may eat and drink at my table, and, seated upon thrones, judge the twelve tribes of Israel. But mark: the kings of the people rule over them as dictators, and the dictator it is whom they call benefactor. But thus shall it not be with you. For the greatest among you, let him be the least, and the master be as your servant! For who is greater, he who sits at the table or he who serves? What say you, my Disciples? I am in the midst of you as one who serves. *(He lays aside His upper garment, girds Himself around with a white linen towel, and pours water in a basin.)* Now, be seated, beloved Disciples.

THE APOSTLES. What will He do now?

CHRIST. Peter, reach me forth your foot!

PETER. Lord, would you wash my feet?

CHRIST. What I do, you may not now understand, but afterwards will it all be plain to you.

PETER. Master! Never will I let you wash my feet!

CHRIST. If I do not wash you, then will you have no share with me.

PETER. Master, if such be the case, not only my feet, but also my hands, my head!

73

CHRIST. He who is washed already, need but bathe his feet, for he is quite clean. *(Washes the feet of each Disciple; afterwards He replaces His outer garment, and, standing in their midst, looks around.)* Ye are now clean, but not all. *(Seats Himself.)* Know you what I have done unto you? You call me Master and Lord, and you say well, for so I am. If now, I, your Master, have washed your feet, so should you also do likewise unto each other. For I have given unto you an example, that you may so do as I have done. Verily, verily, the servant is not greater than He who sent him. If you know these things, blessèd are you if you do them. *(Rising again.)* Children, not much longer shall I be amongst you. But that my memory may never die, I shall leave behind me an everlasting symbol of my eternal presence. The Old Covenant between my Father and Abraham, Isaac, and Jacob is at an end. And I say unto you: A New Covenant now begins, which I consecrate with mine own blood, as God the Father commanded of me. And this shall endure until all is fulfilled. *(He takes the bread, blesses and breaks it.)* Take and eat! This is my body, which will be sacrificed for you. *(Gives each Disciple a small piece.)* This do in remembrance of me! *(Lifts the chalice of wine and blesses it.)* Take this and drink therefrom, for it is the cup of the New Testament in my blood which is shed for you and others — shed for the forgiveness of sin. *(Hands the cup to each one.)* So often as ye do this, do it in remembrance of me. *(Seats Himself.)*

JOHN. Best of Teachers, never will I forget your love. You know that I love you. *(Bows his head upon the breast of Christ.)*

THE APOSTLES *(with the exception of Judas)*. O Thou who art so full of love, eternally will we be bound to Thee.

PETER. This holy meal of the New Testament shall be perpetuated forever in conformity with Thy will.

MATTHEW. And so often as we celebrate it, will we think on Thee!

ALL. Belovèd Teacher! O Divine One! O best of friends!

CHRIST. My children, abide in me, and I will abide in you. Even as the Father has loved me, so have I loved you. Remain in my love! But, — alas! must I say it? The hand of my betrayer is here with me at this table.

DISCIPLES *(severally)*. How, a betrayer amongst us?

PETER. Is it possible?

CHRIST.   Verily, verily, I say unto you: One among you shall betray me.

ANDREW.   Master, one of us twelve?

CHRIST.   Yea, one of the twelve! — one who has dipped his hand into this very dish with me, shall betray me. The Scriptures will be fulfilled: Whoso eats bread with me, his foot against me shall be raised.

THOMAS AND SIMON.   Who can this faithless creature be?

MATTHEW.   Master, you can look into all hearts. You know it is not I.

THE TWO JAMESES.   Declare him openly, the infamous traitor!

JUDAS.   Master, is it I?

THADDEUS.   Rather my life than such a step!

BARTHOLOMEW.   Rather would I sink into the earth for shame!

CHRIST *(to Judas)*.   Thou hast said it. *(To all.)* The Son of Man now goeth as it is prophesied; but woe unto him through whom the Son of Man is betrayed! Better for him had he never been born!

PETER *(leaning toward John.)* Of whom does He speak?

JOHN *(leaning toward Christ)*. Master, who is it?

CHRIST *(to John)*. It is he to whom I give the bread that I have soaked.

MANY APOSTLES.   Who might that be?

CHRIST.   *(after He has passed the bread to Judas)*. What you do, do quickly! *(Judas hastens from the room.)*

THOMAS *(to Simon)*.   Why does Judas leave so suddenly?

SIMON.   Probably the Master has sent him to buy something.

THADDEUS.   Or to distribute alms among the poor.

SECOND SCENE

CHRIST.   Now will the Son of Man be glorified, and through

Him, God the Father also. If God through Him is glorified, then will God glorify Him in Himself. Little children of mine! But yet awhile am I among you. You would seek me, but, as I have said unto the Jews: Whither I go, there can you not come. Thus say I now unto you.

PETER. Master, whither do you go?

CHRIST. Whither I go, there can you not now follow me; but later shall you come.

PETER. Why not now? For you would I fain give my life!

CHRIST. Would you give up your life for me? Simon, Simon, Satan would claim you, that he might sift you as wheat is sifted. But I have interceded, that your faith may not fail you. And when you are saved, then strengthen your brothers. This night will you all be offended by me, for it already stands written: I will smite the Shepherd, and the sheep of His flock will be scattered.

PETER. Even though others be offended, I will not. Lord, I am ready to go with you to prison, — yea, even unto death!

CHRIST. Verily, verily, I say unto you: Peter! to-day, even this night before the cock crows twice, will you three times deny me.

PETER. Though I should die with you, yet would I never deny you!

ALL. Master, everlastingly will we remain true unto you. None amongst us shall betray you.

CHRIST. When I sent you forth without purse or pouch or shoes, were you lacking aught?

ALL. No, nothing!

CHRIST. But now take each one his own purse, and likewise his pouch. And whosoever has no sword, let him sell his coat and buy one. For there begins a time of trial, and I say unto you: In me must be fulfilled that which stands written: He was reckoned among the transgressors.

PETER AND PHILIP. Behold, Lord, here are two swords!

CHRIST. Enough! Let us arise and pronounce thanksgiving. *(With His Disciples.)* Praise the Lord, all you people! Praise Him, all the Nations of the earth! for His compassion is established over us. The truth of the Lord is everlasting. *(Goes to the foreground, and remains standing for a while with His face raised towards heaven. The Apostles stand on either side, with troubled look upon Him.)* My children, why are you so sad, and why look upon me thus grieved? Trouble not your hearts. You believe in God; believe also in me. In my Father's house are many mansions, and I go even now to make ready a place for you; then I will come again, and take you unto myself, that you also may be where I am. I leave you not as orphans. I leave with you peace; yea, mine own peace do I give unto you, but not as the world bestows it. Keep this my commandment: That you love one another, as I have loved you! Thereby shall all know you as my Disciples. Hereafter will I not hold much speech with you. For the Prince of the World cometh, although he hath naught to seek in me. But that the world may know I love the Father, thus will I do even as the Father has commanded me. Let us depart from this place. *(They go.)*

END OF ACT

ACT VI. REPRESENTATION

The Betrayer

PROLOGUE.   His foes have bereft Him!
　　　　　　False friend, thou hast left Him—
　　　For silver thou turnest away to thy ruth!
　　　　　　Thy conscience will cloy thee,
　　　　　　Thy error destroy thee,
　　　The heart of a fool never holds to the truth.

　　　　　　Ungrateful you leave Him,
　　　　　　In shame you deceive Him,
　　　You traffic in souls for your profit and gain!
　　　　　　For silver betray Him,
　　　　　　For silver you slay Him,
　　　A traitor's reward is your price for His pain!

　　　　　　'T was thus that a brother
　　　　　　Was sold to another—
　　　His value was weighed in the scales of the mart!
　　　　　　No love could withhold them,
　　　　　　No mercy enfold them,
　　　These wild sons of Jacob were hardened in heart!

Let silver but bind you,
Let gold ever blind you!
Then honour and love and man's word have an end!
The idol will claim you—
Nor conscience will shame you—
For silver or gold you would barter your friend!

SOLO.   Oh, Judas, art thou blinded quite?
Is gold so loving to thy sight
That thou wouldst sell thy Master so,
Without a shudder let Him go?
Thy doom is laid upon thy head.
Already has the Master said:
"Amongst you one shall me betray."
Thus spake He thrice. And yet, oh, stay,
Is there no fervour in thy trust?
Art thou so deeply dyed in lust?

CHORUS.   Ah, Judas, Judas, do not sin;
Bethink the crime thou wouldst be in!
Yet no! By greed turned deaf and blind,
He goes to serve the Council's mind!
The self-same evil is their plan,
Which once took place in far Dathan!

TABLEAU: *For twenty pieces of silver the sons of Jacob sell their brother Joseph. Gen. 37 : 28. This scene typifies the treachery of Judas, who unto the Pharisees delivers his Master for thirty pieces of silver.*

SOLO.   "What am I bid," the brothers cry,
"For this fair boy you seek to buy?"
The life and blood of Jacob's son
They fain would sell to anyone—
And now for twenty silver pence,
They would for that commit offence.
"What will you give? — and how reward—
If I to you betray the Lord?"
Iscariot spake, and then agreed
To serve the Council's bloody need—
They gave him silver for the deed!

CHORUS.   Behold, this picture to our eyes,
Reminds us we are worldly wise,

78

And often sell our friends like this—
Betraying with a traitor's kiss!
Ye curse the sale of Jacob's son,
And him who sold the holy One,
And yet for envy, hate, and greed,
Destroy the peace and joy you need!

ACTION

Judas comes before the Sanhedrin, and promises for thirty pieces of silver to hand over his Master to the Pharisees: these latter determine on the death of Jesus.

FIRST SCENE

The High Council

CAIAPHAS. Welcome tidings, assembled Fathers, have I to impart unto you. The would-be Prophet out of Galilee, I hope, will soon be in our hands. Dathan, the zealous Israelite has won over to our cause a most trusted companion of the Galilean, who has consented to serve as guide for our night attack. Both of them are already here, and only await the summons of this august assembly.

MANY VOICES. Some one call them in.

JOSUE. I will do so.

CAIAPHAS. Yes, call them. *(Exit Josue.)* And now I would learn your will, holy Brothers, as to the price which shall be given for the deed.

NATHANEAL. The Law of Moses instructs us thereon: a slave shall be valued at thirty pieces of silver.

PRIESTS. Yes, yes, such a slave's price is the false Messiah worth!

SECOND SCENE

Dathan and Judas come before the High Council

DATHAN. Most learned Council! Herewith my errand is complete, for I present to you, Fathers, a man who, in return for a suitable reward, is willing to deliver our enemy which we have in common into your authority. He is an intimate associate of yon Galilean, and knows His ways and His secret haunts.

CAIAPHAS *(to Judas)*. Know you the man whom the High Council seeks?

JUDAS. For a long while I have been of His company; yea, I know Him and also where He is wont to stop.

CAIAPHAS. What is your name?

JUDAS. I am called Judas, and am one of the Twelve.

PRIESTS. Truly, we have seen you often with Him!

CAIAPHAS. Are you now fully determined to aid us in conformity with our will?

JUDAS. I give you my word thereon.

CAIAPHAS. Will you not repent of it? What has moved you to this step?

JUDAS. The friendship between Him and me has been cooling for some time, and now have I quite broken with Him.

CAIAPHAS. What has caused you to take this step?

JUDAS. There is naught more to be had from Him, and upon the whole I am resolved to conform to lawful authority, which is assuredly the best. What will you give me if I deliver Him over to you?

CAIAPHAS. Thirty pieces of silver shall be yours, and that immediately.

DATHAN. Hear, Judas, thirty pieces of silver! What profit!

NATHANAEL. And mark, Judas, that is not all. If you accomplish your work well, then further consideration will be made you!

EZEKIEL. You may become a rich and distinguished man.

JUDAS. I am satisfied. *(To himself.)* Now, indeed, rises my true star of hope.

CAIAPHAS. Rabbi, bring the thirty pieces of silver from the Treasury, and, in the presence of the entire Council, pay them over. Is this your will?

PRIESTS. Indeed it is! *(Rabbi departs.)*

NICODEMUS. How can you conclude such a wicked bargain? *(To Judas.)* And you, base wretch, do you not blush to sell your Lord and Master, you godless, perfidious creature whom the earth shall swallow up? For thirty pieces of silver you would betray your most loving Friend and Benefactor? Stay, ere it is too late! this blood money will cry unto Heaven for vengeance, and will burn into your avaricious soul some day like hot iron! *(Judas stands trembling and undone.)*

JOSUE. Be not annoyed, Judas, by the speech of this zealot. Let him be a disciple of this false Prophet. But you do your duty as a follower of Moses, and at the same time you serve the lawful authorities.

RABBI *(arrives with silver).* Come, Judas, take the thirty pieces of silver and play the man! *(Counts out the money to him, ringing each piece upon the table, so that it sounds lustily; Judas pockets the coins greedily.)*

JUDAS. My word upon it, you may depend on me.

SARAS. Before the Feast the work must be done.

JUDAS. At this moment the most perfect opportunity offers itself. He shall be in your hands to-night! Give me an armed guard so that He may be well surrounded, so that every way of flight may be shut from Him.

ANNAS. Let us send the Temple watch.

EZEKIEL. Yes, yes, order them to go forthwith!

CAIAPHAS. It would seem also advisable to dispatch some members of the holy Sanhedrin.

ALL. We are all ready.

EZEKIEL. The High Priest must choose.

CAIAPHAS. Be that the case, then I select Nathan, Josaphat, Salomon, and Ptolemäus. *(The four stand up.)*

THE PRIESTS. We are ready.

CAIAPHAS. But, Judas, how will the Master be recognized in the dark?

JUDAS. The soldiers shall come with torch and lanterns, and besides, I will give them a sign.

PRIESTS. Excellent! Excellent!

JUDAS. Now, I must hasten ahead and spy upon everything, then return for the armed force.

DATHAN. I will accompany you, Judas, and never leave your side until the work is done.

JUDAS. At the Gate of Bethphage I shall await your men. *(Judas goes with Dathan and the four delegates.)*

THIRD SCENE

The High Council

CAIAPHAS. All moves excellently well, worthy Fathers. But now it were best for us to consider the leading question: What shall we do with this Man, once He is delivered into our hands?

SADOK. Let Him be thrown into the deepest, the darkest dungeon, and kept there, loaded down with chains and well guarded! There, let Him go through a living death!

CAIAPHAS. Who among you can guarantee that His friends would not provoke a riot and set Him free, or that the guard might not be bribed? By means of His atrocious magic, could He not break through His chains? *(The Priests are silent.)* I see clearly you neither know nor understand. Hear then the High Priest. It is better that one man die than that a whole nation go to ruin. He must die! Until He dies there is no peace in Israel, no safety for the Law of Moses, no hour of rest for us!

RABBI. God hath spoken through His High Priest! Only by the death of Jesus of Nazareth can the people of Israel be delivered!

NATHANAEL. For a long while have the same words been upon my lips. And now have they been spoken. Let Him die, this enemy of our Fathers!

PRIESTS *(excitedly)*. Yes, He must die! In His death is our salvation!

ANNAS. By these grey hairs of mine, I swear: I will not rest until our insult is wiped out in the blood of this Seducer.

NICODEMUS. May I be allowed a word, O Fathers?

ALL. Yes, speak, speak!

NICODEMUS. Thus far has the judgement upon this Man been spoken without a hearing, an examination, or a gathering of witnesses. Is this a proceeding worthy of the priests of the people of God?

NATHANAEL. What! dare you accuse the Council of injustice?

SADOK. Know you the holy Law? Compare—

NICODEMUS. I know the Law; and therefore do I also know: Before all testimony is examined, the judge is not allowed to render judgement.

JOSUE. What need is there now for further witnesses? We ourselves have heard His speech and have noted His acts whereby He has outraged the Law.

NICODEMUS. You are all accusers, witnesses, and judges in one. I have listened to His sublime teaching and have seen Him perform His miraculous deeds; they deserve belief and admiration, not contempt and punishment.

CAIAPHAS. What! this scoundrel, Jesus of Nazareth, deserves admiration? Admiration? You believe in the Law of Moses, and yet will justify what the Law condemns? Ha, Fathers, up, the Law demands vengeance!

PRIESTS. Out from our midst if you persist in such speech!

JOSEPH OF ARIMATHÆA. I agree with Nicodemus. Naught has been proven against Jesus which makes Him deserving of death. He has done nothing but good.

CAIAPHAS. You also? Is it not everywhere known how He desecrated the Sabbath, and misled the people by His false speech? In His deception has He not performed His so-called wonders through Beelzebub? Has He not set Himself up as a God, He who is merely a man?

THE PRIESTS. Do you hear that?

JOSEPH OF ARIMATHÆA. Yea, envy and malice have wrongly construed His words and attributed base motives to His worthiest deeds. That He is from God, His godlike acts bear witness.

NATHANAEL. Ha! we know you! For a long time you have been a secret follower of this Galilean! Now you have fully unmasked yourself.

ANNAS.   So, even in our very midst have we traitors to the holy Law — even thus far has the Deceiver cast His net!

CAIAPHAS.   What do you here, you Apostates? Return to your Prophet, hasten after Him, ere His hour strikes when He shall die! That is irrevocably said!

PRIESTS.   Yes, He must die! Such is our decree!

NICODEMUS.   I deplore this resolve; no part whatsoever will I have in this infamous proceeding.

JOSEPH OF ARIMATHÆA.   Likewise will I forswear the place where the innocent are murdered. I swear to God: My soul is clean! *(Exit Nicodemus and Joseph.)*

FOURTH SCENE

The High Council

JOSUE.   At last we are rid of these traitors. Now may we speak freely among ourselves.

CAIAPHAS.   Brothers, it will certainly be necessary for us to sit in formal judgement on this Man; yea, and to examine Him, else the people may believe we persecuted Him out of hate and malice.

JACOB.   The Law requires at least two witnesses.

SAMUEL.   We shall not be lacking as to witnesses; I myself shall take care of that.

DARIABAS.   Our sentence stands as at first determined, but in order to satisfy the timid we must observe the legal forms.

EZEKIEL.   Should these not be sufficient, then must our force of mind and will supply the rest.

RABBI.   What matter if He be guilty, more or less? The public weal demands once and for all that He be removed.

CAIAPHAS.   Moreover, in the fulfilment, it would be far safer if we could bring it about that the Governor of the Province condemn Him to death — then would all responsibility, all blame, be removed from us.

NATHANAEL.   This we might try. And if it does not succeed,

84

there is always left us to have our sentence carried out by our representatives during the excitement of a riot! This could we do, without being openly concerned in the matter.

RABBI.   And in the case of dire failure on our part, we assuredly could find some hand which, in the silence of the dungeon-keep, would rid the Sanhedrin of its enemy.

CAIAPHAS.   Time will show us. And now, let us adjourn. But be ready at any hour of the night. I may have to call you, for there is no time to lose. Our resolve is: He dies!

ALL *(vehemently)*.   He dies, He dies — this enemy of our holy Law!

END OF ACT

ACT VII. REPRESENTATION

Christ on the Mount of Olives

PROLOGUE.   The weight of sin rests on the Saviour now,
    As once on Adam fell the bitter strife-
    His strength exhausted, sweat upon his brow—
    Who fought to expiate his guilt in life.

    The Saviour's head is bowed, His face is white,
    With bloody drops of silent anguish found;
    There, on Gethsemane He fights His fight,
    Heartweary in a sea of sadness bound.

    But hark, the leader of the band draws near—
    Iscariot, the faithless, the untrue—
    In shameless profanation and with sneer,
    Intent upon the work he has to do!

    'T was thus that Joab with unfeighnéd guile,
    Amasa's hand held fast in friendly part,
    And kissed him on the lips with cunning smile,
    And pressed the dagger's blade into his heart!

SOLO.   Lo, Judas took the bit of broken bread,
    Which, at the Sacrament, the Master blessed!
    All doubts within him on the moment fled,
    And thoughts of Satan welled within his breast!

Then spake the Lord, "Oh, Judas, wicked one!
What thou wouldst do, let it be quickly done."
Then Judas turned, and hastened from the room,
And pledged himself unto the Saviour's doom!

The deed accomplished and the aim achieved!
What terror in the thought, the word dismayed!
The Christ by Judas pledged to be deceived!
The Christ by Judas kissed and thus betrayed!

CHORUS.   Now come, ye people, and with Jesus go,
To see Him suffer on the cross, and die!
The night descends, yet in the evening glow,
The sign of hope draws nigh!

TABLEAU: *Adam in bitterness must eat his bread. Gen. 3 : 17. Like
Adam, who for his sin toiled in sweat for his punishment, so Christ
shall on the Mount of Olives be drenched in the cold sweat of
agony, and expiate the sins of Mankind.*

SOLO.   Consuming heat and bitter dread,
In weight descent on Adam's head—
The sweat of anguish and disgrace,
Like drops of blood upon his face!

CHORUS.   Behold, the fruit of sin is there,
God's curse on Nature made aware!
For racking pain and toilsome gain
But little fruit can Nature spare!

SOLO.   Thus our Saviour, sorely yearning,
Bitter anguish in Him burning,
Adam's sin upon Him weighing,
On Gethsemane is praying!

CHORUS.   'Gainst sin He struggles for the world,
'Gainst sin His strength the Lord has hurled—
He quivers, trembles, yet is brave,
And drinks the sorrow of the grave!

TABLEAU: *Joab, pretending to give a friendly kiss to Amasa,
thrusts a dagger into his body. 2 Sam. 20 : 9. The picture recalls
the kiss by which Judas betrayed the Saviour.*

PROLOGUE *(Recit.).*   The scene, once famed in Gibeon's land,
Repeats itself at Judas' hand!

Ye rocks of Gibeon, cry aloud!
Ye rocks, which mists of night enshroud,
Ye once could boast, ye once were proud!
But now, dishonoured, do ye stand—
Ye rocks once famed in Gibeon's land!
Yea, speak that we may understand!

CHORUS *(in the distance).* Away, ye wanderer, away from
    here!
This blood-stained spot, accursed and drear,
Is where Amasa's life was spilled,
In friendly guise by Joab killed.
Oh, curséd be, oh, curséd be!
The curse of curses rest on thee!

PROLOGUE.   The rocks complain!

Revenge the stain!
The blood-soaked earth revenge hath ta'en!
Ye rocks of Gibeon, silence while we tell
What at Gethsemane befell!

Ye rocks of Gibeon, Judas thither came,
Dissembling, lying, restless without shame —
Upon the Master sealed a kiss, and turned
Unto the silver such a deed had earned!

CHORUS.   Accursed they
Whom friends betray,
Who love pass by
With lie on lie!
Who kiss in guile,
With cunning smile.
Curse ye such souls that thus dissemble!
Curse those whom Judas doth resemble!

ACTION

*Christ suffers the bitter death-agony; is betrayed by Judas with a kiss
into the hands of the soldiers who lead Him captive away.*

FIRST SCENE

*In the Neighbourhood of the Mount of Olives. – Judas, Nathan, Josue,
Ptolomäus, Salomon, the Traders, Selpha, Malchus, the Soldiers*

JUDAS. Now take care! We are drawing near to the place where in retirement the Master rests. In this lonely spot for the last time He spends the night.

SALOMON. It would be well to avoid having the Disciples spy us too soon.

JUDAS. They are unconcerned and suspect naught of an attack. Hence we need fear no resistance.

SOLDIER. And should they attempt it, they would soon feel the strength of our arms!

JUDAS. Rest easy. You will capture Him without the use of a sword.

JOSAPHAT. But how will we recognize Him in the dark, so as not to take another instead of the one we desire?

JUDAS. Mark the sign I will give to you. As soon as we enter the garden, then pay close attention! For I will hurry up to Him, and whomsoever I kiss, that is He. Him you must bind.

KORAH. Good! with such a sign we could not go astray.

PTOLOMÄUS *(to the Soldiers).* Do you hear? By the kiss shall you know the Master.

SOLDIER. Indeed! We will not mistake Him!

JUDAS. Make haste! The time has come; we are not so far away from the garden.

JOSAPHAT. Judas, if all goes well with us this night, then shall you reap rich profit from your work.

TRADERS. We also will give you a large reward.

SOLDIERS. Beware, you Stirrer up of the people! Soon will your deserts overtake you! *(They exit.)*

SECOND SCENE

The Mount of Olives

Christ and His Disciples come forward slowly from the background.

CHRIST. Verily, verily, I say unto you: You shall weep and lament, but the world will shout for joy. You shall be sad, but your grief will be turned into exultation. For I will see you again, and your heart will be glad, yea, and your joy no one can take from you. I forsake the world and enter unto my Father.

PETER.   Behold, you speak clearly unto us, and no longer in parables.

JAMES THE ELDER.   Now we realize you know all things and need ask of no one.

THOMAS.   Hence we believe that you are come from God.

CHRIST.   Do you now have faith? But behold! The hour is coming, yea, is already come, when you, each to his own, shall be scattered, and shall leave me alone. Yet still am I not alone, for our Father is with me. Yea, Father! The hour has come! Exalt Thy Son, so that He may glorify Thee! I have fulfilled the work Thou has put upon me to do; I have disclosed Thy name to men, whom Thou gavest me. Holy Father, receive them in Thy name. Hallow them, consecrate them in the Truth. Not alone do I beg for them, but also for those who through Thy word shall believe in me — that all may be one , even as Thou, Father, art in me, and I in thee. Father! I would that wheresoever I am, they may be also — those whom Thou hast given me, that they may behold my splendour which Thou hast bestowed upon me. For Thou didst love me before the beginning of time. *(Reaching the entrance to Gethsemane, Christ turns to the Disciples with infinite sadness.)* Children, rest here, while I go within and pray. — Pray also that you do not fall into temptation. But you, Peter, James and John, follow me! *(Enters with the three Disciples.)*

DISCIPLES *(who remain behind).*   What has occurred to our Master?

BARTHOLOMEW.   Never have I seen Him so sad.

JAMES THE LESS.   My heart also is full of anguish.

MATTHEW.   Oh, that this night were over, with its fateful hours.

A DISCIPLE.   Not without cause has the Master prepared up for this.

PHILIP.   Dear Brothers, let us here settle ourselves until He returns.

THOMAS.   Yes, I am quite weary and weak. *(All sit down.)*

CHRIST. *(in the foreground, to the three Apostles).*   Oh, beloved

Children, my soul is troubled, even unto death. Remain here and watch with me! *(After a pause.)* I will go hence a little ways, that I may strengthen myself through communion with my Father. *(Moves toward the grotto slowly and with faltering steps.)*

PETER *(gazing after him).*   Ah, best of Masters!

JOHN.   My soul suffers with the soul of our Teacher.

PETER.   I am so downcast, so anxious.

JAMES.   Why does the good Master thus separate us now from one another?

JOHN.   Alas, we are to be witnesses.

PETER.   You remember, Brothers, we were witnesses of His transfiguration on the mountain. But now — what is it we must see? *(They gradually fall asleep.)*

CHRIST *(near the grotto).*   In such manner shall the hour come upon me — the hour of darkness! For this, indeed, I was sent into the world. *(Reaching the grotto, He throws Himself upon His knees.)* Father! My Father! If it is possible — and with Thee all things are possible — then let this cup pass from me. *(Falls upon His face and remains awhile, rising to His knees once more.)* Yet, Father, not as I would, but as Thou wouldst, shall it be done! *(Stands, gazes to heaven, then returns to His three Disciples.)* Simon!

PETER *(as in a dream).*   Alas, my Master!

CHRIST.   Simon, are you asleep?

PETER.   Master, see, here am I!

CHRIST.   Could you not watch with me an hour?

PETER.   Master, forgive me!

JOHN AND JAMES.   Rabbi, sleep overcame us.

CHRIST.   Alas, watch and pray, that you fall not into temptation.

THE THREE APOSTLES.   Yea, Master, we will pray and watch.

CHRIST.   The spirit is willing, but the flesh is weak. *(Returns to the grotto.)* My Father, Thy demand is just! Thy decrees are holy. Thou askest this sacrifice — *(Falls on His knees.)* Father, the battle is difficult! *(Bends low and then raises Himself.)* Still, if the cup cannot pass me, without I drink, then, Father, Thy will be done. *(Stands up.)* Holy One, by me shall all be worthily accomplisned. *(Turns toward the sleeping Disciples.)* Are your eyes then so heavy that you cannot watch with me? Oh, my trusted followers, even in you I find no consolation! *(Taking a few steps toward the grotto, He pauses.)* Alas, how dark is everything around me! The pangs of death overwhelm me! The burden of godly judgement rests upon me. Oh, the sins, the sins of mankind! they weigh me down! Oh, the fearful burden! Oh, the bitterness of this cup! *(Reaches the grotto.)* My Father! *(On His knees.)* If this hour may not be taken from me, then Thy will be done, Thy most holy will! — Father, Father — Thy Son — hear Him!

THIRD SCENE

An Angel appears.

THE ANGEL.   Son of Man! Hallow Thy Father's will! Contemplate the eternal bliss which will come out of Thy Passion! The Father has put upon Thee, and Thou has freely taken it upon Thyself, to atone for the sins of Mankind. Do what Thou has set out to do. The Father will glorify Thee.

CHRIST.   Yea, most Holy Father! I reverence Thy will — and by me shall it be consummated — to reconcile, to save, to bless. *(Stands up.)* Fortified through Thy word, O Father, I go joyfully to the fate ordained me as hostage for the sins of the world. *(To the three Disciples.)* Sleep on and rest!

PETER.   What is it, Master?

THE THREE.   Behold, we are ready.

CHRIST.   The hour has come. The Son of Man will be delivered into the hands of the sinners. Arise, and let us go. *(A clank of weapons is heard; the other Disciples waken.)*

DISCIPLES *(in the background).*   What is that uproar?

PHILIP.   Come, let us gather around the Master. We will not leave Him. *(They hasten toward Christ.)*

CHRIST.   Behold! He who shall betray me draws near.

ANDREW.   What means this multitude?

ALL.   Alas! we are undone!

JOHN.   And see, Judas at their head!

91

FOURTH SCENE

JUDAS *(hastening toward Christ.)* Rabbi, greetings be unto you. *(Kisses Him.)*

CHRIST. Friend, why do you come? Judas, with a kiss you betray the Son of Man! *(Advances toward the crowd.)* Whom seek you?

SOLDIERS. Jesus of Nazareth.

CHRIST. I am He *(The leaders bow down.)*

SOLDIERS. Woe unto us! What is this? *(They fall to the ground.)*

DISCIPLES *(joyfully).* One word from Him upsets them!

CHRIST *(to the Soldiers).* Fear not! Stand up!

DISCIPLES. Lord, cast them down, that they may nevermore arise.

CHRIST. Whom seek you?

SOLDIERS. Jesus of Nazareth.

CHRIST. I have already said that I am He. If then you seek me, let these others go.

SELPHA. Seize Him!

PHILIP. Master, shall we strike with our swords? *(Peter cuts off the ear of Malchus.)*

MALCHUS. Woe! I am hurt! Alas, my ear is cut off!

CHRIST *(to the Disciples).* Leave off! No more of this! *(To Malchus.)* Be comforted, for you shall be healed! *(Touches the ear of Malchus, then turns to Peter.)* As for you, put up your sword into its sheath, for all who lay hold on the sword, by the sword shall perish. Shall I not drink from the cup which the Father has given me? or think you not that if I prayed to the Father he would not send to my help many legions of angels? Yet how, then, would the Scriptures be fulfilled? *(To the Pharisees.)* Am I a thief that you come to take me with swords and clubs? And I sat with you daily in the Temple and taught , yet you did not stretch forth your hand and seize me! But this is your hour! Behold, here I am!

SELPHA. Surround Him, and bind Him fast, so that He may not possibly escape!

NATHAN. You will be answerable to the High Council. *(The Disciples slip away.)*

SOLDIERS. Ha! He shall not escape from our hands!

OBIRON *(to the Traders).* Now, Brothers, let us satisfy our revenge!

DATHAN. Remember what He did to us in the Temple!

JOSAPHAT *(to the Pharisees).* We will hasten in advance into the city. The Sanhedrin anxiously awaits our arrival.

TRADERS. But we will not for an instant leave the side of this Scoundrel!

NATHAN. First, we must to the High Priest, Annas. Thither lead Him!

SELPHA. We follow!

JOSAPHAT *(to Judas).* Judas, you are a Man!

SALOMON. You have kept your word!

JUDAS. Indeed, I said to you that this very day you would have Him.

PTOLOMÄUS. The entire High Council have you made bounden unto you. *(Going.)*

SOLDIERS *(urging Christ before them).* Away with you to Jerusalem! There will the sentence upon you be spoken.

SELPHA. Let us hasten! Watch Him carefully.

SOLDIERS. Ha! run now as in the land of Judæa you were wont to run!

SELPHA. Drive Him on. Spare Him not!

SOLDIERS. On with you, else we will drive you with our clubs.

TRADERS. Ha, ha! does Beelzebub then no longer aid you? *(They all exit.)*

END OF ACT

END OF FIRST PART

SECOND PART

From the Arrest on the Mount of Olives to the Condemnation by Pilate

ACT VIII. REPRESENTATION

Jesus before Annas

PROLOGUE.   Oh, night of fear! From place to place,
From judgement seat to judgement seat,
Abuséd to His very face,
The Saviour with contempt they treat!

He spake to Annas but a word-
A rough hand was against Him raised!
The blow received nor look demurred—
The hand that struck besought and praised!

Micaiah, too, was treated so,
When he to Ahab truth proclaimed;
A lying prophet struck the blow,
With jealous wrath inflamed.

For truth most often genders Hate,
Yet naught may break its constant light;
To those who purely contemplate,
The truth will flood the darkest night!

CHORUS.   Oh, Sinners, in your hearts retain
The mem'ry of the Saviour's paid,
Upon Gethsemane begun,
And suffered by the Holy One!
For you He suffered in despair!
For you His Passion and His Care!
Upon Him rested Sorrow's crown,
By terror, torn, with head bowed down;
The sweat of anguish through Him coursed,
Like blood, from Him the sweat was forced!

TABLEAU: *Micaiah, the Prophet, receives a blow in the face
because he speaks the truth of King Ahab. 1 Kings 22:24. An allusion to the first trial of Christ by Annas, the High Priest, where
the Saviour suffers a blow in the face.*

94

SOLO.　Whoso the truth in freedom deals,
　　　The sting of hate he later feels!
　　　Micaiah dealt in truth, and lo!
　　　Upon his face was struck a blow.
　　　"Oh, King!" he said, "should Ramoth fight,
　　　He will o'ercome thee with his might.

　　　"To save thyself from Baal's seer—
　　　Upon false prophets lend no ear!"
　　　'T was thus Micaiah spake the word—
　　　No flattery by Ahab heard!
　　　In fury on him rushed a liar,
　　　And smote him, such his hate, his ire!

CHORUS.　Thus hypocrites and liars too,
　　　Pluck laurel leaves without ado!
　　　'T is truth alone must yield its pride,
　　　For truth no flattery can bide!

ACTION

Christ is led before Annas, and is struck in the face.

FIRST SCENE

Annas, Esdras, Sidrach, Misael

ANNAS.　I can find no rest tonight until I learn that this Disturber of our peace is in our hands. Oh, were He only safe in chains! Full of anxiety I await my servant with the welcome news.

ESDRAS.　They cannot tarry much longer, for ample time has passed since they went away.

ANNAS.　In vain has my troubled gaze wandered up and down the street of Kidron. Naught could I see or hear. Go, my Esdras, hasten to the Gate of Kidron and see whether they do not approach.

ESDRAS.　Thither will I quickly go! *(Exits.)*

ANNAS.　It would indeed serve as a thunderclap upon the Sanhedrin if this time the outcome were unsuccessful.

SIDRACH.　High Priest, leave your grieving!

MISAEL.　There is truly no doubt of our success.

95

ANNAS. They have perchance changed their way and are returning by the Siloa Gate. I must keep an eye on that place also.

SIDRACH. If the High Priest so wishes it, I will to the Siloa Gate—

ANNAS. Yes, do so! Yet see first whether anyone comes by way of Sanhedrin Street!

SIDRACH. I will not delay. *(Exits.)*

ANNAS. The night advances, and still no certainty. Every minute of this anxious delay seems more than an hour to me. I think — hark! — some one comes! Yes, yes, some one comes! Surely there will be good news.

SIDRACH *(hastening in)*. My Lord, yonder Esdras comes in haste. I saw him running, fleet of foot, along the street.

ANNAS. He must bring gladsome tidings, since he thus makes such haste. I have, indeed, no more doubt as to the death of this Malefactor.

ESDRAS *(rushing in)*. Hail to the High Priest! I have myself seen the Fathers chosen to go with Judas. Everything has occurred in accordance with your desire. The Galilean is in fetters! I have spoken with them, and hurried ahead quickly, so as to bring you instantly the joyful news.

ANNAS. Heavenly intelligence! Blissful hour! A weight is lifted from my heart, and I feel myself born again. For the first time indeed, I, with pride and joy, call myself the High Priest of the Chosen People.

SECOND SCENE

The four delegates of the High Council appear with Judas on the balcony.

THE FOUR PHARISEES. Long live our High Priest!

NATHAN. The wish of the High Counsel is fulfilled!

ANNAS. Oh, I must embrace you for very joy! So then our planning has prospered. Judas! you will receive an honourable place in our chronicles of the year. Even before the Feast, shall the Galilean die!

JUDAS *(terrified)*. Die? — Die?

ANNAS. His death is determined upon.

JUDAS. I will not be held responsible for the life and blood of the Master!

ANNAS. Nor is it necessary. He is now in our power!

JUDAS. I did not deliver Him to you for this!

PTOLEMÄUS. You have done your part; the rest is our concern.

JUDAS. Woe is me! What have I done! Shall He die? No, no! I did not wish that, I will not have it! *(Goes away.)*

THE PHARISEES *(laughing).* Whether you will or no, He still shall die!

THIRD SCENE

The former, without Judas. Directly after, Christ is led on, followed by the leader of the band, Selpha, the Servants, Balbus. All are on the balcony. The soldiers remain below.

ESDRAS. High Priest! The Prisoner is at the threshold.

ANNAS. Let Selpha with the necessary guard bring Him up. The others must wait for Him below. *(Selpha appears with Christ.)*

SELPHA. High Priest! According to your command, the Prisoner stands here before your judgement bar.

ANNAS. Have you brought only Him captive?

BALBUS. His adherents scattered like frightened sheep.

SELPHA. We did not find it worth the trouble to catch them. However, Malchus came near losing his life.

ANNAS. How so? What happened? Speak quickly!

BALBUS. A Disciple struck at him with a drawn sword, hitting his ear, and it was cut off.

ANNAS. How? But it has left no mark.

BALBUS *(mocking).* The Miracle-worker, through His magic, put it back again.

ANNAS. What say you to this, Malchus? Speak.

MALCHUS *(earnestly).* I cannot explain it — a miracle has

97

indeed happened to me.

ANNAS. Has the Deceiver forsooth bewitched you also? *(To Christ.)* Say, by what power have you done this? *(Christ remains silent.)*

SELPHA. Answer, when your Judge questions you!

ANNAS. Speak! Give an account of your Disciples, and of your teaching which you have spread through all Judæa, and by which you have misled the people.

CHRIST. I have spoken openly before the world. I have always taught in the Temple and in the Synagogue, and naught have I said secretly. Why do you ask me? Question those who have heard me. They know what I have said.

BALBUS *(striking Christ).* Is it thus you answer the High Priest?

CHRIST. If I have spoken evil, then show that it is evil! But if I have spoken truth, why do you strike me?

ANNAS. Do you even thus now defy us, when the very power of life and death is in our hands? Take Him away! I am weary of this Imposter!

BALBUS *(to Jesus, as He is led away).* Just wait! Your pride will soon falter!

ANNAS. I will now rest for a while, or rather reflect in silence as to how this fortunate commencement may be brought to as fortunate an end. I shall undoubtedly be called to the Sanhedrin very early in the morning. *(They exit.)*

FOURTH SCENE

Christ in the midst of the Crowd

CROWD. What, is His business already over?

SELPHA.*(who leads Jesus).* Yes, His vindication has ended badly.

BALBUS. Nevertheless, it brought Him a sound slap in the face.

SELPHA. Men, take Him now, and let us hasten with Him to the palace of Caiaphas.

CROWD. Away with Him! Hurry up, you!

BALBUS.   Be of cheer! From Caiaphas you will receive a much better reception.

CROWD.   There, no doubt, the ravens will sing about your ears! *(Christ is led through the streets.)* You will become a laughing stock, an example for the entire nation!

BALBUS.   Hurry! Your Disciples are all ready! They would proclaim you King of Israel!

SOME SOLDIERS.   Is it not true that you have often dreamed of this?

SELPHA.   Caiaphas, the High Priest, will now explain this dream to you.

BALBUS.   Do you hear that? Caiaphas will proclaim your exaltation to you.

SOLDIERS *(with laughter).*   Yes, in truth your elevation between heaven and earth!

SELPHA.   Listen, you fellows! Yonder through the palace of Pilate is our nearest way to the house of Caiaphas. There place yourselves in the courtyard until further orders.

SOLDIERS *(in the mob).*   Your commands shall be fully obeyed!

FIFTH SCENE

Peter and John before the House of Annas. A Priest

PETER.   Alas! How has it befallen our Master! John, I am so anxious about Him!

JOHN.   I fear to approach the place, for undoubtedly He will receive ridicule and have abuse heaped upon Him.

PETER.   It is so still about here.

JOHN.   Inside the palace not even a human voice can be heard. Could they have taken Him away again?

ESDRAS *(stepping out).*   What would you here at this time of night before the palace?

JOHN.   Forgive us. We saw a crowd of people from afar; they came hither through the Gate of Kedron, and so we have come to see what has happened.

ESDRAS. They brough a Prisoner, but He has already been sent to Caiaphas.

JOHN. To Caiaphas? Then we will leave immediately.

ESDRAS. 'T is well, for otherwise I must have you taken up for night brawlers.

PETER. We will raise no disturbance and will go away silently. *(They exit.)*

ESDRAS *(looking after them).* Perhaps they are Disciples of the Galilean. If I but knew! Still, they are not against our people, since they hasten to the palace of Caiaphas. The whole band must be destroyed, otherwise the people will never be brought to obedience! *(Exit.)*

END OF ACT

ACT IX. REPRESENTATION

Jesus before Caiaphas

PROLOGUE. His enemies are judges, and before them now He stands,
The Lord in silence, patiently, behold, with folded hands!
He hears the words condemning, and the lies on every breath,
While the rod of accusation thrusts Him nearer unto death!

As did Naboth in his goodness meet the persecutor's rod,
Heard false witnesses proclaim him a blasphemer of his God,
So the Lord, whose fault is goodness, finds a like sad recompense.
For His truth and for His love and for His kind beneficence!

Soon, before you, to your sorrow, will you see Him bent and bound—
While the servants set to guard Him, His dear person will surround.
Oh, the cries of sharp derision, and the blow that cometh after!
Oh, the harsh and bitter jeering, and the wild, inhuman laughter!

100

Thus did Job bow 'neath affliction in the days of long ago,
Laden down with heavy sorrow, every friend become his foe;
He foreshadowed in his anguish what was later to take place,
And in him, proclaimed the likeness of the Saviour's patient
    face!

(Recit.)   In pity bleeds my heart
For Him who stands before the judgement seat!
He bears the sinner's part,
Betrayed and scorned and dragged from street to street.
Oh, men, your faces hide!
The Christ is touched by hands that desecrate!
He will be crucified!
Behold the scene which shadows forth His fate!

TABLEAU: *The innocent Naboth is condemned to death by false
witnesses. 1 Kings 21 : 8, 13. As Naboth was, so will the innocent
Saviour be condemned to death before the High Priest, Caiaphas,
through false testimony. As on patient Job all imaginable scorn
was heaped, so will the same be done unto the Saviour.*

CHORUS.   "Naboth, O King, shall die!
He dared his God blaspheme, and thee abuse.
Let him effacéd be from Israel!"
Thus was proclaimed the lie—
Bribed were the Jews
By the wicked Jezebel!

SOLO.   Upon the innocent revenge they take!
Upon the innocent their thirst they slake—
Their thirst for vengeance in unrighteous cause!
False rogues who scorn the sacredness of laws!
Deceit and Hate against the Christ are bent,
While Malice seeks to crush the Innocent!

CHORUS.   Lords of the earth, beware, beware-
Of worldly rule ye have your share!
Forget not, in your regal dower,
A higher Judge, a greater Power.
The rich, the poor, the peasant-bred,
The nobly born, the underfed,
Are one to Him who rules above
In justice measured by His love!

101

TABLEAU: *The suffering Job is affronted by his wife and relatives. Job 2 : 9.*

Ah, what a man!
A Job in pain,
In ridicule, in mockery to judgement ta'en
Thence to be slain!

Ah, what a man!
Beneath the burden of a cross He bends,
Scorned by His friends,
Yet His trust in God never ends—
Ah, what a man!

No noise of grief,
No supplication to be brief,
Amidst the mockery of unbelief;
Ah, what a man!
All ye whose hearts in pity break,
Shed tears of love for His dear sake!
Ah, what a man!

ACTION

Christ is taken to Caiaphas, before whom He is tried, and upon Him the sentence of death is imposed. He is denied by Peter, and is scoffed at as well as maltreated by the servants.

FIRST SCENE

Caiaphas in his Bedroom. The Priests and Pharisees

CAIAPHAS. Our fortunate beginning portends the happiest realization of our wishes. I thank you, noble members of the Sanhedrin, for your zealous and wise co-operation!

JOSAPHAT. Our greatest gratitude is due the High Priest.

CAIAPHAS. Now, let us proceed without delay! All is ready. The Council shall immediately be assembled. Samuel has already brought hither the necessary witnesses. The trial of the Prisoner will be taken in hand without delay. Then shall judgement be rendered, and careful provision made for its execution. The quicker we are, the surer our success.

NATHAN. It would be best were the thing done before our adversaries have given much thought to the matter.

CAIAPHAS. That is my idea. Trust me, my friends, I have a plan which I hope to carry out.

SADOK. The wisdom of our High Priest deserves our fullest trust!

ALL. The God of our Fathers bless his steps!

SECOND SCENE

The foregoing. The Soldiers bring in Christ. The False Witnesses

SELPHA *(who is the leader of the guard).* Most exalted High Priest! Here is the Prisoner!

CAIAPHAS. Bring Him nearer, that I may look Him in the face and question Him.

SELPHA *(to Christ).* Step forward, and respect the head of the High Council.

CAIAPHAS. So, you are He who would attack our Synagogue and would bring about the fall of the Law of Moses? You stand accused of inciting the people to disobedience, of scorning the sacred traditions of the Fathers, of repeatedly violating the divine regulations of the Sabbath, and of allowing yourself many times to utter blasphemous speeches and to do blasphemous deeds. Here stand some trusty men who are ready to vouch for the truth of these accusations with their evidence. Listen to them, — that you may answer them if you can!

FIRST WITNESS *(Nun).* I testify before God that this Man has incited the people, openly denouncing the members of the Council and the Scribes as hypocrites, as hungry wolves in sheep's clothing, as blind leaders of the blind, and, moreover, has proclaimed that no one should follow their decrees.

SECOND WITNESS *(Eliab).* I also agree to this, and, furthermore, can add that He has warned the people not to pay tribute to the Emperor.

FIRST WITNESS *(Nun).* Such ambiguous speech have I also heard Him utter!

CAIAPHAS *(to Christ).* What say you to this? Are you silent?

103

— Have you naught to say in return?

THIRD WITNESS *(Gad).* I have often noted how He, with His Disciples, in defiance of the Law, has gone to the table with unwashed hands; how He has had friendly intercourse with the publicans and sinners, and has even entered their houses and eaten with them.

THE OTHER WITNESSES. We have also seen this.

THIRD WITNESS *(Gad).* I have heard from trustworthy sources that He even has spoken with Samaritans, and has dwelt with them for days at a time.

FIRST WITNESS *(Nun).* I also have been witness to what He has done on the Sabbath without fear — though forbidden by the Law of God. He has healed those seized with sickness, with the pest; He has urged others to desecrate the Sabbath; He even ordered a man to carry his bed to his house.

SECOND WITNESS *(Eliab).* I have seen that too!

CAIAPHAS *(to Christ).* How can you refute this? Have you nothing to say?

THIRD WITNESS *(Gad to Christ).* You have, for I was present, taken unto yourself the power to forgive sins — a power belonging only to God. You have thus blasphemed God!

FIRST WITNESS *(Nun).* You have called God your Father, and have dared to name yourself as one with the Father. You have thus made yourself equal to God.

SECOND WITNESS *(Eliab).* You have raised yourself above our Father Abraham, and have dared to assert that you were, before Abraham was.

FOURTH WITNESS *(Raphim).* You have said: "I can destroy the Temple of God, and in three days build it up again."

FIFTH WITNESS *(Eliezer).* You have said: "I will destroy this Temple built by the hand of man, and in three days will I set up another which is not built by the hand of man."

CAIAPHAS. You have thus boasted of a superhuman, divine power! These are hard accusations; and they are lawfully attested. Contradict them if you can! I see, you believe by your silence you will be able to save yourself! You dare not admit before the Father of the people and before your Judge what you have taught. Or do

104

you dare? Then hear: I, the High Priest, adjure you by the living God! Tell us, are you the Messiah, the only begotten Son of God—are you divine?

CHRIST. You have said it, and it is so. But I say unto you: From now on it will come to pass that the Son of Man shall sit upon the right hand of God in power and shall come out of the clouds of Heaven.

CAIAPHAS. He has blasphemed God! What need we further with witnesses? Behold, you yourselves have heard the blasphemy! What think you?

ALL. He deserves death!

CAIAPHAS. He is thus declared unanimously to be deserving of death. Still, neither I nor the High Council, but the holy Law itself, pronounces the sentence of death upon Him. You teachers of the Law! I bid you give me answer! What says the holy Law of him who is disobedient to the ordained authorities of God?

JOSUE *(reads).* "Whosoever is presumptuous and does not hearken to the commandments of the High Priest, or to the opinions of the Judges, shall die, and the evil be uprooted from Israel." *(Deut. 17 : 12.)*

CAIAPHAS. What does the Law prescribe for him who profanes the Sabbath?

EZEKIEL *(reads).* "Keep thou my Sabbath, for it is holy. Whoso profanes it shall be put to death! Whoso does any work thereon, that soul shall be cut aloof from the people."

CAIAPHAS. What punishment does the Law impose upon the blasphemer?

NATHANAEL *(reads).* "Say unto the children of Israel: He who blasphemes his God shall carry his offence! And whoso slanders the name of the Lord shall be put to death. The whole congregation shall stone him, be he born in the land or a stranger. Whoso blasphemes the name of the Lord shall be put to death!"

CAIAPHAS. Accordingly is the sentence spoken over this Jesus of Nazareth, in conformity with law, and it shall be carried out as soon as possible. In the mean time let the condemned be guarded. Away with Him, watch Him well, and in the early morning bring Him before the great Sanhedrin!

SELPHA.   Then come, you Messiah! We will show you to your Palace!

BALBUS.   There will you receive befitting homage! *(They lead Him away.)*

THIRD SCENE

CAIAPHAS.   We are nearing our goal! But now, the matter demands resolute proceedings!

ALL.   We shall not rest until He is brought to death!

CAIAPHAS.   At the break of day we will gather together again. Our intention must be secretly announced to the High Priest, Annas, and to the others. *(Cries of: "It shall be done without delay!")* Then shall the judgement be confirmed by the whole Assembly, and the Prisoner immediately thereafter led before Pilate, in order that he may sanction our act and allow its execution.

ALL.   Grant that the hour will soon come when we are rid of our enemy! God hasten the hour! *(They all depart.)*

FOURTH SCENE

JUDAS *(alone).*   Fearful presentiments drive me hither and thither! Those dreadful words: He shall die! Oh, the thought pursues me everywhere! It is terrible! No, it must not come to that! They cannot go so far! It would be horrible if they — my Master — No — and I — I — guilty of it all! No! Here in the house of Caiaphas, I shall probably find how it goes with Him. Shall I enter? I can no longer bear this doubt, and yet it terrifies me to know the truth! My heart is breaking with anguish — still the truth must be some time! *(Enters.)*

FIFTH SCENE

Hall. Agar, Sara, Melchi; then Panther, Arphaxad, Abdias, Levi; later, John, Peter; finally, Christ, led by Selpha, Malchus, and Balbus

AGAR *(to Melchi, outside).*   You men, come in here.

SARA.   It is more comfortable inside!

MELCHI.   True, good children! *(Calls out.)* What ho, comrades, come in here! It is better for us to lie down in the hall. *(The men-at-arms enter.)*

ARPHAXAD.   This pleases me! Would, though, we had come in sooner! How foolish! We always stand outside in the open and freeze. But where is there any fire?

PANTHER.   Go, Sara, fetch us fire, and wood to lay thereon.

AGAR.   Surely!

SARA.   That shall you have. *(They both go.)*

SOLDIERS.   Will the trial soon come to an end?

MELCHI.   It may last longer, until all the witnesses are heard!

PANTHER.   And the Accused will no doubt resort to a flow of rhetoric so as to free Himself.

ARPHAXAD.   Still, that would be of no help to Him; He has offended the priesthood too deeply. *(Agar and Sara re-enter.)*

AGAR.   Here is fire for you.

SARA.   And wood and tongs.

SOLDIERS.   Thank you, girls!

PANTHER.   Ah, that is good! Now let us see to it that the fire does not go out! *(Some sit around the fire, while others stand in groups. Sara brings them bread and drink.)*

AGAR *(to John, who appears on the threshold).*   John, do you come hither also in the middle of the night? Enter! Here you may warm yourself at the fire! Is it not so, you men, that you would not grudge a place for this young man?

SOLDIERS.   To be sure! Come on!

JOHN.   Good Agar! There is also with me a travelling companion. May he not be allowed to enter too?

AGAR.   Where is he? Let him come in also! Why does he stand outside in the cold? *(John steps aside, but returns alone.)* Well, where is he?

JOHN.   He waits on the threshold; but he does not trust himself inside.

AGAR.   Come hither, good Friend, have no fear!

SOLDIERS.   Yea, Comrade, come amongst us and warm yourself! *(Peter timidly draws nigh to the fire.)*

107

ARPHAXAD. Still do we see naught and hear naught of the Prisoner.

ALL. How long must we wait?

PANTHER. Probably He will return from His trial — a man doomed to death.

ARPHAXAD. I am curious to know whether His Disciples will not also be sought after.

SOLDIERS. That were indeed a pretty piece of work, if we had to capture all!

PANTHER. It would not be worth the trouble. Once the Master is safely away, then will these Galileans take flight, and they will never again show themselves in Jerusalem.

ARPHAXAD. At all events, one of them shall receive severe punishment — he who in the Garden took a weapon and cut off the ear of Malchus.

SOLDIERS. Yes, it should be as ordained: An ear for an ear, ha, ha, ha! *(Peter, restless, goes away from the fire.)*

PANTHER. A good idea! But the application is of no value here. Malchus' ear is whole again.

AGAR *(to Peter)*. I have been looking at you for some time. If I mistake not, you are one of the Disciples of the Man from Galilee. Yes, yes, you were with Jesus of Nazareth.

PETER. No, woman, I was not. I do not know Him, neither do I by any chance understand what you say. *(He draws back, and comes near Sara.)*

SARA. Look, this one was also with Jesus of Nazareth.

SEVERAL. Perhaps you are one of His Disciples?

LEVI. Yes, you are one!

PETER. I am not, on my soul! I know naught of them. *(The cock crows.)*

ABDIAS *(to the others in his circle)*. Look at yonder man. Truly he was also with Him!

PETER. I know not what you would with me. What does He mean to me?

SEVERAL.   Yes, yes, you are one of them; indeed, you are a Galilean. Your speech betrays you.

PETER.   God be my witness that I do not know the Man of whom you speak. *(The cock crows a second time.)*

MELCHI.   What! Did I not see you with Him in the Garden, when my cousin Malchus had his ear cut off?

SOLDIERS *(standing by the fire).*   Ha! See! They bring in the Prisoner! *(Selpha enters with Christ.)*

PANTHER *(to them as they advance).*   How has it gone?

SELPHA.   He is condemned to death.

SOLDIERS *(jeering).*   Oh, poor King! *(Christ looks upon Peter sorrowfully.)*

SELPHA.   Forward, Comrades! Until the dawn of to-morrow we must keep watch over Him.

SOLDIER.   Come, He shall help us pass the time away!

SIXTH SCENE

In the Proscenium. Peter and afterwards John

PETER.   Alas, my Master! Oh, how far have I fallen! Oh, woe is me, a weak and wretched man! My dear Friend and Protector, I have denied you thrice! I do not understand how I could have so far forgotten myself! A curse upon my faithlessness! My best Master! Have you still grace for me? My heart will repent of this contemptible cowardice! Oh, Lord, if you feel mercy toward me — a perfidious one — then show it me now! This once, hear the voice of a contrite soul! Oh, my sin is done! I cannot undo it! But ever and ever more will I regret it and expiate it. Never again shall I leave you, O most kind! At least, you will not reject me; you will not scorn my bitter remorse! No, the kind, compassionate look which you cast upon your deeply fallen Disciple bids me hope: you will forgive me! Dearest Teacher, this comfort I have from you, and the whole love of my heart from this moment I dedicate to you. I shall fast, I shall cling to you — ah, naught shall ever again have the power to take me from you! *(Exits.)*

JOHN *(coming from the other side).*   Where can Peter have gone? In vain I searched for him in the crowd. Surely naught of ill could

109

have befallen him. Perhaps I might yet meet him on the way. I will now go toward Bethany. But ah, dearest Mother, how will your heart feel, when I tell you of the terrible scenes — the Innocent wronged and by the the miscreant condemned! What will your soul go through! Judas, Judas, what a frightful deed is thine! *(Exits.)* *(Exits.)*

SEVENTH SCENE

Christ, surrounded by servants and guards, is seated on a stool.

LEVI.   Is not this too poor a throne for you, great King?

PANTHER.   Hail, new-born Ruler!

MELCHI.   But sit steadier, otherwise you might fall off. *(Pressing Christ down.)*

LEVI.   Truly you are a Prophet, so they say. We would test your craft.

MELCHI *(striking Him in the face).*   So tell us, great Elias, who has struck you?

ABDIAS *(striking Him).*   Was it I?

MELCHI.   Do you not hear? *(Shaking Christ.)* I almost believe you are asleep. He is deaf and dumb — a pretty Prophet! *(Strikes Him from the stool, so that He falls at full length.)*

LEVI.   Oh, woe, woe, our King has been upset from His throne!

ABDIAS.   Oh, woe, woe, what is now to be done? We have no more King!

MELCHI.   You are surely to be pitied — so great a Magician and now so powerless and weak!

PANTHER.   What is now to be done with Him?

ALL.   We will help Him again to His throne.

PANTHER *(lifting Christ).*   Raise yourself, O mighty King, and receive a new our homage!

MESSENGER *(Dan, one of Caiaphas's men, entering).*   Now, how goes it with the new King?

ALL.   He neither speaks nor makes a sign. We can do nothing with Him.

DAN.   The High Priest and Pilate will soon make Him speak. Caiaphas has sent me to fetch Him.

SELPHA.   Up, comrades!

LEVI *(taking Christ by the ropes).*   Stand up, you! You have been King long enough.

ALL.   Away with you! Your kingdom has come to an end! *(All exit.)*

END OF ACT

ACT X. REPRESENTATION

The Despair of Judas

PROLOGUE.   Why wanders Judas in the tortures of despair?
Alas, an evil conscience on him turns!
The blood-guilt in his soul he has to bear,
While the awful flame of sin within him burns.

Weep, Judas, for the deed that thou has done!
Oh, let repentant tears blot out thy sin!
Implore for mercy from the Holy One!
Salvation's door is open. Go thou in!

Alas, alas, in woe though deeply bowed,
No ray of hope doth over Judas shine!
"Too great my sin," the sinner cries aloud,
As Cain once cried, "too great this sin of mine!"

Impenitent and unconsoled like Cain,
A mighty fear o'er hapless Judas falls;
The just reward of sin is racking pain,
Toward such a fate we hasten when it calls!

TENOR SOLO AND CHORUS.   "Oh, woe to the man who betrays me,"
Cried the Lord, "to the traitor who slays me!
'T were better for him he had never been born
Than wander in terror and tremble 'neath scorn!"
Such words follow Judas in tortuous pain,
Pursuing his footsteps, beclouding his brain.

CHORUS.   Vengeance falls on Judas' head,
He shall not go unpunishéd!
By frenzy torn, by conscience cowed,
By furies scourged, in madness bowed—
He wanders, and his peace is oe'r;
He knows no rest forever more,
Until despair his being rends—
Until his worthless life he ends!

TABLEAU: *The brother-murderer, Cain, tortured with remorse,
wanders a fugitive on the face of the earth. Genesis 4 : 10 - 17.
Abel is the symbol of the dying Messiah. Abel, the upright, was
hated by his brother, Cain, even as Christ was despised by
His brothers, the Jews. Even as Cain became a fugitive so the
Jewish Nation shall be expelled from its kingdom, and dispersed
over the whole earth.*

SOLO.   'T was thus that Cain, ah, whither sped!
To drown his thoughts, ah, whither fled!
You cannot from your conscience hide—
The shadow trembles at your side;
And though you hasten here and there,
The pains of Hell you have to bear!
The scourge will fall, the wound will bleed,
You cannot now escape the deed!
Ah, Judas!

CHORUS.   Behold, this picture you shall see,
It will the sinner's mirror be!
Though vengeance cometh not to-day,
It yet will come, and so repay
In double-fold upon the morrow—
Full vengeance on the Man of Sorrow!

ACTION

*The assembled High Council confirms the death sentence pronounced
upon Christ. Judas appears in remorse before the Assembly,
throws down the thirty pieces of silver, departs in anguish, and
hangs himself.*

FIRST SCENE

JUDAS *(alone).*   My anxious foreboding has become a horrible
certainty! Caiaphas has condemned the Master to death, and the

112

Council has sanctioned his judgement. It is all over - no more hope of rescue! Had the Master wished to save Himself, He would have made them feel the force of His power a second time in the Garden of Gethsemane. As He did not do it then, He will not do it now. What am I able to do for Him, — I, the most wretched, who have delivered Him into their hands? They shall have the blood-money back — and in return they must set my Master free! I will go instantly and let them know my demand. Yet — will He be saved thereby? Oh, vain, empty hope! They will ridicule me, I know it! Accurséd Synagogue! You tempted me through your agents, you deceived me, and concealed from me your bloody purposes — until you had Him in your clutches! Unjust judges that you are, I will heap upon you my bitter reproaches. I will know naught of your devilish design. No part will I have in the blood of this innocent One! Oh, the anguish of Hell racks my innocent being! *(Exits.)*

SECOND SCENE

The High Council

CAIAPHAS.   Assembled Brethren, I thought we could not wait until morning to send the Enemy of the Synagogue to His death.

ANNAS.   I also could find no moment's rest, so eager was I to hear the sentence of death pronounced.

ALL.   It is decided. He must, He shall die!

CAIAPHAS.   Last night I did not think it necessary to have all the members of the Sanhedrin come hither. There was the required number of judges to pass sentence in conformity with the regulation of the law. The Accused was unanimously declared worthy of death, for all present heard with their own ears how this Man slandered God in the most horrible manner, daring to set Himself up as the Son of God!

PRIESTS AND PHARISEES *(who were present at the former gathering)*.   Yes, we were witness to what was said. We indeed heard the blasphemy against God from His own mouth.

CAIAPHAS.   Once more will I have the Criminal brought before you, that you yourselves may be convinced of His being worthy of death. Then the whole Council assembled may pass judgement upon Him!

THIRD SCENE

JUDAS *(rushing in)*.   Is it true? Have you condemned my Master to death?

RABBI.   Why come you, unbidden, into the Assembly? Get out! We will call you if we need you.

JUDAS.   I must know. Have you sentenced Him?

ALL.   He must die!

JUDAS.   Woe, woe, I have sinned! I have betrayed the Righteous! Oh, and you, you bloodthirsty judges, you condemn and murder the Innocent!

ALL.   Judas, peace! or —

JUDAS.   No longer any peace for me! And none for you! The blood of the Innocent cries aloud for vengeance!

CAIAPHAS.   What troubles your soul? Speak, but speak with reverence, for you stand before the High Council.

JUDAS.   You would deliver this One up to death, Him who is guiltless of every fault? You dare not do it; I protest against it! You have made me a traitor. Your accursèd pieces of silver—

ANNAS.   You yourself offered to do it, and concluded the bargain.

JOSAPHAT.   Bethink you, Judas! You have obtained what you most desired. And if you bear yourself properly, you may still —

JUDAS.   I will have no more of it! I cut loose from your infamous bargain! Give me back the Innocent!

ALL.   Clear out, you mad one!

JUDAS.   I demanded the Innocent back! My hands shall be clear of blood.

RABBI   What, you infamous traitor! Will you forsooth dictate laws to the High Council? Know, your Master must die and it is you who have delivered Him up to death!

ALL   .He must die!

JUDAS *(with wild and frightened look)*.   Die? I am a traitor? He must die? I have delivered Him over to die? *(Breaking forth.)* Then may ten thousand devils from Hell rend me to pieces — crush me!

114

Here, you bloodhounds, take back your accursèd bloodmoney! *(Throws down the bag of silver.)*

CAIAPHAS. Why did you allow yourself to be made use of in a transaction which you had not beforehand well weighed?

ALL. That was your lookout!

JUDAS. Thus shall my soul be damned, my body rent asunder, and you—

ALL. Silehce — and away from here!

JUDAS. You shall sink with me to the lowest Hell! *(Rushes out.)*

FOURTH SCENE

CAIAPHAS *(after a pause).* A fearful man!

ANNAS. I suspected something of the kind.

ALL. It is his fault.

CAIAPHAS. He has betrayed his Friend, we have condemned our Enemy. I remain steadfast in my resolve, and if there be any one here who is of another opinion, let him come forward.

ALL. No! What has been determined on shall be carried out!

CAIAPHAS. What shall we do with this silver? As blood-money, we dare not lay it back in the sacred coffers.

ANNAS. If it is agreeable to the will of the High Council, it might be put to some useful end.

SARAS. True! A burial place for strangers is needed. With this a field might be purchased for such a purpose.

ALL. We agree with you!

CAIAPHAS. Is such a field to be had?

SARAS. A potter in the city has for sale a piece of ground at just this price. *(Pointing to the bag.)*

CAIAPHAS. Then close the bargain. Now, let us delay no longer in passing final sentence on the Prisoner.

RABBI. I will immediately have Him brought in. *(Exits.)*

ANNAS. I will now see whether the obstinacy which He

showed toward me has not somewhat abated. A real satisfaction will it be for me to hear the death sentence: He dies!

FIFTH SCENE

Christ before the High Council

SELPHA *(leading Christ in)*. Show better respect to the High Council than you did before! Venerable Fathers, here we bring the Prisoner, as we were ordered.

CAIAPHAS. Lead Him forward into our midst.

BALBUS. Step forth. *(Pushes the Prisoner.)*

CAIAPHAS. Jesus of Nazareth, do you still hold to the words you spake before your judges during the night?

ANNAS. If you be the Anointed One, tell us so!

CHRIST. If I tell you, still will you not believe me, and if I ask you, you will neither give answer nor set me free. But henceforward the Son of Man shall sit on the right hand of Almighty God.

ALL. You are then the Son of God?

CHRIST. You say it, and so I am.

ANNAS. That is enough! Why do we need further witnesses?

PRIESTS AND PHARISEES *(who had attended the night session)*. Now we have heard it again from His own mouth.

CAIAPHAS. Fathers of the People of Israel! It now rests with you to pronounce the final legal verdict as to the guilt and punishment of this man.

ALL. He is guilty of blaspheming God! He deserves death!

CAIAPHAS. Therefore we will lead Him before the judgement seat of Pilate.

ALL. Yes, away with Him! Let Him die!

CAIAPHAS. But Pilate must be prepared beforehand, so that he may issue the verdict before the Feast.

RABBI. Should not some one from amongst us go before in order to sue for speedy audience?

CAIAPHAS. You yourself, Rabbi, together with Dariabas and

Rabinth, — you go ahead, and we will immediately follow. *(The three exit.)* This day shall rescue the religion of our Fathers, and exalt the honour of the Synagogue so that the echo of our glory will be transmitted to later generations.

ALL. Men will speak of us for centuries to come!

CAIAPHAS. Now lead Him away! We follow!

ALL. Death to the Galilean! *(Exit.)*

SIXTH SCENE

Proscenium

The three Ambassadors of the High Council before the House of Pilate

RABBI. Now we may breathe again more freely. We have been insulted quite enough!

DARIABAS. It is indeed high time for the Synagogue to put an end to it. His following was very large.

RABBI. Now there need be no further fear of Him or His followers. The Traders have, these past days, displayed the most commendable activity; they have won over a crowd of most resolute folk. You shall see: if it amounts to anything, these will set the tone for the others. The waverers will accord with them, while the followers of the Nazarene will find it to their advantage to be silent, yea, even to recant.

RABINTH. How shall we bring our suit before Pilate? We dare not enter the house of the Gentile to-day, else we shall become unclean for the Passover.

RABBI. We will send our petition through one of his people. I am known in the house; let me knock at the gate. *(Does so.)* Certainly some one is within. Yes, someone is coming.

QUINTUS *(opens).* Welcome, Rabbi! Just step in!

RABBI. We are not allowed to do so to-day because of our Law.

QUINTUS. Indeed? Can I, perchance, do the errand for you?

RABBI. We are sent hither by the High Priest to lay a petition before the noble representative of Cæsar, requesting that he receive

117

the High Council, who will bring before him a criminal for the confirmation of the death sentence.

QUINTUS. I will immediately notify my Lord. In the mean time wait here. *(Exits.)*

RABINTH. It is disgraceful that we must knock at the door of a Gentile in order to have the sentence of the holy Law ratified.

RABBI. Be of good courage! When once yonder Enemy is removed from our path, then, who knows whether we may not also very soon free ourselves from this stranger?

RABINTH. Oh, may I yet live to see the day which will bring freedom to the Children of Israel!

QUINTUS *(returning).* The Governor greets you! Will you inform the High Priest that Pilate is ready to receive the petition of the Sanhedrin?

RABBI. Our thanks for your kindness! Now let us hasten to inform the High Priest of the outcome of our visit.

RABINTH. Will Pilate agree to the demand of the Sanhedrin?

RABBI. He must. How can he oppose it when the Sanhedrin and the people unanimously clamour for the death of this man?

DARIABAS. What does the life of one Galilean mean to the Governor? Were it only to please the High Priest, who is worth much to him, he would not hesitate to approve of the execution. *(The three exit.)*

SEVENTH SCENE

The End of Judas. Woodland

JUDAS. Where shall I go to hide my shame, to escape the torture of my conscience? No dark forest is deep enough quite, no cavern black enough. O Earth, open up and devour me! I can no longer exist. Alas, my Master, the best of all men, — I have sold you, given you up to every abuse, to the martyr's painful death! I, the abominable traitor! Oh, where exists a man on whom such blood-guilt rests! Alas, nevermore shall I be able to appear before the Disciples as a brother! An outcast, everywhere hated, everywhere abominated; even by those who led me astray, branded as a traitor, alone I wander here and there, with this burning fire in my soul. Ah,

118

could I but once more gaze upon His countenance — I would cling fast to Him, the only anchor! But He lies in prison, and is perhaps already slain through the madness of His enemy. Alas, by my fault, my fault! I — I am the infamous being who sent Him to prison and have brought Him to death! Woe is me — the outcast! For me there is no hope, no more deliverance. My crime is too great; through no atonement can it be expiated. He is dead! and I — I am His murderer!Unhappy hour when my mother brought me into the world! Must I drag on for much longer this martyr's life, and bear these torments — fleeing from men as one who is tainted — shunned and despised by all the world? No, never will I suffer this! Not a step further shall I go! Here, accursèd life, will I put an end to thee. On this branch let hang the accursèd fruit! *(Tearing off his belt.)* Ha, come, thou serpent, grip me strangle the traitor! *(Makes all preparations to hang himself, as the curtain falls.)*

END OF ACT

ACT XI. REPRESENTATION

Christ before Pilate

PROLOGUE.   "Death to the foe of Moses!" The cry is heard,
Echoed by many voices. "Death" is the word!
For the blood of the guiltless they thirst,
With a wild desire accurst!

Impatiently for the sentence they cry:
"Pilate, heed us, for He must die, must die!"
Before the judge their grievances they bring
In eloquence; accusation on accusation fling!

A thousand-voicèd sound 'gainst Daniel rose,
"Great Baal hath he destroyed — a thousand woes!
Away with him, unto the lions' den!
Let him be food for beasts — accurst of men!"

Ah, when deceit hath entered in the heart,
Man of himself destroys the better part.
Injustice lurks a virtue in his eyes,
While sin disports as truth in dark disguise!

(Recit.). "God hath He blasphemed in blindness,
    So no other witness need we!
Condemned He is by holy Law,
    His crucifixion speed we!"
The priest-band thus His death demanded,
And then away to Pilate came they.
What accusations do they utter?
    Hark, what legal judgment claim they?

TABLEAU: *The Governor of the Province impeaches Daniel be-*
fore King Darius, and urges that he be thrown into the lions' den.
Dan. 6 : 4, 13. Even as Daniel was accused without foundation, so
in the same way the High Priest brought forward before Pilate the
most preposterous accusations against Jesus and demanded His
death on the cross.

CHORUS.   Behold this picture, every one.
    Falsely accused was God's own Son,
    As Daniel once in Babylon.
    "Let us, O king, our grievance tell!
    The foe of God is Daniel—
    He hath destroyed the mighty Bel;
    The priests and dragon slain as well!"
    "O King, before thy person stand they—
    All Babylon enraged; demand they
  That if from ruin yourself would save,
    Then haste this Man unto the grave.
    For God whom He by deed defiled,
    Through death alone is reconciled."

SOLO.   The holy Council passionately cry,
    As to the throne of Pilate they draw nigh;
    The blood of Jesus vehemently demand.
    What blinds them that they take this awful stand?
    What is it that their arguments presage,
    So dark their passion and so wild their rage?

CHORUS.   Envy which no pity knows!
    Fire of Hell that inward glows,
    Hath a brand in fury burned,
    Goodness into evil turned!
    Naught is holy in its sight,
    Right is wrong, and wrong is right!
    Woe to those whom Envy trips!
    Woe to those whom Envy grips!

Guard the way unto your soul—
Let not Envy's strength control!
For 't is Satan's joy in part,
To set evil in the heart!

ACTION.

Christ is led before Pilate and is accused by the Priests. Pilate declares Him innocent, but allows Him to be led before Herod.

FIRST SCENE

Before the House of Pilate. To the left, the High Council, the Traders, and Witnesses; to the right, the Guards with Jesus

ABDIAS *(to Christ).* Ha! Know you where you are going?

CROWD. Away with you to death, false Prophet! Ha! Are you afraid, that you do not go forward?

LEVI. Soon you will have your merited reward.

SELPHA. Push Him on!

MELCHI *(striking Him).* Go on! The way is not much more. Shall we have to carry you?

LEVI. This is your last journey.

CROWD. Only on to Calvary. There you may rest comfortably on the cross.

CAIAPHAS *(at the Palace of Pilate).* Be quiet. We must announce ourselves. *(Rabbi advances to the gate and knocks.)*

QUINTUS *(comes out).* What does this crowd want here?

RABBI. The High Council has come.

QUINTUS. I will immediately announce you. *(Exits).*

RABBI *(to the Council Members).* Do you hear! He will not delay announcing our presence.

CAIAPHAS. Members of the High Council! If you have at heart your holy tradition, your honour, the peace of the whole land, then ponder well this moment. It holds us and this Deceiver in the balance. If you are men in whose veins flows any of the blood of your Fathers, then stand firm in your resolve! An immortal monument will be raised to your memory.

121

MEMBERS OF THE COUNCIL. Long live our Fathers! Death to the Enemy of the people!

CAIAPHAS. Do not rest until He has been removed from the quick — until He is on the cross!

ALL. We will not rest! We demand His death, His blood!

CROWD. Do you hear that — you King — you Prophet?

SECOND SCENE

Pilate appears on his balcony with attendants.

CAIAPHAS *(bowing).* Viceroy of the great Emperor at Rome!

ALL. Happiness to you — blessing on you.

CAIAPHAS. We have a man, whose name is Jesus, and whom we have brought hither to your judgement seat, that you may ratify the death sentence pronounced upon Him by the High Council.

PILATE. Lead Him forth! What accusations have you against this Man?

CAIAPHAS. Were He not a great evil-doer, then would we not have handed Him over to you; rather would we have punished Him ourselves according to the regulations of our Law.

PILATE. Now, of what evil deed has He been guilty?

CAIAPHAS. In various ways He has grievously violated the sacred Laws of the people.

PILATE. The take Him away and judge Him according to those Laws!

ANNAS. He has already been judged by the holy Sanhedrin, and has been declared worthy of death.

PRIESTS. For, according to our law, He has deserved death.

CAIAPHAS. But we are not allowed to execute the death sentence on anyone. Therefore we come to the Governor of the Emperor with the request that the sentence be sanctioned.

PILATE. How can I condemn a man to death without knowing his offence and before I have been convinced that his crime is deserving of death? What has He done?

RABBI. The sentence of the High Council against this Man was

122

unanimously given, and was based upon a close examination of His crimes. For that reason it does not seem necessary for the Governor to take upon himself the annoyance of another examination.

PILATE. What, you dare to suggest to me — the representative of the Emperor — that I become a blind instrument for the working of your decree! Far be it from me! I must know what law He has broken, and in what way He has overstepped it.

CAIAPHAS. We have a law; and according to it He must die. For He has represented Himself as the Son of God.

ALL. We have every one of us heard the blasphemy from His own mouth.

ANNAS. Therefore we must insist that He suffer the awful punishment of death.

PILATE. On account of such speech, which at best is only the fruit of a fanciful imagination, a Roman can find no one guilty of death. Who knows whether this Man may not be the Son of God? If you have no other crime to lay to His charge, then do not think that I will perform your desire.

CAIAPHAS. This Man has been guilty of dreadful offence, not only against our Law, but also against the Emperor himself. We have found Him to be an agitator of the people.

ALL. He is a misleader, an insurgent!

PILATE. I have indeed heard of one Jesus, who goes hither and thither through the land, teaching and performing exraordinary deeds. But never have I heard aught of any riot provoked by Him. If anything had occurred of such a nature, I should assuredly have learned of it before you, — I who am the justice of peace in the land and who am apprised of every movement, every deed of the Jews. Yet tell me, when and where has He stirred up a disturbance?

NATHANAEL. He assembled around Him hosts by the thousands, and not so very long ago He gathered together just such a crowd to make a solemn entrance into Jerusalem.

PILATE. I know it, but nothing of a seditious nature occurred.

CAIAPHAS. Is it not treachery when He forbids the people to pay tribute to the Emperor?

PILATE. What proof have you?

CAIAPHAS. . Sufficient evidence, indeed, for He proclaims

Himself the Messiah, the King of Israel. Is not that a challenge threatening the downfall of the Emperor?

PILATE. I admire your suddenly awakened zeal for the authority of the Emperor! *(To Christ.)* Do you hear what severe accusations these people bring against you? What have you to say? *(Christ remains silent.)*

CAIAPHAS. See, He cannot deny it. His silence is a confession of His guilt.

ALL *(in an uproar).* Now, condemn Him!

PILATE. Patience! There is time enough! I will examine Him alone. *(To his attendants.)* Perhaps, when He is no longer overawed by the crowd and by the anger of His accusers, He will speak and give me answer. Lead Him here. *(To the servants.)* Go, my guards will take charge of Him. *(To the members of the Council.)* And you — once more reflect well the foundation or the falsity of your griev-ances, and decide carefully whether these grievances are not born of an ignoble source. Then let me learn your intention. *(He turns from them.)*

JOSUE. Everything has already been thought over and proven. The Law deems Him worthy of death!

RABBI *(to the others).* This is an unfortunate delay!

CAIAPHAS. Do not lose courage! Victory belongs to the resolute! *(Exits.)*

THIRD SCENE

Pilate and his attendants. Christ is brought on to the balcony.

PILATE *(to Christ).* You have heard the accusations of the Council lodged against you. Give me answer as to them! You have, so they say, named yourself the Son of God. Whence are you? *(Christ is silent.)* Do you not even speak to me? Do you not know that I have the power to crucify you as well as to set you free?

CHRIST. You could have no power over me, if it were not given you from on high. Hence he who has delivered me unto you has done a greater sin.

PILATE *(aside).* A candid word! Are you the King of the Jews?

CHRIST. Say you thus to me of your own accord, or because of

124

what others have said to you of me?

PILATE. Am I a Jew? Your people and your priests have handed you over to me. They have accused you of wishing to be the King of Israel. What causes them to do so?

CHRIST. My kingdom is not of this world. For if my kingdom were of this world, then truly would my subjects have fought for me, that I might not have fallen into the hands of the Jews. But my kingdom is not here.

PILATE. Then you are a king?

CHRIST. You say so. I am a king and I came for that purpose into the world, that I might be evidence of the truth. Whoso lives in truth always, he shall hear my voice.

PILATE. What is truth?

FOURTH SCENE

Quintus, the servant of Pilate, enters quickly.

QUINTUS *(excitedly).* My Lord, your servant Claudius is here. He has urgent news to impart to you from your wife.

PILATE. Let him come! Lead him hither at once! *(To Claudius, who enters, after Christ is led away.)* What news have you from my beloved wife?

CLAUDIUS. My Lord, your wife greets you, and begs you earnestly, for her sake as well as for your own, have naught to do against the just and innocent Man who before your judgement seat has been accused. On His account, in the past night, she has suffered the anguish and fear of a terrible dream.

PILATE. Go back to her, and tell her that she may rest without uncertainty. I personally will have naught to do with the machinations of the Jews, but instead shall exert every means to save Him. *(Claudius exits.)*

FIFTH SCENE

PILATE *(to his companion).* I would that I had nothing to do with this business. What do you think, my friends, of these accusations of the Jewish priests?

MELA. It seems to me that envy and jealousy alone have driven them to do this. The consuming hate tells in their words, and in the very expressions of their faces.

SYLVIUS. The hypocrites act as though the authority of the Emperor lay close to their hearts, whereas it is only because they believe their own authority is endangered by this Teacher among the people.

PILATE. I believe you. I cannot imagine that this Man has any criminal plans in mind. He possesses so many lofty qualities — in His features, in His bearing, and His speech is such evidence of His lofty frankness and high talents that, to me, He seems much more a wise Man. Perhaps too wise indeed for these evil men to tolerate the light of wisdom! And the ominous dream of my wife on His account! — If He were really of divine origin? — No, I will positively refuse to meet the demands of the priesthood! *(To his servants.)* Let the High Priest come hither again; and lead forth the Accused once more from the Judgement Hall. *(Servants exit.)*

SIXTH SCENE

The former. Members of the High Council beneath the Balcony.

PILATE. Here again you have your Prisoner. He is without blame!

ANNAS. We have the Emperor's word that our Law shall be upheld. How is He guiltless who rides roughshod over this very Law?

ALL. He is worthy of death!

CAIAPHAS. Is He not also punishable by the Emperor, when He wantonly violates that which through the will of the Emperor has been granted us?

PILATE. I have already told you: If He has transgressed your Law, then punish Him according to that Law, as far as you are empowered to do so. I cannot pronounce the death sentence over Him, because I find nothing in Him which, according to the law by which I am to judge, is deserving of death.

CAIAPHAS. If any one proclaims himself a king in the provinces of the Emperor, is he not a rebel? Does he not merit the punishment of a rebel — the sentence of death?

PILATE.   If this Man has called Himself a king, even then can I not through such ambiguous claims bring myself to condemn Him. It is generally taught among us in Rome that every wise man is a king. But you have not brought forward any evidence, furthermore, which points to His having claimed sovereign power for Himself.

NATHANAEL.   Is there not sufficient evidence in the facts that through Him the people have been thrown into turbulence, and that He has carried His teaching through all Judæa — from Galilee, where He first drew to Him His disciples, even here to Jerusalem?

PILATE.   Is He from Galilee?

ALL.   Yes, He is a Galilean.

RABBI.   His home is in Nazareth, in the province of King Herod.

PILATE.   Ah, if that be so, then I am relieved of judging Him. Herod, the King of Galilee, has come hither for the Feast: he may now render judgement on his subject! Take Him away, and fetch Him before His King. My own bodyguard shall lead Him thither. *(Exits, with his attendant.)*

CAIAPHAS.   Away, then, to Herod! Through him, who himself holds the belief of our Fathers, shall we find better protection for our holy Law!

ANNAS.   And if a thousand hindrances presented themselves, still must the punishment be measured out to the Offender!

ALL *(to Christ).*   An hour sooner or later, still must you come to the end, and at that, this very day! *(All exit.)*

END OF ACT

ACT XII. REPRESENTATION

Christ before Herod.

PROLOGUE.   New anguish falls upon the One we love;
To Herod brought, to that vain worldly prince,
His miracles and second-sight He will not show.

The wisest oft by fools are badly treated!
In garments white, exhibited to view,
This One is sneered at by King Herod's men.

127

In such wise Samson stood — the youthful hero,
Bereft of sight, and fettered and despised —
Because of weakness scorned by Philistines!

But He who now seems weak, will yet be strong!
And He who humble stands, will yet be King!
And He who now is scorned, will yet be loved!

CHORUS.   In vain the High Priests show consuming hate,
Demanding judgement from the heathen's throne;
Yet Herod sits unmoved by all their threats!

SOLO.   Ah, see them drag the Christ to Herod's throne!
The Saviour seems to them a heedless jest!
Alas, His anguish is most terrible!

TABLEAU: *Samson, imprisoned and ridiculed by the Philistines,
rends asunder the pillars to which he is chained. The Philistine
princes are entertained by Samson. Judges 16 : 25. This picture
symbolises the insults and ridicule heaped on Christ by Herod.*

CHORUS.   Yonder is Samson, see how strong his hand,
Yet chains of slavery is he forced to wear!
This hero — Samson — once a thousand slew,
But suffers now the stigma of a slave.

Once dreaded by his enemies, he serves
As target, now, for all their bitter scorn!
The Philistines upon him turn their ire,
Make merry of his weakness and his pain!

'T is thus that Jesus stands, the Son of God!
To haughty foes a pleasing sight He seems,
With insults heaped, and clad in garments white,
Derided and weighed down and sore abused!

ACTION.

*Fall of Herod. Herod, Naasson, Manasses, Courtiers; Zabulon,
Servant*

HEROD.   What? Is it the famous Man from Nazareth whom
they bring here a prisoner to me?

ZABULON.   Certainly, my Lord! I have seen Him, and on the
instant recognised Him.

HEROD.   For a long time I have wished to see this Man, about whose acts the whole land speaks so loudly, to whom the people, as if won by magic stroke, flock in thousands. *(Seats himself).* Could He not very easily be John raised from the dead?

NAASSON.   Oh, no! John performed no miracles. But of this One they relate deeds truly wonderful, if the tales be not magnified.

HEROD.   Since I have so unexpectedly come to see Him, I am most eager to test His magic art.

MANASSES.   He will be very willing to satisfy you therein, in order to gain your favour and protection.

HEROD *(to Zabulon).*   Tell the priests that they may come in with the Prisoner. *(Zabulon exits.)*

MANASSES.   They will likely come with complaints against this Man, since they have been deserted by the people.

HEROD.   They must lodge such before Pilate: Here I have naught to do, naught to judge.

MANASSES.   Perhaps they have been refused by the Governor, and now seek another outlet.

HEROD.   I will not meddle in their quarrels; I will only see Him and test His miraculous powers.

SECOND SCENE

The foregoing. Caiaphas, Annas, Rabbis. The four Priests. Christ, led by the Soldiers of Herod

CAIAPHAS.   O most mighty King!

THE PRIESTS.   Peace and blessings to thee from on high!

CAIAPHAS.   We have brought you here a prisoner from the Council — a criminal, that you may inflict upon Him the penalty of the Law.

NATHANAEL.   The Law demands His death.

ANNAS.   May it please the King to countenance the sentence of the Synagogue.

HEROD.   How can I be judge in a foreign land? Take Him before your Governor; he will render you justice.

CAIAPHAS. Pilate sent Him hither, because, being a Galilean, He is your subject.

HEROD. Is this Man from my district? Who is He?

PRIESTS. He is Jesus of Nazareth.

CAIAPHAS. Hence, Pilate said: Go to King Herod; let him pronounce sentence upon his own subject.

HEROD. And did Pilate speak thus? Wonderful! *(To his courtiers.)* Pilate sends this Man to me? Grants me judicial power in his own territory?

NAASSON. It would seem that he wishes to draw nigh unto you again.

HEROD. This shall be evidence of his renewed friendship! *(To Christ.)* Much, very much have I heard of you through report, and for some while have I wished to see a man over whom the entire land seems astounded.

RABBI. He is a deceiver, an enemy to the holy Law!

HEROD. I have heard that you can solve the mystery of man, and perform deeds exceeding the bounds of nature. Give us proof; let us have evidence of your knowledge, of your high art! We will then believe in you with the people, and likewise we will honour you.

SADOK. O King! Do not allow yourself to be led astray. He is in league with Beelzebub.

HEROD. That is all one to me. Hear you: I had a wonderful dream last night. Can you tell me what it was I dreamed? If so, I will exalt you as a profound interpreter of hearts. *(Christ remains silent.)* You are not able to go so far? Well, then, perhaps you will explain the dream if I tell it to you. I dreamt: I stood on the battlements of my palace at Herodium, and saw the sun go down. Suddenly before me stood a man who stretched out his hand and, pointing to the evening glow, said: "Behold! yonder in Hesperia is Thy bedroom!" Scarcely had the words been spoken, when his form melted away in the mist. I was startled and awoke. If you are inspired as Joseph when he stood before the King of the Egyptians, explain this dream now to your King. *(Christ remains silent, with sad gaze upon Herod.)* Are not you skilled in this special branch, either? Well, then, show us some evidence of your famous magic. Make sudden darkness fall upon this room! — or raise yourself, and go from us without touching the floor! — or change the scroll on which your death sentence is written into a serpent! You will not? Or is it that you cannot? It should be an easy task for you. Much greater marvels do they tell of you! *(To the courtiers.)* He is silent; He does not move! Ah, I see! The reports which have made Him so very famous are naught but empty people's tittle-tattle. He knows nothing and can do nothing!

NAASSON.   It is easy to dazzle the eyes of stupid people sometimes. But it is otherwise — a far different thing — to stand before a wise and powerful king.

MANASSES.   If it is really true that there is something in you, why in this instance keep your learning silent? Why does your power disappear before the eyes of your King, like a bubble?

HEROD.   There is nothing in Him. He is a conceited Man whose head has been turned by the applause of the multitude. *(To the Priests.)* Let Him go! He is not worthy the trouble you take!

CAIAPHAS.   O King! trust not this crafty man. He pretends to be a fool so as to gain, under such pretence a milder sentence from you.

ANNAS.   If He is not put out of the way, then even the person of the King himself is in danger; for He has dared to proclaim Himself as King!

HEROD.   This one? A king? A king of fools, indeed! That is more credible, and as such He deserves to be acknowledged. Therefore I will give Him the gift of a king's mantle and set Him up formally as the King of all fools. *(Signs to his servants.)*

PRIESTS.   Not that — for He deserves death!

CAIAPHAS.   Our King! Upholder of our holy Law! Remember your duty to punish the transgressor as the Law ordains.

HEROD.   What have you really against Him?

RABBI.   He has violated the Sabbath of the Lord.

NATHANAEL.   He is a blasphemer of God.

PRIESTS.   As such, the Law proclaims Him deserving of death!

EZEKIEL.   He has furthermore spoken scornfully of the Temple which your Father so magnificently restored to us: He declared, forsooth, that on that very ground He would build another Temple more beautiful still, and all in three days!

131

HEROD *(laughing).* Now, that assuredly proves Him to be king of all fools!

JOSUE. Of you, also, has He spoken insultingly. Oh, insolent words! He has dared to call you — you, His Lord and King — a fox!

HEROD. Then, in faith, He has attributed to me a quality which He Himself lacks utterly. *(Servants enter with a mantle.)* Clothe Him! Bedecked in this strikingly beautiful king's robe, He will play His role well before the people.

ZABULON *(after having clad Christ).* Now, for the first time you will make a mighty sensation, you great Miracle-worker!

PRIESTS. Death! Death! He shall die!

MANASSES. Many a fool in the land would account himself in honour to be such a king!

FIRST SOLDIER. Come, now, you Wonder-king, let us escort you!

SECOND SOLDIER. What luck for me to walk by the side of such a great Lord! *(They lead Christ away.)*

THIRD SCENE

As before, without Christ and the Soldiers

CAIAPHAS. You are now yourself convinced, O King, that His alleged great deeds are only falsehood and deceit whereby He has duped and misled the people. Render, therefore, the verdict!

PRIESTS. Pronounce the sentence of death upon Him, as the Law requires!

HEROD. My decision is: He is a simple-minded Man and is not capable of the misdeeds of which you accuse Him. If He has done aught or spoken anything illegal, then it must be attributed to His simplicity.

CAIAPHAS. O King! take care that you do not deceive yourself!

ANNAS. I fear that you will yet repent of it if you now let Him go unpunished.

HEROD. I fear naught! One must deal with a fool as a fool; He has already suffered for His follies and will avoid them in future.

Consequently the trial is at an end.

RABBI.   Alas! then is it all over with our Law and religion, with Moses and the Prophets!

HEROD.   I hold to my decision. I am tired and will no longer vex myself with this affair! Pilate may yet decide according to his official duty. Back to him! Present him with greetings and friendship from King Herod! *(The Priests exit.)*

FOURTH SCENE

Herod, Naasson, Manasses

HEROD *(stepping down from his seat)*.   This time the result has not come up to our expectations. I promised myself the great enjoyment of every conceivable miracle and of eloquent speech, but we saw only an ordinary man before us, and heard no sound from His lips.

MANASSES.   How false rumour colours that which on near approach appears to be nothing!

HEROD.   Friends! That is not John! John at least spoke, and spoke with vigour and in wisdom — all of which one must esteem. But yonder Man is as dumb as a fish!

NAASSON.   I only wonder that the Priests persecute Him to death.

HEROD.   Since I have seen Him here myself, I think there is so much less reason for them to get rid of Him. Besides, Pilate would not have sent Him here to me if He had been found guilty of any great crime. It were folly indeed to revenge oneself on such a Man. We have, nevertheless, my friends, sacrificed quite enough time to this troublesome affair. Let us go and make up for lost moments with a more agreeable pursuit. *(They exit.)*

END OF ACT

ACT XIII. REPRESENTATION

The Scourging and The Crown of Thorns

PROLOGUE.   Ah, what a sight to place before their eyes—

133

The followers of Christ are bowed in woe!
The body of the Lord with wounds is marked,
Where countless scourge-strokes cut into His soul!

His head is circled with a crown of thorns,
The sharp spikes drawing drops of sweat and blood!
His face scarce recognised, so great the pain!
Ah, who would not some tears of pity shed!

When Jacob once beheld his loved-one's coat
With blood bespattered, how he trembled then!
How wept he, crying in his sudden grief,
Heart-rending lamentations and deep woe!

Thus let us weep when we behold our Friend—
Our Friend who in such agony is found!
Our sins upon Him have been visited,
And for our sins they wound His loving heart.

SOLO.   As yet they have not ceased their brutal rage;
Their thirst for vengeance is not satisfied!
Their thoughts are bent on murder, while they brood—
This reckless band which Satan's grasp confines!

CHORUS.   Can nothing seem to soften these hard hearts,
Not even when they see His body torn-
His body seared with wounds innumerable?
Is there no hope to waken them to love?

TABLEAU: *Joseph's coat besprinkled with blood. Gen. 37 : 31,
32. The body of Christ is cruelly lacerated by scourge strokes.
Isaac symbolises the sorrowful and dying Messiah. Isaac, the
child of promise, the only son of Abraham, himself carries the
wood over which he shall be sacrificed on Mount Moriah. Jesus,
likewise a child of promise and the only Son of God, drags the
cross to Calvary, in accordance with the old tradition, even a part
of the self-same lofty march. A ram, sacrificed in Isaac's stead,
typifies that Christ shall shed blood when the crown of thorns is
put upon Him.*

Oh, what a scene! what shuddering scene is this!
Behold, the coat of Joseph stained with blood,
While Jacob's cheeks turn pale and in his eyes
Hot tears of deepest sorrow slowly well!

134

SOLO. "Where is my Joseph — my one joy in life,
On whom depended an old father's hope?
Ah, woe! the blood of Joseph stains his coat!
Alas, the blood of Joseph, my dear son!

"A wild beast hath his body rent asunder!
My Joseph, after thee I soon shall follow,
For naught on earth shall comfort me in sorrow!"
So Jacob mourned, and so did he complain,
And nevermore did he his son behold!

CHORUS. 'T is even thus as happened long ago,
The flesh of Jesus shall be torn in rage;
Thus will His precious blood, in anguish spilled,
In streams flow down from every gaping wound!

TABLEAU: *The ram intended for the Sacrifice is entangled in the thorn-bush. Gen. 22 : 13.*

PROLOGUE *(Recit).* Ah, stay thy father's hand and kill him
not,
Abraham, Abraham!
In thy great faith, thy son was given up!
Thus spake Jehovah: "Abraham,
Thy only son whom thou wouldst sacrifice,
Shall, for the Nation's weal, live on with thee!"

SOLO. A ram entangled in a thicket stood,
Which Isaac's father quickly sacrificed,
Since thus Jehovah chose for him to do!

TENOR. A mystery this picture represents,
'T is veiled in sacred shadow, yet behold!
Thorn-crowned stands Jesus, ready with His life,
To make, according to the Father's will,
A sacrifice in payment for our sins!

CHORUS. Oh, where may one encounter any love
Which ever to this love will equal be!

ACTION

Christ is led once more before Pilate, who offers the choice between Him and Barabbas, and allows Jesus to be scourged.

FIRST SCENE

Caiaphas, Annas, of the High Council. Traders and Witnesses appear with Christ again led before Pilate's place, flanked on each side by soldiers.

CAIAPHAS. Now then, Pilate must be pressed importunately, and if he does not judge according to our will, then we must threaten him with impeachment before the Emperor.

ANNAS. Shall I still in my old age see the Synagogue overthrown? Alas, no! With faltering tongue I shall call down blood and death upon the criminal, and not until I see this scoundrel die upon upon the cross will I descend into the grave of my Fathers.

RABBI. Rather would we ourselves be burned beneath the ruins of the Temple than swerve from our resolve.

PHARISEES. We shall not give up until He is dead.

CAIAPHAS. Whoever does not hold to this resolve, let him be cast out from the Synagogue!

ANNAS. The curse of the Fathers fall upon him!

CAIAPHAS. Time presses. The day advances. Now, now, must we set all plans in motion, so that before the Feast our will shall be done.

SECOND SCENE

Pilate appears on the balcony with his attendants.

CAIAPHAS. Once more we bring before your judgement seat this Prisoner, and now we demand His death in all earnestness.

THE PRIESTS AND PHARISEES. We insist upon it! He shall die!

PILATE. You bring me this Man as an inciter of the people, and behold, I have heard your complaints, I have myself examined Him, and have found nothing about Him wherefore you could accuse Him.

CAIAPHAS. We remain firm in our charges. He is a criminal deserving death.

PRIESTS. A criminal against our Law and against the Emperor.

136

PILATE. I sent Him to Herod, because He was a Galilean. Have you there registered your complaints?

CAIAPHAS. Yes, but Herod would not judge Him because you have to command — you are in authority!

PILATE. He also has found nothing in Him which deserves death. However, I will now, in order to meet your wishes, have this Man punished with scourge strokes, but afterwards I shall set Him free.

ANNAS. That will not do.

CAIAPHAS. The law prescribes for such a criminal, not punishment by the scourge, but the punishment of death.

PRIESTS. To death with Him!

PILATE. Is your hatred of this Man so deep, so bitter, that it cannot be appeased with blood from His wounds? You force me to say frankly to you what I think: Driven by ignoble rage, you pursue Him, because the people are more attached to Him than to you! I have heard enough of your despicable complaints. I will now hearken to the voice of the people! Shortly a tremendous crowd will assemble here, according to an ancient custom, to beg the release of one prisoner at the Feast of the Passover. Then I shall see whether your spleen is the reflection of popular sentiment or only your own personal vengeance!

CAIAPHAS *(bowing)*. Events will show, O Governor, that you have unjustly thought evil of us.

JOSUE. Truly, it is not thirst for vengeance, but holy zeal for God's Law — the Law of our Fathers — which incites us to seek His death.

PILATE. You know of the murderer, Barabbas, who lies in chains, and of his infamous deeds. Between him and Jesus of Nazareth I will let the people have choice. Whichever one they choose, to that one will I give freedom.

ALL. Then release Barabbas, and to the cross with the other!

PILATE. You are not the people! The people themselves must pass sentence. Meanwhile I will have this Man scourged. *(To the servants.)* The soldiers shall lead Him forth, and, according to the Roman law, shall scourge Him. *(To his associates.)* Whatever He may have done in any way will thus be sufficiently compensated for,

137

and perhaps the sight of the scourging may soften the blind wrath of His enemies *(Exits with attendants.)*

THIRD SCENE

The Priesthood, etc., under the Empty Balcony

CAIAPHAS.   Pilate calls upon the voice of the people. Well, we also appeal to them. *(To the Traders and Witnesses.)* Now, good Israelites, your time has come! Go hence into the streets of Jerusalem! Summon your friends, our loyal folk, to come hither; gather them together in compact crowds. Kindle their hearts with glowing hate against the Enemy of Moses. The waverers you must strive to win by means of promises and through the strength of your words. Intimidate the followers of the Galilean by a concerted attack upon then, through ridicule, threats, and, if it must be, by means of violence. Act in such manner that none of them will dare show himself here, much less open his mouth!

TRADERS AND WITNESSES.   Indeed, we will hasten and soon return!

DATHAN.   Each of us at the head of an enthusiastic crowd!

CAIAPHAS.   We will assemble in the street of the Sanhedrin. *(The Traders and Witnesses exit. The Priests call after them: "Hail, faithful followers of Moses!")*

CAIAPHAS.   Now let us no longer defer! Let us reach the multitude, exhort them, inflame them!

ANNAS.   From every street in Jerusalem we will lead them before the Court!

RABBI.   If Pilate would hear the voice of the people, he shall hear it!

CAIAPHAS.   He shall hear it — the united cry of a Nation: "Release Barabbas, to the cross with the Galilean!"

ALL.   Release Barabbas! To the cross with the Galilean! *(Exit.)*

FOURTH SCENE

Christ is undressed, His hands tied to a short post and around Him the soldiers.

138

CASPIUS.   Now He has had enough! He is quite dripping with blood!

DOMITIUS.   You pitiable King of the Jews! Ha, ha, ha!

SABINUS.   But what kind of a king is this? He holds no sceptre in His hand, He wears no crown upon His head!

DOMITIUS.   What is not, may yet be easily remedied.

CASPIUS.   Hold, I will fetch immediately the insignia of a king. *(Exits.)*

MILO.   You will now in truth be a king!

SABINUS.   Patience, my Lord; just a little while and you shall be a king.

CASPIUS *(returning with a scarlet mantle, a crown of thorns, and a reed).* Here! This is assuredly a most appropriate attire for a King of the Jews! Is it not true that you have expected such an hour as this? Come let us hang this royal robe upon you.

SABINUS.   But sit down. A king should not stand!

MILO.   And here a royal, spiked crown! *(Forces it upon His head.)* King of the Jews, let us see you! *(General laughter.)*

DOMITIUS.   But that it may not fall from your head, we must set the crown firmly. Lay hold, Brothers, help me! *(Four soldiers seize the ends of two rods, and press therewith upon the crown. Christ quivers in pain.)*

SABINUS.   And here is the sceptre! Now you need nothing more!

CASPIUS.   What a king! *(Kneeling before Him.)* Hail to Thee, most mighty King of the Jews, — ha, ha, ha!

QUINTUS *(the servant of Pilate, entering.)*   The Prisoner must be brought immediately to the Court!

SABINUS.   You arrive inopportunely. You interrupt our homage.

CASPIUS.   But we shall come on the instant. *(Quintus exits.)*

MILO.   Stand up! We will lead you around as a spectacle.

SABINUS.   There will be jubilation among the Jews when their King appears before them in such splendour.

CASPIUS.   Take Him; we cannot delay! *(They exit with Christ.)*

END OF ACT

ACT XIV. REPRESENTATION

Jesus condemned to Death on the Cross

PROLOGUE: Behold the abject figure of the Lord!
Pilate himself, with pity touched, protests!
Have you no mercy, you deluded folk?

No, for in madness they still cry,
"The cross for Him — to torture and to death!"
And then they shout: "Barabbas must be free!,,

How differently in Egypt Joseph stood,
While songs of exultation people raised—
As Saviour of the land was he proclaimed!

But round the Saviour of the world there beats
The fury of a blinded Nation's rage,
Which stays not till the Judge bids crucify.

Ah, see the King, behold how He is scorned!
Behold Him crowned, alas, with such a crown,
And such a sceptre held within His hand!
Upon His shoulders they have purple hung,
In tattered folds to please the executioners mood!
Is such a festive robe designed for kings?
Ah, what a Man!
Where lurks divinity in such a garb?
Ah, what a Man!
Divinity is made a plaything of the hour!

TABLEAU: *1.   Joseph is presented to the people as ruler. Gen. 41 : 41. As Joseph was set free from prison and was raised to the throne of the Egyptians as the Saviour of the Land, so Jesus rose from the grave and established Himself as the world's Saviour. The tableau symbolises the manner in which the Jews preferred the murderer, Barabbas, to Christ.*

CHORUS.   "Behold what a Man!"
'T was in compassion thus that Pilate cried.

140

Behold, what a Man!
A shout of joy was that which Joseph heard!

Through Egypt shall the tidings now go forth,
"Long life to Joseph, honour be to him!"
A thousand-fold shall it be made to sound!
Father, Protector, and Defender is he!
Let all unite in happy exultation!
Father of Egypt — thus was Joseph hailed!

SOLO.   The eyes of Egypt rest upon thee!
As Saviour Egypt long shall praise thee!
On thee they now will all their trust bestow,
To thee they will their homage render—
Through Egypt shall it be proclaimed! *(Rep.)*

TABLEAU: 2.   *The symbol of the two kids, one of which is let
go the other of which is killed for the sins of the people. Lev. 16 : 7.*

SOLO.   The ancient covenant the Lord demanded—
Two goats — and one for sacrifice was chosen.

CHORUS.   Jehovah, Lord! because we spill this blood,
Be Thou unto Thy people good again!

SOLO.   No more the blood of goats the Lord will have,
But purity must mark the sacrifice.

CHORUS.   From every stain the sacrifice must be,
And pure the emblem also which they raise!
The Lord would have the first-born of the flock;
Already are the cries of vengeance heard;
The Lamb will rise and fall and rise again!
PEOPLE *(behind the curtain).*   Let Barabbas be
From fetters free!

CHORUS.   No, no! 't is Jesus must be free!
How wild, alas, it sounds — the murderer's cry!

PEOPLE *(behind the curtain).*   To the cross, to the cross,
To the cross with Him!

CHORUS.   Ah, look on Him!
Ah, look on Him!
What evil has He done?

PEOPLE *(behind the curtain).*   If you release this wicked Man,
Then are you no more Cæsar's friend!

CHORUS. Jerusalem! Jerusalem!
The blood of Jesus will the Lord avenge!

PEOPLE *(behind the curtain)*. Upon us and our children let it fall!

CHORUS. Then, let it be indeed upon you all!

ACTION.

Pilate brings the scourged and thorn-crowned Christ before the people, who demand His death and the release of Barabbas. Pilate's former resoluteness wavers, and he frees Barabbas, at the same time pronouncing upon Jesus the sentence of death.

FIRST SCENE

From three sides, representing as many streets in Jerusalem, come three groups of shouting people, headed by Priests and Pharisees. Nathanael and Ezekiel to the right and left; while in the midst of the centre group stand Caiaphas and Annas. The priests inflame the crowd which stretches far back. The groups come together in one mob, crying to Pilate, amidst threats, for the release of Barabbas and the death of Christ.

NATHANAEL. Moses, your Teacher, calls upon you. His holy Law cries out to you for vengeance!

PEOPLE A. We are and shall always be the followers of Moses. We will have naught to do with any other teacher!

PEOPLE B. We are faithful to our Priests! Away with any who would rise against them!

PEOPLE C. You are our Fathers, as heretofore. We answer for your honour.

ANNAS. Come, children, throw yourselves into the arms of the Sanhedrin. Let it protect and serve you!

EZEKIEL. Shake it off — shake it off — the yoke of the Deceiver!

PEOPLE D. We would be free, free of this false Teacher; we would have nothing more to do with Him — this Nazarene!

PEOPLE A. The people applaud you!

THE FOUR RINGLEADERS *(Caiaphas, Annas, Nathanael,*

Ezekiel). The God of your Fathers will receive you again into His favour. Once more you are to Him a holy People!

ALL. In you we recognise our truest friends. Long live the holy Sanhedrin! Long live our Teachers, our High Priest!

ANNAS. And death to the Galilean!

CAIAPHAS. Up! Let us hasten to Pilate!

ALL. Away to Pilate! The Nazarene shall die!

CAIAPHAS. He has falsified the Law! He has defied Abraham, Moses, and the Prophets; He has blasphemed God!

ALL. To death with this false Prophet!

PEOPLE B. Death on the cross!

PEOPLE C, D. Pilate must have Him crucified!

NATHANAEL. On the cross He shall expiate His crimes.

PEOPLE B, C. We shall not rest until the sentence is given. *(The crowds flow towards the background.)*

CAIAPHAS *(leading the mob by look and gesture).* Hail to you, Children of Israel! You are indeed still the true descendants of the holy father Abraham. Oh, exult that you have escaped the unspeakable ruin that this Deceiver would have brought upon you and your children!

ANNAS. The ceaseless efforts of your Fathers have kept the Nation from the abyss.

ALL. Long live the High Council! Death to the Nazarene!

PRIESTS. Curse him who does not aid in His death!

ALL. We demand His death!

CAIAPHAS. Let Him be cast out from the heritage of our Fathers!

ALL. Let Him be cast out!

CAIAPHAS. Pilate will give you the choice between this Blasphemer and Barabbas. Let us stand resolute for the release of Barrabbas!

ALL. Let Barabbas be free! And down with the Nazarene!

ANNAS. You Fathers! Be praised! Our wishes are heard!

ALL. Pilate must give his consent. It is the will of the Nation!

CAIAPHAS. Most glorious day for the people of Israel! Children, be firm!

PRIEST. This day restores honour to the Synagogue and freedom to the people.

CAIAPHAS *(as they draw near to Pilate's house)*. Now, let us demand the death sentence, let us threaten Him with general riot.

ALL *(tumultuously)*. We demand the death, the blood of our Enemy!

SOLDIER *(coming through the door)*. Tumult and insurrection!

ALL. The Nazarene shall die!

CAIAPHAS. Show courage! Remain undaunted! A righteous cause protects us!

ALL. Pilate, pronounce the death sentence!

POMPONIUS *(Pilate's servant, on the balcony)*. Quiet! Peace!

ALL. No, we will not rest until Pilate has given the death sentence!

POMPONIUS. Pilate will come immediately. *(Exits.)*

ALL. We demand the death of the Nazarene!

CAIAPHAS *(to the Priests)*. Now may Pilate learn the temper of the people, as he wished!

SECOND SCENE

The same. Pilate and his attendants come on to the balcony. The thorn-crowned Christ is likewise led forward by two soldiers.

ALL. Now judge you, and pronounce the sentence upon Him.

PILATE *(pointing to Jesus)*. Behold, what a man!

PRIESTS AND PHARISEES. To the cross with Him! To the cross!

PILATE. Can this pitiable plight win no compassion from your hearts?

ALL. Let Him die! To the cross with Him!

PILATE. Then take Him, and crucify Him at your own peril! I will have nothing to do with it, for I find no fault in Him.

CAIAPHAS. Hear, O Governor of the mighty Emperor, hear the voice of the people! Behold, it accords with our feeling, and calls for His death.

PEOPLE. Yes, we demand His death!

PILATE *(to the soldiers).* Lead Him down! and bring Barabbas hither from prison! Have the gaoler hand Him over immediately to the head lictor.

ANNAS. Let Barabbas live! Upon the Nazarene pronounce the sentence of death!

ALL. To death with the Nazarene!

PILATE. I do not understand these people! A few days back, shouting in approval and for joy, they followed this Man through the streets of Jerusalem. Is it possible that to-day these self-same people cry death and destruction upon Him? It is contemptible vacillation!

CAIAPHAS. The good people have at last come to see that they have been deceived by an adventurer who has presumed to call Himself the Messiah, the King of Israel.

NATHANAEL. Now the eyes of these people have opened wide, and they see how He cannot help Himself, — He who promised to bring freedom and happiness to the Nation.

EZEKIEL. Israel will have no Messiah who allows Himself to be caught and bound and treated with such scorn!

PEOPLE. Death to the false Messiah! To the Cheat!

PILATE. Listen, men of Judæa! It is customary for me to free a prisoner on the Feast day. Behold these two: the one with the gentle countenance, worthy bearing, the ideal of a wise teacher whom you have long honoured as such, convicted of no wicked deed, and already humbled through sore chastisement; the other a culpable, lawless man, a convicted robber and murderer! I appeal to your better judgment, to your human sympathy. Choose! Which would you that I should let go, Barabbas, or Jesus, the Christ so called?

PEOPLE. Free Barabbas!

PILATE. Would you not rather that I should liberate the King of the Jews?

PEOPLE.   Away with Him! Set Barabbas free!

CAIAPHAS.   You have promised to give freedom to him whom the people choose.

PILATE *(to Caiaphas).*   I am accustomed to keep my promise without needing a reminder! *(To the Crowd.)* What shall I then do with this King of the Jews?

PRIESTS AND PEOPLE.   Crucify Him! Crucify Him!

PILATE.   How! Shall I crucify your King?

PRIEST.   We have no king, — only an Emperor!

CAIAPHAS.   As Governor, you alone are answerable for the consequences.

PILATE.   No! I cannot condemn this Man, for I find in Him no guilt. He has been sufficiently disciplined. I cannot, I dare not, condemn the guiltless!

PRIESTS.   If you release Him, then you are no friend of the Emperor.

CAIAPHAS.   He proclaimed Himself King!

PRIESTS.   And whosoever proclaims Himself King is a traitor to the Emperor!

NATHANAEL.   And shall this rebel remain unpunished, and be allowed to continue scattering abroad the seeds of His heresy?

PEOPLE.   It is the Governor's duty to get rid of Him!

CAIAPHAS.   We have done our part as subjects of the Cæsar, for we have delivered this Agitator to you. If you do not heed our accusations, and the demands of the people, then we are free from all blame.

ANNAS.   If general insurrection results on account of this Man, then we shall know who is to blame, who should be made to bear the guilt of it, and we shall take care that the Emperor is told of it!

PEOPLE.   The Cæsar shall hear of the matter!

EZEKIEL.   In astonishment, the people in Rome will hear that the Governor has taken under his protection a person guilty of high treason — a person whose death was demanded by all of us.

146

PEOPLE.   You must crucify Him, else there will be no peace in the land!

PILATE.   Why, what evil has He done?

CAIAPHAS.   Allow me to ask a question. Why should you take such care in judging this man? Quite recently, because of a few seditious outcries, you had hundreds, in groups and singly, massacred by your soldiers without trial, without sentence. *(Pilate starts.)*

PEOPLE.   You dare not befriend this One now, if you are a true servant of the Emperor!

PILATE *(in agitation)*.   Bring me water!

CAIAPHAS.   The people will not leave here until you have pronounced the death sentence.

PEOPLE.   No, we will not go until the death sentence is given!

PILATE.   Thus you compel me through your violence to consent to your demands. Take Him away and crucify Him; but know *(makes a gesture)*: I wash my hands of it. I will not be guilty of the blood of this innocent, this righteous Man. You must answer for it!

PEOPLE.   We take it upon ourselves. His blood upon us and our children!

PILATE.   Let Barabbas go free according to the will of the people. Lead him away — outside the city gate, that he may nevermore set foot therein.

HEAD LICTOR.   Take him away and follow me! *(Soldiers lead Barabbas away.)*

PRIESTS *(to Pilate).*   Now you have judged rightly!

PILATE.   I have only yielded to your violent pressure, so as to prevent any greater evil. But I will have no share in the blood-guilt. His blood — let it fall upon you and your children!

PEOPLE.   Well, let it be so.

ANNAS.   We and our children will bless the day, and cry out with thanksgiving and joy: Fortune and happiness to the Governor, Pilate! Long live Pilate!

PEOPLE.   Long live our Governor, Pontius Pilate!

PILATE.   Bring forth the two murderers who are in prison.

147

They have deserved death more, very much more than the Accused here. Let the head lictor hand them over to the guard.

HEAD LICTOR. Drive them on, the infamous pair! *(They come into view.)*

RABBI. Behold! What a worthy company yonder for the Messiah on His last journey!

PILATE. Now let the death sentence be known. *(To the Scribes who have been writing steadily during the time the head lictor was driving the thieves forward. Then turning to the thieves.)* Of you and your horrible deeds, the earth shall be well rid to-day. You are to die on the cross! *(To the Scribes.)* Read on!

SCRIBE. I, Pontius Pilate, Governor of the province of Judæa, and under the mighty Emperor, Claudius Tiberius, pronounce in accordance with the importunate clamours of the High Priests, the Sanhedrin, and all the people in Judæa, the sentence of death upon one Jesus of Nazareth, so known, who stands accused of having incited the people to rebellion, of having forbidden them to pay tribute to the Emperor, and of having proclaimed Himself King of the Jews. This same Jesus shall, outside the city walls, be crucified between two evil-doers, who, because of many robberies and murders, have likewise been condemned to die. Done at Jerusalem, on the eve of the Passover.

PILATE *(breaking the staff)*. Now, take Him away and — crucify Him! *(Exits hastily.)*

CAIAPHAS. Victory! The triumph is ours! The Enemy of the Synagogue is overthrown!

ALL *(Priests and people)*. Away with Him to Golgotha! Long live the Synagogue! Long live Moses and the Nation!

ANNAS. Hasten, that we may return home in time!

ALL. We will keep this Passover joyfully, even like our Fathers in Egypt!

CAIAPHAS. Let us triumph through the streets of Jerusalem!

RABBI. Where are the friends of the Nazarene — His Disciples? They are invited to join in the triumph — to cry Hosanna!

PEOPLE *(crying as they go)*. Up and away! — Off to Golgotha! — Come and see Him as He faints on the cross! Oh, happy day! The Enemy of Moses is overthrown! — Ha! Now He has His reward! —

148

Thus let it be done to every one who defies the law! He deserves death on the cross! — Oh, most happy Passover! Now joy will return unto Israel! It is all over with the Galilean! *(Exit tumultuously.)*

END OF ACT

END OF SECOND PART.

THIRD PART

From the Condemnation by Pilate until the Glorious Resurrection of the Lord

ACT XV. REPRESENTATION

The Way to the Cross

PROLOGUE. The sentence has been forced, and now they go
Unto Golgotha, called the Mount of Skulls,
While Jesus staggers, burdened with the cross.

'T was thus that Isaac on his shoulders bore
The sacrificial wood unto the heights
Where he himself as offering was doomed.

So, willingly, the weight does Jesus bear,
The cross which through the power of His lover
Shall for us come to mean the Tree of Life.

For, as the brazen serpent long ago
Did once bring healing in the wilderness,
So from the cross will happiness be born.

TABLEAUX

CHORUS. Worship and give thanks, for He who from the Cup
Partook of Sorrow goes unto His death,
And seeks thereby to reconcile the world with God!

1. *Isaac, dedicated to the sacrifice, ascends Mount Moriah, laden with wood. Gen. 22 : 1 - 10. So, likewise, Christ ascends Calvary, carrying the heavy wooden cross.*

SOLO. As the wood for offering
Was carried once by Isaac to Moriah,
So, staggering with the cross,
Jesus toward Golgotha laden goes!

CHORUS. Worship now!

2. *Moses raises a brass moulded serpent upon a cross-bar. Num. 21 : 8 - 19. The brazen serpent is a symbol of the crucifixion of Christ. Every one is aided by sight of the serpent raised by Moses. Christ will be raised on the cross, and he who gazes upon Him will be*

healed of a wounded soul.

PROLOGUE *(Recit.).* The Son of Man is nailed unto the cross,
And will be raised on high!
The symbol of the cross in Moses' rod
You now shall see.

CHORUS. Worship, worship!

ACTION

*Christ bowed down by the weight of the cross, is led toward Golgotha,
and meets His afflicted Mother. Simon of Cyrene is forced to take
the cross from Him; some women of Jerusalem weep for Jesus.*

FIRST SCENE

*The Holy Women, with John and Joseph of Arimathæa, on their Way
from Bethany*

MARY *(to John).* John! Alas, dear Disciple! How do you think
it has gone with my Jesus since you saw Him last in the house of
Caiaphas?

JOHN. If the Priests could do as they would, then already
would He be counted among the dead. But they dare not carry out
the sentence without permission from the Governor. And Pilate, I
hope, will not condemn Him, since He has done no evil, but only
good always.

MARY MAGDALENE. May the Almighty prompt the heart
of the Governor to righteousness, that he may protect the innocent
from intrigue and malice!

MARY. Whither do we go, friends, ah, whither? That I may once
more see my Son? I must see Him! Yet where shall I find Him? Perhaps, alas, He languishes in a dark prison!

MARY MAGDALENE. Woe! The dearest of Teachers in
prison!

JOHN. No one is to be seen from whom we might inquire.

JOSEPH. The best thing for us to do is to go to Nicodemus;
from him we shall assuredly learn how it passes with the dear
Master.

151

MARY. Yes, let us go there! My sorrow and my doubt as to the fate of my Son increase with every moment.

JOHN. Come, our Mother, be strong in your belief! Whatever happens — it is God's will. *(The cry, "On, on with Him!" is heard in the distance. The crowd drives Jesus forward, and He sinks beneath His load.)*

JOSEPH. What is that? — that terrible noise?

SALOME. As though a thousand voices! What does it mean? *(They listen intently.)*

SECOND SCENE

The Procession of the Cross-bearing. Priests, Pharisees, people, soldiers moving through the Street of Annas. The scene is one of motion. A captain, with his staff of command; a horseman, with a Roman banner. Christ painfully drags the cross, four execution-ers close behind Him.

PEOPLE. Away with Him! He dies, and all who hold with Him must give way!

AGRIPPA *(executioner).* Oho! Is the burden already too heavy for you?

PRIESTS AND PHARISEES. Drive Him on by force, that we may reach Calvary!

FAUSTUS *(executioner).* Stop, He will sink! *(Meanwhile the group in Pilate Street are still in ignorance as to what is the matter.)*

JOSEPH. What shall we do? Amidst this sinister crowd of people we dare not risk ourselves within the city.

SALOME. I tremble!

MARY MAGDALENE. What may this noise mean?

MARY. Has it aught to do with my Son?

JOSEPH. A riot seems to have broken forth.

JOHN. We will remain here until the storm has blown over.

SIMON OF CYRENE *(bearing a basket, comes hastily and uneas-ily from middle stage to front).* I must hasten that I may reach the city, for the eve of the great Feast advances. I have only a short while in which to purchase the necessities and to make ready all things, so that I may return home in time.

PRIESTS AND PEOPLE *(as yet unseen by Simon).* Don't let Him rest! On! Drive Him forward with blows!

SIMON. I hear noises — the cry of men: what could have happened in the city? I will remain here for a little; perhaps my ear has deceived me.

CATILINA *(executioner).* It is of no use to waver! *(Speaking to Christ.)* You must move on towards Golgotha.

AHASUERUS *(rushing out of his house, to Simon).* Away from here! This is no place for rest!

SIMON. The noise grows louder. I must hurry and see what it is. Ah! what is yonder? I cannot go into that. I will await the issue. *(He moves toward Annas Street.)*

THIRD SCENE

The procession with Christ finally comes into view. Meanwhile, from the depth of the middle stage, Veronica and the women of Jerusalem draw near.

JOSEPH. I believe the multitude is coming from the city gates.

JOHN. It looks as though some one were being led toward Calvary for execution.

MARY *(discovering Jesus).* Ah, God! It is He! It is my Son! My Jesus! *(Her companions support her.)*

CENTURION *(to Jesus, who has thus far staggered along, but now has fallen).* He holds us back. Here, strengthen yourself! *(Hands a flask. Jesus takes it, but does not drink.)*

JOHN, MARY MAGDALENE, SALOME *(holding Mary).* Mother, dearest Mother!

MARY. Alas, thus do I see Him being led to His death, like a miscreant between evil-doers!

JOHN. Mother! It is the hour which He prophesied. Such is the will of the Father!

CENTURION. Will you not drink?

PHARISEES. Drive Him on!

153

NERO *(executioner, striking and shaking Jesus)*.   Stir yourself —
you lazy King of the Jews!

FAUSTUS.   On, on! Pull yourself together! We must get on!

MARY.   Oh, where is the sorrow equal to my sorrow!

CATILINA *(as Jesus staggers)*.   He is so very weak. Some one
must help Him, else —

RABBI *(pointing to Simon)*.   Here, that stranger yonder!

PHARISEES.   Lay hold on him!

CENTURION *(captian)*.   Come here you! You have broad
shoulders for carrying!

SIMON.   I? No — I must — I —

NERO.   Certainly you must, or be beaten into doing it!

SIMON.   I know not —

CENTURION.   You will know soon enough; do not refuse!

FAUSTUS.   If you do, you shall come to feel the strength of my
arm!

PHARISEES.   Strike him, if he refuses.

SIMON.   I am indeed innocent, I have done no crime!

CENTURION.   Be silent!

SIMON *(being dragged along)*.   Not with such force! *(Seeing
Christ.)* What do I behold? Yonder is the holy Man from Nazareth.

FAUSTUS.   Your shoulders here! *(They take the cross from
Jesus and put it upon Simon.)*

SIMON.   Out of love for you will I carry it. Oh, if I only could
thereby make myself of use to you!

CHRIST *(standing to one side, exhausted)*.   God's blessing upon
thee and thine!

CENTURION.   Now, forward! *(To Simon.)*   Follow us with
the cross-beam!

AGRIPPA *(to Christ)*.   Now you can move along more rapidly.

FAUSTUS *(laying hold of Jesus by the nape of the neck and shaking
Him)*.   Something still keeps you back? Even though the cross has
been taken from you?

CATILINA.   Are you still further in need?

CENTURION.   Let Him be. We will rest now for a while, so that He may have time to recover before He climbs the hill of death — to Calvary. *(Veronica and the women of Jerusalem draw near.)*

CAIAPHAS.   Another delay! When shall we ever come to Calvary? Make haste!

VERONICA *(kneeling before Jesus and offering Him her handkerchief).*   Oh, Lord, how your face is covered with blood and sweat! Will you not take my handkerchief and wipe it dry?

CHRIST *(taking the cloth from her, and, after making use of it, returning it).*   Compassionate Soul, the Father will requite thee for this!

SARA *(three women draw near with their little ones).*   Our good Teacher!

REBECCA.   Oh never to be forgotten Benefactor!

SUSANNA.   Most noble Friend of Mankind! Alas, thus are you rewarded!

REBECCA.   How we pity you! *(They weep.)*

CHRIST.   Daughters of Jerusalem, do not weep over me, but weep ye over yourselves and your children! For behold, I say unto you: The days are coming in which they shall say: Blessed are the barren and the wombs that never bear, and the breasts that have never given suck. Then will they call aloud to the mountains: Fall upon us; and to the hillocks: Shelter us! For if that is done in the green wood, what will be done in the dry?

RACHEL.   Alas, how will it come to pass in the future for us and for our children? *(The women weep.)*

CENTURION.   Remove these womenfolk! It is time for us to go forward.

AGRIPPA.   What use are your tears? Back!

CATILINA.   Back!

FAUSTUS, NERO *(to Christ).*   Away with you to the hill of death!

PEOPLE.   Quickly — forward to Calvary!

RABBI.   At last we are moving!

155

NATHANAEL. The Centurion is much too considerate.

PRIEST. Don't spare Him anything! *(The procession is in motion when the servant of Pilate arrives.)*

FOURTH SCENE

SERVANT. Stop! It is the command of the Governor that the Centurion appear before him as quickly as possible to obtain further orders. *(The procession stops.)*

CAIAPHAS. What does this mean? Why new orders? The death sentence has been pronounced and must be executed without delay.

CENTURION *(severely)*. No, it will not be until I have heard the commands of the Governor! *(To the soldiers.)* Keep guard meanwhile, and proceed with the condemned to Golgotha. Then *(pointing to Simon)* dismiss this man, and await my return. *(Exits with the servant. The procession again moves on in the direction of the middle stage, back.)*

PEOPLE *(wildly shouting to one another)*. Away, away to Golgotha! To the cross with Him! To the cross! Hail, Israel! The Enemy is conquered! His death is our happiness! We are free! Long live the Synagogue, the Sanhedrin!

SUSANNA. These cries pierce to Heaven! *(The women move away, weeping.)*

JOHN. Mother, shall we not return to Bethany? You will not be able to bear the sight!

MARY. How can a mother forsake her child in his last and most bitter need?

KLEOPHA. But evil and harm might befall you also, if they recognised you as His Mother.

MARY. I will suffer with Him, and with Him share scorn and insult — yea, with Him die!

JOHN. If only the strength of the flesh does not succumb!

MARY. Fear nothing! I have prayed to God for strength. The Lord has heard me! Let us follow!

156

ALL.   Best of mothers! We follow you! *(They move with the procession.)*

ACT XVI. REPRESENTATION

Jesus upon Golgotha

The Chorus, grief-stricken, appears, clad in black.

PROLOGUE *(Recit.)*.   Ye pious souls, arise and with me go
    Unto Golgotha in remorse and pain!
    Behold, ye pious souls, what there befell—
    The Intercessor between Sin and God
    Made thus to suffer the atonement death!

    In nakedness, His wounds are what you see—
    He yonder lies in anguish on the cross.
    'T is vengeance wantonly makes sport with Him,
    While, for the love of sinners, He is still,
    And shows forgiveness, — suffers and endures.

    Hark, do you hear? His limbs are rent and torn,
    As from their sockets they are rudely dragged!
    Who would not quake to hear the hammer strokes
    Which cruelly cut, alas, through hands and feet, —
    The nails through each limb pressed unerringly!

(There is heard behind the curtain a dull, penetrating sound of hammer blows.)

    Oh, come, ye souls, and raise your countenances,
    Unto the cross compassionately turn!
    Yonder, behold the tender Lamb of God,
    Who blood and life for you has sacrificed!
    Behold, between two murderers He hangs—
    The Son of God — beneath the weight of scorn!

    Would you not dedicate your tears to Him?
    Behold, how now He opens His mouth and begs
    That pardon for the murderers be given;

And unto God He utters His last prayer,
While through His side someone a spear has thrust,
Which leaves exposed His sacred heart to view!

Who of us can such high love comprehend,
Which animates a tender heart like this—
A love which ever unto Hate gives Good,
Which for the world its life would sacrifice?
Ah, bring to this Belovéd on the cross
Your heart's clean impulse as an offering!

ACTION.

*Jesus is raised and fastened to the cross. The crowd jeers at Him. Jesus'
last words, and His death. Precautions taken by the Jews for
guarding the grave. The burial of the body of Jesus.*

FIRST SCENE

The scene is set on the middle stage. As the curtain ascends, the crosses of the two thieves are in the act of being raised. Christ on His cross, is still flat on the ground. Lictors, executioners, High Priest, Pharisees, people. In the background, the holy women, with John, Joseph, and Nicodemus.

EXECUTIONERS *(pointing to the thieves, after they have been raised).* We have finished with these. Now must the King of the Jews be raised on His throne!

PHARISEES. No King, but a Betrayer! Traitor!

CENTURION. First, however, by command of the Governor, this incription must be fastened to the cross. Faustus, put it on!

FAUSTUS. A sign! Ha, that is indeed very regal! *(Fastens on the inscription.)*

CENTURION. Take hold, now, and raise the cross! — Only, not carelessly.

CATILINA. Up! Double your strength, man! Heave to! *(They pull.)*

NERO. All right now! The cross stands firm!

CENTURION. The painful duty is accomplished!

158

CAIAPHAS.   And quite excellently done!

PHARISEES.   Thanks — we thank you!

PEOPLE.   Thanks and our approval!

CAIAPHAS.   For all times shall this be a Feast day to us!

PHARISEES.   Yes, and most solemnly shall it be celebrated.

ANNAS.   And now right willingly will I be gathered unto my Fathers, because I have lived long enough for the joy of seeing this Wretch on the cross! What is the inscription? What is its meaning? Is it not very short?

RABBI *(stepping near).*   That is ridiculous! Truly an insult for us and for the people!

CAIAPHAS.   What is written thereon?

AMAN.   The Rabbi is right. The Council cannot countenance this!

RABBI.   It reads: Jesus of Nazareth, King of the Jews. *(The four executioners lie down beneath the cross.)*

CAIAPHAS.   Truly, that is an insult to our Nation!

PHARISEES.   The inscription must go. Tear it down!

CAIAPHAS.   We dare not ourselves lay hands upon it. Have patience! *(To two Priests.)* Rabbi and Saras! Hasten to Pilate, and, in the name of the High Council and of all the people, demand the alteration of this inscription. It should be written that *He has said:* I am the King of the Jews. At the same time petition Pilate to have the bones of the crucified broken before the eve of the Feast, and their bodies taken from the crosses. *(Rabbi and Saras exit.)*

CATILINA.   Now, comrades, let us divide our spoils! *(Takes up Christ's coat and mantle.)* Look, this mantle can be divided first. *(The four executioners seize the cloth and tear it with a jerk into four parts.)* But the coat is not sewn together. Shall we, however, cut it to pieces?

FAUSTUS.   No, better throw lots for it!

AGRIPPA.   Here are the dice. I will try my luck immediately. *(Throws.)* That is too little. I have no chance.

CATILINA *(glancing toward Christ).*   Hi there, you! If you can work any miracle on the cross, then favour my throw! *(Throws.)*

159

THE OTHERS. What has He got to do with it? Lost!

NERO. Shall I be more lucky? Fifteen! Nearly enough. Now it is your turn, Faustus.

FAUSTUS. I must have it! *(Throws.)*

CATILINA *(examining the dice).* Eighteen! That is the best!

AGRIPPA. It is yours! Take it away!

NERO. You are forsooth not to be envied.

RABBI *(returning).* Our mission was in vain.

SARAS. He would not hear us!

CAIAPHAS. Did you not receive any answer?

RABBI. This only: What I have written shall remain as it was written.

ANNAS *(aside).* Ha! Intolerable!

CAIAPHAS. And what instructions did he give you with regard to the breaking of the bones?

RABBI. Concerning that, he said he would send his orders to the Centurion.

JOSUE *(to Christ).* So, then, it remains written: King of the Jews! Ei! If you are King of Israel, then come down now from the cross, that we may see and believe. *(Laughter.)*

ELIAZAR. You who would tear down the Temple of God in three days, and would built it up again in three, help yourself now!

CAIAPHAS. Ha! Others has He helped, but He cannot help Himself!

NUN. Come down! For verily, you are the Son of God! Have you not indeed claimed so?

ANNAS. He has trusted in God. Let God save Him now, if it so pleases Him!

NERO. How? Do you not hear?

AGRIPPA. Show your power, worthy King of the Jews!

CHRIST *(whose head has the while hung motionless, now raises it with a look of unutterable anguish).* Father, forgive them, for they know not what they do!

160

GESMAS *(thief to Christ's left).*   Truly, if you are the Saviour, save yourself now, and us with you!

DISMAS *(thief to Christ's right, addressing the other thief).*   Do you not fear God, since you are condemned to the self-same punishment as myself? We are punished justly; we are being rewarded deservedly for the misdeeds we have done, but yonder One has not committed evil. *(To Christ.)* Lord, remember me when you come unto your Kingdom!

CHRIST.   Verily, I say unto you: To-day will you yet be with me in Paradise. *(Mary and John draw near to the cross.)*

CAIAPHAS.   Listen! He still acts as though He had power over Paradise!

RABBI.   Has His pride not yet weakened, even while He hangs there helpless on the cross?

CHRIST *(showing signs of the end).*   Mother, behold your Son! Son, see your Mother!

MARY.   Even in dying, you yet trouble yourself about your Mother.

JOHN.   Lord, your last will is sacred to me!

CHRIST.   You, my Mother, and I, your Son! I thirst!

CENTURION.   He suffers thirst and calls for drink!

FAUSTUS.   I will hand Him some quickly. *(Takes a pole with a sponge at one end, on which the Centurion has poured from his flask. Christ sips.)*

CHRIST *(in agony).*   Eli, Eli, lama sabachthani!

PHARISEES.   Hear, He calls on Elias!

CAIAPHAS.   Now we shall see whether Elias comes down to help Him!

CHRIST *(breathing heavily).* It is over! Father, into Thy hands my spirit I commend. *(His head drops forward, and He dies. On the instant, a deafening noise is heard, and it grows suddenly dark.)*

ENAN.   What is that? The earth shakes!

HEBRON.   It was an earthquake! Horrible!

AHIRA.   Hear you the crash of falling rocks? Woe unto us!

ENAN.   It is God's hand upon us!

CENTURION.   Verily, this Man was a righteous man!

SOLDIERS.   By this very sign of nature the God on high bears Him witness.

CENTURION.   Oh, His patience in the midst of violent pain — His noble calm, His godly cry to Heaven at the moment of His death — all that foreshadowed something of His high origin! Verily, He is the Son of God!

OZIEL.   Come neighbour; I will stay no longer on this terrible spot!

HELON.   Let us go home. God be merciful unto us!

OTHERS *(striking their breasts)*.   Jehovah! Lord! Almighty God! We have sinned! Show us indulgence! *(The people disperse in remorse and anguish.)*

ZOROBABEL *(servant of the Temple, enters in haste)*.   High Priest, and you members of the Council! Within the Sanctuary a frightful scene has come to pass. Alas, I tremble in every limb!

CAIAPHAS.   What is it? Not the Temple —

ANNAS.   Fallen? Destroyed?

ZOROBABEL.   Not that! But the veil of the Temple has been rent asunder. I hastened here with faltering steps, dreading the while that the whole world was split by the shock.

CAIAPHAS *(pointing to the dead Jesus)*.   All this has yonder Wretch done to us through His magic! Fortunate that He is out of the world, else would He have brought all the elements against one another!

PHARISEES.   Cursed be the allies of Beelzebub!

CAIAPHAS.   Let us now hasten home, and see what has happened. Then hither will we immediately return. For I cannot rest until I have seen that the bones of this fellow are broken, and that His body is flung into the grave for criminals. *(They exit.)*

SECOND SCENE

NICODEMUS *(to Joseph of Arimathœa)*.   Shall the holy body of Him sent by God be thus dishonoured and thrown into the grave of evil-doers? Is there no way to prevent it?

JOSEPH. Listen, friend. I will go straighway unto Pilate, and will beg him fervently to give unto me the dead body of Jesus. This favour he will not refuse me. Friend, then we will render the last honour to our dear Teacher!

NICODEMUS. Do that and make haste! I will bring spices with which to embalm Him. *(They exit.)*

CENTURION *(to the holy women).* Fear not, good women! No harm shall befall you! Come forward and look upon the body of your Friend.

MARY MAGDALENE *(embracing the cross).* My dearest Master! My heart hangs with you on the cross!

SERVANT OF PILATE *(enters and turns to the Centurion).* My Lord commands that the legs of the crucified shall be broken, and that then immediately their bodies shall be taken down. Before the eve of the great Feast all must be over.

CENTURION. It shall be done on the instant. Up with you, men, and first break the bones of yonder thieves!

CATILINA. Come, let us do the work quickly! *(Ascends.)*

FAUSTUS. Strike, so that he dies!

CATILINA *(on the ladder, with blows breaks the bones of the thief on the right).* This one will nevermore awake!

NERO *(who climbs to the thief on the left).* The other will I send from out this world. *(Strikes.)*

MARY. *(shuddering).* My Son! Surely they would not treat your holy body so cruelly!

NERO *(to the thief on the left).* Do you still move? No, now at last he has his reward!

MARY MAGDALENE *(as the executioner moves with his club toward Jesus).* Ah, at least spare Him, spare Him!

CATILINA *(looking up at Jesus).* See! He is already dead! No longer is it necessary to break His bones.

FAUSTUS. But that we may be quite sure, I will pierce His heart with this lance. *(Thrusts the lance into the side of Jesus, and the blood gushes forth.)*

THE HOLY WOMEN. Ah! Alas! Woe!

163

MARY MAGDALENE. Oh, dearest Mother! That stab also enters your heart!

CENTURION. Now take the bodies from the cross!

AGRIPPA. What shall we do with this One?

CENTURION. As we are commanded — into the grave with the thieves!

MARY. What words to wound my heart again!

NERO. Ladders here! They will soon be taken down.

MARY MAGDALENE *(going to the Centurion).* Alas! May we not even now show the last honours to our Friend?

CENTURION. Unfortunately, it rests not in my power to grant you your wish.

FAUSTUS *(to his associate on the lower rung of the ladder).* Go on up; I will hold the ladder.

CATILINA. And I will care for the other. *(They drag the thieves away.)*

THIRD SCENE

The Priests return to Golgotha.

CAIAPHAS *(approaching at the head of the Priests).* The more pleasing will it be for us to see the body of this evil-doer thrown into a shameful grave, after we have beheld the destruction which He has caused in the Temple.

ANNAS. Oh, it would be delight to my eyes to see His limbs torn asunder by wild beasts!

CAIAPHAS. Ha! Look! They are already being taken down. Now we shall see our desires forthwith fulfilled.

SERVANT OF PILATE *(entering with Joseph of Arimathœa. To the Centurion).* The Governor has bid me come and see whether Jesus of Nazareth be really dead, even as this man informed him.

CENTURION. It is so. Behold for yourself! To be absolutely certain, He was also pierced through the heart with a lance.

SERVANT. Then I am commanded to inform you that His body is to be handed over to this man as a gift from Pilate. *(Exits.)*

164

HOLY WOMEN. Oh, comforting words!

RABBI *(looking toward Joseph of Arimathœa).* The Traitor! He has again interposed a barrier!

ANNAS. And our joy spoiled!

CAIAPHAS *(to the Centurion).* Nevertheless, we will not allow His body to be laid elsewhere than with the transgressors.

CENTURION. Inasmuch as the body is given to this man, it is understood that he may bury it how and where he will. No objecttion can be raised. *(To the soldiers and executioners.)* You men, our business is at an end; we will return! *(Exit.)*

ANNAS *(to Joseph of Arimathœa).* Do you still persist in your terrible sin? Are you not ashamed to honour even the cold body of a malefactor who has died on the cross?

JOSEPH. I honour the most virtuous of men, sent by God. — Him who, without guilt, was murdered.

NICODEMUS. Envy and pride were the motives prompting His condemnation. The judge himself was convinced of His guiltlessness, and would not be party to the bloody deed.

CAIAPHAS. The curse, pronounced by the holy Law, will destroy thee, you enemy of our Fathers!

RABBI. Do not anger yourself, High Priest! They are wholly blind!

CAIAPHAS. The curse of the whole Council rest upon you! Honour taken from you, you shall nevermore dare enter our midst!

NICODEMUS. That we do not wish to do. *(The High Priest and Pharisees come forth.)*

ANNAS. Now that the corpse is in the hands of friends, we must be on our guard. For the false Teacher said, while He yet lived, that in three days He would rise again.

RABBI. How easily could a new deception be imposed upon us and the people, and a new embarrassment be prepared for us! His Disciples could secretly steal His body, and then spread the report that He had risen!

CAIAPHAS. Then would the last error be worse than the first. Let us go immediately to Pilate, therefore, and ask him for a guard with which to watch the grave until after the third day.

ANNAS.   A wise thought!

RABBI.   Thus will their schemes be frustrated! *(Exit.)*

FOURTH SCENE

The Descent from the Cross and the Burial

MARY MAGDALENE.   They have finally gone, the madmen! Console yourself, dear Mother! Now are we alone with our friends; the derision and abuse are silenced, and a holy evening stillness surrounds us.

MARY *(to the women).*   Oh, my friends! What my Jesus suffered, this Mother's heart suffered also! Now has He done His work. He has entered into the rest of His Fathers. The peace and comfort of Heaven are lodged in my heart. We shall see Him again; for so He has said, and His word is Truth.

MARY MAGDALENE.   Yea, we shall see Him again! His word is Truth!

MARY *(to the men who took the bodies from the crosses).*   Bring me the body of my dear Child!

SALOME.   Companions, come, help me get ready the linen which shall hold our dead. *(The women seat Mary on a stone, and spread out the winding-cloth at her feet.)*

MARY MAGDALENE.   Mother, will you not rest here a little, until we have made ready His linen for Him?

JOSEPH *(taking the body of Jesus upon his shoulders).*   Oh, you sweet, holy burden, come to my shoulders! *(Receives the body.)*

NICODEMUS *(stretching forth his arms to receive the dead).*   Come, holy body of my only Friend! Let me embrace you! *(The body is placed so as to lean against Mary.)* How the madness of your enemies has lacerated you!

JOHN.   Here shall the best of sons once more rest on the bosom of the best of mothers!

MARY.   Oh, my Son, how your body is covered with wounds!

JOHN.   Mother, from these wounds flow salvation and blessing for all mankind!

MARY MAGDALENE.   Behold, Mother, the peace of Heaven

166

rests on His pale countenance!

NICODEMUS. Let us anoint His holy body and wrap it in this clean winding-sheet.

JOSEPH. Yonder in my new grave within the rocky grotto of my garden shall He find rest.

SALOME. Best of Masters! One more hot tear of love on your lifeless body!

MARY MAGDALENE. Oh, let me once more kiss the hand that so often blessed me!

JOSEPH. We shall see Him again. *(To Nicodemus.)* My friend, help me bear Him into the garden.

NICODEMUS. A fortunate one am I, for I am able to lay the sheath of Him sent by God to rest. *(They bear the body in the direction of the grave.)*

JOHN. Let us follow to the place where the treasure of our sorrow will be laid.

MARY. It is the last service which I can render to my Jesus. *(They all start; in the background is discovered the grave.)*

ALL. *(as Joseph and Nicodemus come from the grave in which they have placed the body of Jesus).* Friend, rest quietly in your rocky grave!

JOHN. Let us go: Mother, come! *(They pass through the garden gate; the women follow.)*

JOSEPH. With this stone will we close the grave. *(They roll the stone to the opening.)*

NICODEMUS. After the Feast we will finish our work of love!

JOSEPH. Come, friend, let us mourn the death of our beloved Teacher.

NICODEMUS. Oh, this Man of Spirit and Truth — how did He deserve such a fate! *(The two exit through the garden gate.)*

END OF ACT

167

ACT XVII. REPRESENTATION

The Resurrection

PROLOGUE.   Now all is over! To us peace and joy,
Life and freedom hath He brought through death,
While in the hearts of those He saved is love!

The Holy One lies buried in the grave;
His rest is short, for His anointed flesh
Defying death — alive — shall rise again!

In three days Jonah from the fish's maw
Returned, while safely through the sea
Engulfing others, moved victorious Israel.

So will the power of the Lord o'ercome
The darkness of the tomb, and in the light
Appear once more in godlike excellence!

TABLEAU: *1. Jonah cast by the whale upon dry land.*

CHORUS.   Rest peacefully, Thou holy body,
Within the stillness of the rocky grave;
From burning pain, Thou holy body rest!
Repose Thou, in the bosom of the earth.

Until the hour Thou art glorified!
Never shall Thy holy body come to be
The victim of the grave and of decay!

TABLEAU.   *2: The people of Israel cross the Red Sea; their enemies meet with ruin.*

Great is the Lord! His goodness great!
Triumph — the dead shall rise again!
The darkness of the grave no more enshroud Him,
For through His power shall He soon go forth!

ACTION.

*Jesus rises. The watch at the grave lose self-possession. More women
seek the grave. An angel announces to them the resurrection of
Jesus, which the High Council seeks to discountenance. The resurrected One appears before Mary Magdalene.*

168

FIRST SCENE

Garden with the Rocky Grotto. Titus, Pedius, Rufus, Kajus, some sitting and others lying around the Hillock by the Grave.

TITUS *(who has been asleep, awakens).* Brothers, how is't with you? To me it seems much too long to sit here thus as a death watch.

RUFUS. Show patience; it is the last night. Only for three days was the watch to last.

PEDIUS. We will soon be free!

TITUS. Truly, it is laughable how the people still fear the dead.

RUFUS. This Man of Nazareth, so the rumour goes, has said that on the third day He would return from the dead; hence the fear.

TITUS. If He is really such a superior being,will He heed us? And were there a hundred of us, we could not stop Him.

KAJUS *(who has been asleep, now wakens).* Brothers, is not the night almost over?

TITUS. Soon it will be. Already in the east the sky begins to redden. A beautiful spring day is about to smile upon us. *(Earthquake.)*

PEDIUS *(springing up).* Immortals! what a frightful shock!

RUFUS. The earth is splitting asunder! *(Thunder and lightening.)*

TITUS. Away from the rock! Away! It wavers! It crashes in! *(An angel rolls the stone away. Christ rises.)*

PEDIUS. Ye gods! What do I see?

TITUS. I grow blind. Alas, a fire from Heaven has seized me! *(They fall upon their knees, some covering their faces, others bowing their heads to the earth.)*

KAJUS *(after a while, still on his knees).* Brothers! What has befallen us!

RUFUS. Not an instant longer will I remain here!

TITUS *(looking).* The Apparition has disappeared. *(Takes his weapon and stands up).* Brothers, be of courage! We have naught to fear, having done no wrong. *(They all stand.)*

PEDIUS. I saw the figure of a Man at the grave; His face shone like the lightning, and His dress was whiter than the snow.

KAJUS.   I saw the figure also. Here a higher power governs!

TITUS *(at the entrance to the garden).*   The garden gate is closed.

KAJUS *(who has neared the grave).*   And lo, the stone is rolled away! The grave is open! *(All move toward the grave.)*

RUFUS *(looking within).*   I no longer see a corpse.

PEDIUS *(venturing further in).*   Here is the winding-sheet, however,which served as a covering for the body. He has gone from the grave!

TITUS.   He must have risen. No man came here.

RUFUS.   So, what the priests most feared has happened!

TITUS.   He has fulfilled His word!

RUFUS.   And we? What is there now for us to do?

PEDIUS.   Nothing more. But let us hasten and inform the Pharisees of what we've seen.

ALL.   That we will, indeed! *(They exit toward Annas Street.)*

SECOND SCENE

Mary Magdalene, Salome, Johanna, Kleopha, Jacobe, the Holy Women, and an Angel. They enter from the right.

MARY MAGDALENE.   How joyful my heart to show this honour to our belovéd Teacher! *(They hasten toward the grave, Mary Magdalene in advance.)*

KLEOPHA.   Yet who will roll the stone away?

JACOBE.   Is it then so very big?

SALOME.   Yes, indeed! Our strength would not suffice!

JOHANNA.   Perhaps Joseph's gardener is not far away.

MARY MAGDALENE *(returning quickly).*   Sisters, what have I seen! The Master has been taken out of the grave — He has been taken away from us! Who knows where they have taken Him?

WOMEN.   Oh, God!

MARY MAGDALENE.   I will hasten to Peter and John, and

170

tell them the sad news! *(Exits weeping.)*

SALOME.   Thus is our last consolation taken from us!

JOHANNA.   Do not lose courage; perhaps —

JACOBE.   If only the enemies of the Master have not stolen His body so as to inflict further insults upon Him!

KLEOPHA.   Let us see for ourselves! *(They go to the grave.)*

JACOBE *(at the garden entrance).*   It is true. The stone is from the hole.

SALOME *(looking within).*   I do not see the holy body! Oh, oh! What is it I do see? *(Recoils, terrified.)*

JOHANNA.   The clothes are here, but the body is not. *(Hastens from the tomb.)* I am afraid!

ANGEL *(appearing at the entrance of the tomb).*   Fear not! You seek Jesus of Nazareth, Him who was crucified? He has risen, and is here no more. Behold the holy place where they laid Him. But go and say unto His Disciples, and to Peter in particular, that He has gone before you into Galilee! There will you see Him as He has said. *(Beside this Angel appear two others; then all three disappear.)*

JACOBE.   Oh, I tremble with fear! We will go from here. *(They hasten away).*

SALOME *(outside the garden).*   Now let me collect myself, for I came near to fainting.

KLEOPHA.   So did I. Yet, sisters, what a heavenly message it was to us! The Lord is risen! We shall see Him again in Galilee!

JOHANNA.   My fear has gone! In rapture beats my heart. He lives again. Friends, bethink you! He lives! Our dear Teacher! *(They are excited. Johanna embraces Kleopha.)*

JACOBE.   Sisters, let us hasten to announce the Angel's message to the Disciples!

KLEOPHA.   All our sadness has been turned to joy!

ALL.   And no one can take it from us! *(They exit).*

THIRD SCENE

Caiaphas, Annas, Rabbi, the Pharisees, and the four guards. They enter from the left.

CAIAPHAS.   It is impossible to keep back what the watchers have told us. *(Goes quickly to the grave).* Yes truly, the stone is rolled away; the grave is empty!

ANNAS.   It is not unlikely that some people came here.

CAIAPHAS *(to the watch).*   How did it happen? Confess, or the worst punishment awaits you!

TITUS.   As we told you, so did it happen. We can tell you nothing more.

PHARISEES.   You lie!

RUFUS.   How do you think it possible for any one to come here? The garden gate was closed and we sat around the grave.

CAIAPHAS.   You are all confederates in this!

ANNAS.   You have been bribed!

WATCHERS.   What? You would question our honour! We will not have such slander put upon us.

ANNAS.   Why did you not immediately raise an alarm?

PEDIUS.   How could we, when a thunderbolt laid us low!

CAIAPHAS.   You say this only to escape punishment.

RUFUS.   Ha! You might say that to a Jewish soldier, but a Roman will not slip out by lying!

WATCHERS.   We will complain before Pilate, demanding satisfaction for such insult.

CAIAPHAS.   Tell us: where is the body now?

RUFUS.   We do not know.

TITUS.   He rose, as you feared.

CAIAPHAS.   Be silent with your Resurrection tale!

PEDIUS.   Even though you do not believe it, still is it none the less true! I tell what I myself saw.

172

ANNAS.   Now, what did you see? Perchance the Disciples who stole His body?

PEDIUS.   No, on my honour! I saw Him rising from the grave. The light which shone around Him struck me low.

TITUS.   We will go to Pilate; he shall decide.

RUFUS.   And over all Jerusalem shall the news be published—

PEDIUS.   That He has risen!

CAIAPHAS. *(aside to the Pharisees).*   We must prevent any such move. *(To the watch.)* Believe what you will; but it is best for us that the story be not spread abroad. Your silence will be adequately rewarded.

RUFUS.   Even though we remain silent, it will still become known that the body is no longer to be found in the grave.

TITUS.   Pilate would call us to account.

ANNAS.   Leave that to us!

CAIAPHAS *(showing them a full purse).*   See this gold! It will all be given for your silence!

PHARISEES.   Take it, and leave it to the High Council to settle the affair.

ANNAS.   We will stand by you before Pilate.

TITUS *(to his companions).*   They only ask silence of us. That we can give!

WATCH.   We'll do it!

CAIAPHAS *(handing over the purse to Titus).*   Mark you: deep silence!

RUFUS.   But if one should question us?

CAIAPHAS.   Then say this only: The Disciples came while we slept and stole Him from the grave.

TITUS.   No! Take back your money!

PHARISEES.   Nothing will be done to punish you.

CAIAPHAS.   I promise you in the name of the whole Council!

PEDIUS.   Well, if you will promise that, then we will do it.

PHARISEES.   Fear nothing!

173

CAIAPHAS.   Now then: be silent!

THE WATCH.   We will. *(They exit.)*

CAIAPHAS *(to the Pharisees)*.   Now, friends, let us take care to spread among the people the report that the body has been stolen by His Disciples.

ANNAS.   This Man gives us trouble, even in death!

NATHANAEL.   And must something always intervene, that we cannot rejoice in our victory undisturbed?

CAIAPHAS.   Do not grieve over this! The best is won! Our Enemy is dead! Let His body rest where it will! A short time hence — and the name of this Nazarene will be forgotten - or uttered only with insult, as an evil-doer who was crucified. His work is at an end!

PHARISEES.   Hail to the Synagogue! At an end is the work of our Enemy! *(They exit with haughty confidence.)*

FOURTH SCENE

John, followed shortly by Peter and Mary Magdalene. Then Christ and an Angel

JOHN *(enters from the right)*.   I must convince myself whether or no Mary has rightly told us. *(He goes quickly to the grave and, stooping, looks within.)* Truly, the body has disappeared! Still, the clothes are there.

PETER *(coming with Mary Magdalene)*.   Is it so? Have you already been in the rocky grave?

JOHN.   It is empty! I have looked within; but a godly fear prevents me from entering!

PETER.   We must examine closer. *(Goes into the grave, but immediately returns to the entrance.)* See for yourself, John; see how orderly the linen clothes lie within. The head cloth is laid, separated from the others. *(John enters.)*

MARY MAGDALENE.   Alas! where is my Friend? Shall I not even see His body again?

PETER *(coming out with John)*.   If the enemy had carried Him off, then they would have taken Him as He was, wrapped in linen.

JOHN.   And had they dragged the body about, the linen would

174

certainly be strewn around the place.

PETER. But everything is very orderly, as though some one had risen from a sleep and laid his night raiment in order.

JOHN. Simon, what presentiment your speech awakens in me! Perhaps the Lord has risen from death, as though from a gentle sleep. Yes, I believe it! He who called forth Lazarus, could He not likewise bring Himself from the grave? And did He not prophesy to us that on the third day the Son of Man would — Oh, Simon, to-day is the third day!

PETER. My God! If it were so!

JOHN. I do not doubt it. We shall soon see Him again!

PETER. John, let us go to our Brothers, and impart to them what we here have seen! *(To Mary Magdalene.)* Mary, will you not come with us?

MARY MAGDALENE. Leave me here! Oh, let me grieve alone! Let me weep! I cannot stir from this place until I have satisfied my heart's need!

PETER. Do not stay long. In Mark's house you will find us. *(Exits with John.)*

MARY MAGDALENE. Now, my tears, have your way! To weep is the only consolation for a heavy heart. *(Weeping violently, she rests her head upon the rock at the entrance.)*

ANGEL *(appearing, after a while, inside the entrance).* Woman, why weep you?

MARY MAGDALENE. They have taken away my Lord. I know not where they have put Him. *(Turns, weeping, from the grave.)*

CHRIST *(appears on the side of the hillock, between trees).* Oh, woman, why weep you? Whom seek you?

MARY MAGDALENE. If you have taken Him away, then tell me where you have put Him.

CHRIST. Mary!

MARY MAGDALENE. Oh, that is His voice! *(Hastens to Him, and falls before Him.)* Rabbi! *(Would embrace His knees.)*

CHRIST. Do not stop me! Not yet have I entered unto my

175

Father. But hasten and say to my Brothers: I go to my Father and to your Father; to my God and to your God!

MARY MAGDALENE *(bending low)*. My dearest Teacher! *(Looks up.)* He has disappeared. *(Stands, full of rapture.)* Still, I have seen Him! I have heard His dear voice. Oh, blesséd sight! Away from me, grief! The ecstasy of Paradise fills my soul! Ah, as though borne on wings, I will hasten to His Disciples, and tell them of the Resurrection, and give them greetings from their Lord! Oh, could I proclaim it through the whole world, that mountain and vale, and rocks and woods, and heaven and earth might resound with the tidings: Hallelujah! He has risen! *(As she exits, an echo comes from every side: "Hallelujah! He has risen!")*

CLOSING SCENE

Hallelujah

PROLOGUE. Christ is risen! Rejoice, ye heavens!
The Christ is risen! Rejoice, ye mortals!
The lordly leader of the Tribe of Judah
The serpent's head 'neath His heel has crushed!

Firm stand the faithful, while hope the happiest
Within us wakens, through sign and token
Of our future — our resurrection!
In jubilation cry: "Hallelujah!"

We saw Him enter into Jerusalem,
Weighed down and humble, humiliated!
Ah, let us witness, before we leave here,
The Christ victorious, the Christ triumphant!

He now approaches glorification,
With regal power enters Jerusalem,
Where He will gather unto His person
Those whom His Passion hath saved from sin!

With such divine love, with spirit strengthened,
Oh, friends, turn homeward, your joy renewed
For Him who loved you in all His trials,
Throughout His Passion — through time eternal!

176

And round the Saviour, where sounds the chorus,
"The Lamb be praised, which once was offered" —
Oh, let us gather within the future,
Oh, let us gather and meet again!

HALLELUJAH CHORUS. The might of the enemy He hath overcome, yea hath He overcome! In the shadow of the grave new life hath He found! Sing unto Him songs of jubilation, before Him strew palms of victory! The Lord is risen! Shout unto Him, ye heavens above! Praise Him, ye earth below! Hallelujah unto the Resurrected! Hallelujah!

Adore ye the Saviour! The Lamb who was slain! Hallelujah! Him who from the grave ascends victorious to life on high! Hallelujah! Hallelujah! He hath conquered!

Praise Him, the Victor over death! Him who on Gabbatha was condemned! Praise Him, the Saviour of all Sinners, who for us on Golgotha died! Praise Him! Hallelujah! Halleluhah! He hath conquered!

Let us unto the Victor bring leaves of bay! Unto Him who is resurrected and eternal lives! Unto Him who from the grave ascends to life on high! Hallelujah! Hallelujah! He hath conquered!

Ye heavenly hosts, your praises bring, your praises sing! Excellence be unto the Lord! And glory be and power evermore! Honour unto the Lord from eternity unto eternity without end! Hallelujah! Hallelujah! He hath conquered!

(The closing tableau represents Christ's Ascension, as He stands on the Mount of Olives, surrounded by His Disciples and the holy women.)

THE END

177

The Crucifixion (after Tintoretto)

The Entombment (after Van Dyck)

THE ACTORS AND THE THEATRE

Two years before the Passion Play season is due to begin the Burgomaster convenes a meeting of the village, at which he reminds them of the vow of 1633 and asks for their support in staging the next season of plays. The 24 members of the Passion Play committee are then elected. Traditionally the Burgomaster is nominated as its chairman, the parish priest as his deputy, with places for the 16 members of the village council, leaving only 6 seats for outside people. The director of the play is chosen from the members of the committee.

The allocation of the parts takes place in the September preceding the Passion Play. Following a service in the parish church the chairman calls upon his fellow members to elect the 1,200 performers needed for the play. The actors are chosen by secret ballot, with the eagerly-awaited results written up outside the theatre.

To be eligible for a part an actor must have lived at least 20 years in the village. Before World War II it was necessary to have been born and lived all one's life in Oberammergau to take part in the play, but the influx of refugees and the founding of the international children's village has led to this rule being relaxed. The potential candidates for the principal parts are quietly screened and become well-known to the committee by taking part in the 'training plays' which fill in the years between Passion Play seasons.

After being selected, the male actors let their hair and beards grow, as wigs and make-up are not allowed, and nine months of rehearsals get under way. As women who take part in the play must be under 35 and unmarried there is usually a flurry of weddings after the Passion Play season. Although the religious and devotional nature of the play is always being emphasized, and the cult of the star is strongly discouraged, some performances have become legendary, setting standards that succeeding generations seek to emulate and even encouraging younger members of the family to follow in a certain role. Some of the older Oberammergau families almost appear to have had a hereditary interest in the principal parts. Although not one of the original Oberammergau families (they did in fact originate in the Tyrol and moved across some 250 years ago), the Langs have been very important in the more recent

182

history of the Passion Play. The outstanding figure was the woodcarver, Georg Johann Lang, who was involved in one form or another with the play for some seventy years. He was a colossus of a character who was the director from 1922 - 1970; He had a walk-on part in 1900 and had been stage-manager in 1910. The Lang family has several branches so it is not surprising that they tend to crop up often in cast-lists, but they have provided several actors and actresses of rare renown. Jesus Christ was played for five cycles by first Anton (1900 - 10 - 22) and then Alois (1930 - 34). Anton's Christ emphasised mildness and calm in contrast to his predecessor, the fiery passionate, Joseph Mayr. When he was too old to play Christ, Anton Lang was elected to the part of the Prologue in the following productions. In the middle of the 19th century female members of the family dominated the two principal roles of Mary (1830 - 40 - 50) and Mary Magdalene, which was played by Helena (1850), Josapha (1860 - 70) and Maria Lang (1880). The role of Caiaphas, the High Priest, was played by Peter Lang for the first four series of the 19th century (he became director in 1830), to be followed by Johann who took over the role in 1860 and was to retain it until the end of the century.

A glance at the cast-list for the last completed season of 1980 shows the present ascendancy of the Zwinks — a very old established Oberammergau clan. No fewer than eight people bearing the name were involved in the play: Franz, Luise, Heinrich, Werner, Anton, Markus (bass soloist) and Rudolph, who played Jesus and has been re-elected to the part in 1984, which he will share with Max Jablonka. The Zwinks are no strangers to this part since Jakob had performed as Christ for the four seasons from 1800 - 1820, following these exhausting seasons with the older part of Peter in 1830 - 40. His kinsman Johann preceded his three appearances as Judas (1890 - 1900 - 10) with two seasons as John (1870 - 80), a rare break in the Bierling tradition, and was on stage with his daughter Ottilie, who played Mary, in 1910. His son portrayed Judas during the tercentenary season.

Another family well represented in an early Passion Play was the Rutz family, who took five parts in 1680. Although many members of this prestigious family have had roles in the play, it is really in the female parts that they have distinguished themselves. The more important of the roles is Mary Magdalene (Therese in 1815, Viktoria in 1840), but often reputed to have been the greatest actress seen in the Play was Anni, who portrayed the Virgin Mary in the 1930's. It is difficult for a girl to make an impression on the history of the play because of the scarcity of roles and the severe restrictions on age and

183

marital status: Anni, however, is still remembered fondly by older members of the community for her Mary.

Other families have traditions almost as impressive; the Lechners, who portrayed Judas from 1815 to 1880; the Stuckls; the Mayrs; the Rendls; the Preisingers, with Anton, the owner of the famous Alte Post hotel, the Christ in 1950 and 1960. Perhaps though it is the countless other families whose involvement in the play, generation by generation, has been limited to minor parts and crowd scenes, but whose commitment is just as important, which helps to make Oberammergau such a unique event.

Although tradition is the hallmark of Oberammergau, the village in its staging of the Passion Play has kept pace with modern development. The fame of the play and the increased attendance meant that by the end of the 19th century it was time to replace the collapsible stage and the Passion Meadow by a permanent theatre. Designed by Ludwig Lang the first theatre had a long arched roof, which for the first time gave covered accommodation to the 4,000 strong audience, although the stage was still an open-air one. By 1922 it was already felt that this theatre was inadequate, and plans were begun for a new theatre, which was opened in time for the 1930 season. Covered by a glass roof it cleverly allows gradations of light, giving the audience the feeling of being out in the open-air with the actors — that is until it rains. The acoustics, enhanced by the use of panelling are superb, so there is no need for the use of concealed microphones.

The theatre is constantly being modernised: the stage has been enlarged, the audience has recently been increased from 5,000 to 6,500, and a large foyer with exhibition glass cases has been erected, while the wooden steps have given way to a broader stone stairway. Although somewhat spartan, the wooden tip-up seats, are a vast improvement from the previous wood benches.

The Bavarian Alps provide a stunning backdrop for the play. The actors perform regardless of the weather — one of the reasons why every major part has two actors assigned to it. As the orchestra pit is in front of the stage, they can shelter under it during inclement weather. Off-stage the performers are provided with very good facilities, including dressing rooms, with an intercom system, which can accommodate 700 people.

Some of the costumes are exquisite and date back to 1830 when the community began purchasing its own costumes. More than 2,000 costumes are painstakingly maintained by a whole host of village women. When there is no Passion Play season these and the props can be inspected by the visitor during the tours of the theatre

184

organised by the community. Particularly interesting are the three types of wooden cross used during the play: the heavy cross on which Jesus is crucified, which is erected with the aid of electrical equipment, and has a footrest, invisible straps and bent nails to give the actor some support; the smaller, hollow cross, which weighs about 85 lbs and is carried through the streets toward Calvary by Jesus and Simon; and the crosses on which the thieves stand. The spear used to pierce the side of Christ is 300 years old, and has a mechanical retractible point with a device for ejecting a substance resembling blood. The table used for the Last Supper scene dates back to the 18th century, and is a further example of the enduring nature of everything connected to the Oberammergau Passion Play.

PART II

Bavaria became part of the Roman province of Rhaetia after the first inroads into S. Germany were made in 15BC and legions had been established at Regensburg ("Castra Regina") and Augsburg. Its main importance to the Empire was most probably as a transit route, commercial and military, linking north and south, since not more than a couple of thousand people appear to have been in occupation at any one time. When the Romans arrived they encountered pockets of resistance from the Celts, much as in Britain, who were almost certainly the earliest inhabitants of the region. Various remaining place-names in Bavaria bear witness to Celtic origins: towns and districts with the typical endings of "ing" and "lingen" abound (e.g. Nordlingen, Unterhaching).

With the decline of the Roman Empire around the fifth century AD, Bavaria was subject to growing Barbarian attacks and the Roman militia was driven south by Alemanni and Juthungi. They in turn were quickly subdued by the Franks pushing into S. Germany, who granted a certain amount of independence to the first known ruler of Bavaria, Duke Garibaldi I. By all accounts, Garibaldi was a tempestuous character whose attitude did little to unify the different claims to the rulership and whose legacy to the people of Bavaria was a whole series of violent disputes over who should rule. After a century and a half of this infighting the Franks once again intervened. Until the advent of the Wittlesbach dynasty in 1180 the story of this part of Germany is very much one of periods of crushing overlordship alternating with relative independence, much as in later centuries it would be periods of quiet prosperity interspersed with the folly of involvement in European power-politics.

In 730 the grandfather of Charlemagne and the Frankish king, Charles Martel ("The Hammer"), became the supreme overlord. It was during this time that Christianity took root in the region, reinforced by the arrival of St. Boniface in 734, after the initial seeds were sown by Ruprecht, the Bishop of Worms, at the turn of the century. While the pagan chiefs were involved in their own efforts to establish order, Christian monks using Augsburg as their base were quietly going about their own business of establishing churches and monasteries.

With the death of Charles Martel in 741, twenty years of struggles were followed by the same period of peace and Bavaria remained relatively independent, but in Europe another great power was already coming to the fore and in 781, the Bavarian ruler, Duke Tassilo, along with many of his contemporaries was forced to recognise the sovereignty of Charlemagne. Just seven years later, the Duke of Bavaria had been deposed and his territories added to Charlemagne's empire, officially becoming part of the Eastern Frankish Empire in 843 with the signing of the Treaty of Verdun.

The next three hundred years saw many changes in Bavaria's ruling figures and families, but in Europe as a whole the dominant force in its early years was the Holy Roman Empire. On Christmas Day in 800 Pope Leo crowned Charlemagne with the title 'Emperor of the Holy Roman Empire'. He gained nothing in the way of territory (as the Frankish king of thirty years already, he was ruler of a huge area of Europe, and he kept his capital in Frankish Aachen, or Aix-la-Chapelle), but the title was an indication of the allegiance in temporal matters which the pope had transferred to him. On Charlemagne's death, the empire was split into several different parts and the imperial authority was all but lost, although the title was borne on occasions by rival princes with a claim to Carolingian descent. In the 10th century, the concept was revived with the coronation of Otto I, which was considered to give him both spiritual and political authority over the whole of Christendom. It was looked upon at the time as the restoration of the old empire of Charlemagne, itself claiming descent from the Caesars, but since large parts of the old domain such as France and southern Italy were not included, the 'universal' supremacy of the new emperors rested on a theoretical basis.

Although the Holy Roman Empire is the traditional name of the German Empire until 1806 and its dissolution during Napoleonic times, the empire was for the most part one in name only. In theory the German king had to be elected by the leading figures of six German tribal duchies. In practice, however, the choice was restricted to members of the ruling dynasty, and in most cases they had already been 'designated' so that the election was less a choice than a confirmation. The procedure was to show itself open to abuse as the principalities gained power and influence in later years, since it became possible to extort benefits from the 'emperor-to-be' in exchange for help in securing the Electors' votes. The new German king automatically became King of Lombardy, Burgundy and Rome, until the moment arrived when he was crowned Holy Roman Emperor. By the middle of the 13th century the loss of Italy restricted the empire to Germany alone: it was soon to be called, somewhat absurdly, 'The Holy Roman Empire of the German Nation'. At the same time, the participants in the electoral college and successors to the original tribal duchies were the six 'Electors': the three Rhenish archbishops of Mainz, Trier and Köln, and the three main officers of state (the High Steward or Count Palatine, the Chamberlain or Margrave of Brandenburg and the Marshal or Duke of Saxony). Soon after, a seventh Elector was created: the King of Bohemia, who had previously been denied a say in the elections because he was not a German. The main objector was Bavaria, whose own claim was denied, since the Wittelsbach family, rulers of the duchy, would then control two of the Electorships. The electoral procedure was quite simple: the Archbishop of Mainz acted as convener and chairman of the meetings, which took place in Frankfurt, and a majority decision was necessary from a quorum of four. No doubt the election had already been the subject of lengthy discussions beforehand.

The ceremonial facade of the Holy Roman Empire served to keep up the pretence of its own importance long after it had disappeared. The Electors' main objective was to keep the monarchy as important as possible by the choice of the weaker candidates. Frequent changes in ruling dynasty took place, among which were the houses of Wittelsbach and Hapsburg, the upholders of the faith. As time passed, the Hapsburgs became the natural, if nominal, emperors, and the princes had become virtually independent. When the Holy Roman Empire was dissolved in 1806, after the blows of the Reformation, the Thirty Years War and the Napoleonic struggles - all of which undermined the unity of the empire and strengthened the individual princes — there were ten Electors and a Hapsburg ruler, Francis II, who already in 1804 had assumed the title of 'Emperor of Austria' as if in preparation for the sad demise of the impressively named, but by now irrelevant, Holy Roman Empire.

Although very necessary as an aid to understanding the affairs of the whole of Germany, the Holy Roman Empire is of less importance to our understanding of Bavaria than the Wittelsbach family. After the many years of fighting between different families, even fighting within the families themselves, it is with some relief that the year 1180 sees the advent of a dynasty which, in name at least, was to outlast the mighty Hapsburgs in terms of longevity. For 738 years the Wittelsbachs ruled Bavaria until their somewhat inevitable demise with the Great War of 1914 - 1918: in good company, however, as the Hapsburgs, Hohenzollerns and Romanovs also failed to survive this crushing blow to the system. Three different branches contributed to the Wittelsbach family, not of all whom were taken with Bavaria: in the 1770's one such ruler was so unimpressed with his new southern domain that he wished to return to his Palatinate

190

home and sell Bavaria! Fortunately this was not to be a typical reaction, as most of the rulers of Bavaria settled down to concentrate on upholding and furthering the Catholic faith in the face of the Protestant threat, consolidating and adding to the Bavarian territories, and ensuring that the succession remained safe (the latter encouraged by the adoption of the law of primogeniture, or inheritance by the first-born, in 1506).

It is time to look at events on a broader scale and move away from Bavaria to Germany as a whole. Every so often a figure appears on the scene and provokes a fundamental reassessment of what has gone before. It is difficult to have any insight into the turbulent century to follow without reference to one such figure: Martin Luther (1483 - 1546). An Augustinian monk, he became Professor of Theology and after years of striving, he found in the Holy Scriptures the answer to the problem of salvation for which he had been searching: "Man justifies himself by his faith, not by the workings of the law". Faith alone therefore was seen as justifying the existence of man. At this time Luther began inveighing against the sale of indulgences, which were being used to finance the new building of St. Peter's in Rome, and the methods being used by his enemy, the Dominican Tetzel, to collect them. His teachings against the established church and threat which he posed to the young Emperor Charles V's authority, the upholder of the faith, struck a chord with the spirit sweeping through large parts of Germany: his famous deed of attacking church corruption in his theses, which he nailed to the door of the Wittenberg church in 1517, acted as a catalyst around which the German people forged their resistance to papal authority.

Luther was denounced by the court of Rome, but refused to retract his criticisms. In 1520 he burned the papal bull threatening him with excommunication and published a denunciation of the claims of priests to primacy in the spiritual domain. He also criticised the sacraments minutely and the institutional and hierarchical establishment of the church. Luther was summoned under safe conduct to the Diet of Worms in 1521 which had been convoked by Charles V, but did not give way. As arrangements were being made to exile him to the outer reaches of the empire and an edict proclaimed which both condemned his works to be burnt and instituted an ecclesiastical censorship of all books printed in Germany, Martin Luther was "abducted" by the Elector of Saxony, Frederick the Wise, one of his supporters, and lodged for nearly a year in Wartburg Castle. Here he began his translation of the scriptures into German. The New Testament was completed by 1522, the Old Testament by 1534. This is often referred to as the first true German work of literature, and the importance of the printing press enabling Luther's arguments to be circulated in the vernacular (as can be seen by the flood of pamphlets) cannot be underestimated.

In spite of the ban, the Reformation progressed in many parts of Germany, although having limited success in Bavaria. In Wittenberg, Garlstadt admitted fanatical preachers from Zwickau and proceeded to revolutionary lengths which resulted in disorder there and elsewhere. Luther was forced to return to preach in 1522 to restore stability to the movement. A visit to Saxony revealed a serious need for church reform; and there, as in other states where the rulers were favourable, worship and order were reorganised in accordance with Luther's teachings. He did not desire separation from the Catholic church but intended a temporary organisation with a view to local freedom in adapting, not dismantling, the "old religion". The settlement proposed at the Diet of Speyer in 1526 was to be adopted for the German Empire after years of struggle in the Peace of Augsburg (1555), where the religion of the ruler was recognised as the religion of the state ("cuius regio, eius religio"). The political aspect of the Reformation encouraged princes to support Luther, often more out of opportunism than faith — indeed Luther's exhortation to the rulers to crush the popular risings of 1524 shows that the rulers rather than the people were to safeguard the Reformation — but it also served to polarise support into two distinct camps, since the Catholic rulers were in turn the subject of Counter-Reformation emissaries and were unlikely to deviate from the faith.

Charles V was not successful in rooting out the "evil" of "revolt within": he was simply too often engaged elsewhere in external matters to be able to turn his undivided attention to the Luther problem. The Peace of Augsburg was therefore little more than an unsatisfactory compromise which encouraged both sides that there was still much to play for. Bavaria remained a Catholic stronghold as a result of the constant vigilance of rulers from William IV to Maximilian I. While much of the rest of Europe was in turmoil caused by the battle for religious supremacy between the Protestant forces of Lutheranism and Calvinism, and the opposing Catholic troops of the Counter-Reformation, brought about by the Council of Trent (1545 - 63) and supported by the Emperor, Bavaria had a period of relative calm. There were the occasional problems, however: about forty or so landowning nobles had to be arrested, tried and dispossessed of their lands because they evinced Lutheran sympathies, and the threat remained in the parts of Bavaria around Oberammergau that Protestant forces, belonging to the Elector of Saxony and operating out of the recently captured town of Augsburg, would once more attack the Ammergau as in 1552 when the monastery of Ettal was plundered and its monks driven away. As a result merchants and pilgrims lost confidence in the route through the Ammer Valley and Oberammergau suffered lean times for many years.

Having learned from the Reformation the importance of concentrating attention on the princes, the popes sent out legates and eloquent members of the new religious orders (like the Society of Jesus) to strategically placed courts, such as Paris, Vienna, Brussels and Munich. Schools for the aristocracy, seminaries for the clergy and spiritual missions for the laity were founded. The result of these endeavours on the part of the Catholic church was to produce a group of rulers whose main driving force was the furtherance of the work of the church. One of the principal figures in this quasi-crusade was the Duke of Bavaria, Maximilian I, who ruled from 1597 to 1651. Remembered mainly as the founder of the Catholic League in 1609, Maximilian attended the Jesuit university of Ingolstadt and became very friendly with Ferdinand of Styria (who was to become Emperor in 1619). Both were inspired by Ferdinand's advisor, Caspar Scioppius, and both came to see themselves as the chosen leaders in the quest to re-Catholicise Central Germany. Maximilian's court encouraged the ablest Catholic preachers and writers and was directed at the increase of the church's influence both outside and inside the state with all the means which the growth of the power of government at the end of the 16th century provided.

In the early 1600's Maximilian ruled over a duchy of 11,000 square miles and a population of well over a million people. He took an active part in the administration of the region and concentrated largely on building up the duchy's finances — it is estimated that his fortune amounted to some 5 million Florins or about £850,000. Within his duchy, the church and state were complimentary: the personnel of the church were appointed and controlled by the ducal government, while attendance at mass was compulsory and before Easter every Bavarian had to secure a certificate to prove that he had gone to confession. Such was the zeal of Maximilian for the salvation of his subjects that early in his reign he tried to institute a system of public guardians of morality, beside which the efforts of the English puritans not long afterwards appear almost fainthearted. He was therefore a formidable figure who had both the will to uphold the Catholic faith and the financial means to do so. Perhaps the best illustration of Maximilian's importance in the power politics of Central Europe is his action over Donauwörth, the imperial free city. The Catholic inhabitants complained to the Emperor of persecution by the Protestant majority. As the neighbouring state and a strong Catholic power, Maximilian's Bavaria was asked by the Emperor to provide protection for the minority. In December 1607 Bavarian troops occupied the city (far exceeding what was allowed under the constitution of the Empire); later the Protestants were expelled and the city annexed. Naturally the reactions of the two different sides were in violent opposition: the Catholics were jubilant, the Emperor turned a blind eye and the German supporters of the faith looked increasingly to Munich for guidance and support, whereas for the Protestants it was no more than confirmation that guarantees would have to be sought for their own protection. The result was a hardening of divisions and the formation of two rival confessional alliances.

The events at Donauwörth had the effect of bringing the Calvinists and Lutherans together as they realised their tenuous position in Germany and the threat posed by the Bavarians. They signed the Evangelical Union on 16th May 1608. It consisted of nine princes and seventeen imperial cities, but real power lay with the Elector Palatine Frederick IV. The formation of a Protestant Union galvanised the Catholics into action and within two years a similar body had been created, or rather revived, to look after their interests. The 1556 Catholic League of Landsberg had been dissolved in 1599 as Maximilian had found that Bavaria alone was footing the bill. Later talks to revive the League had broken down once again over who should finance the League, but in 1609 Maximilian could use the recently-formed Protestant Union to encourage the leading prelates of S. Germany to come into a new League with a standing army of some 25,000 men and with all members contributing to the budget. Formally signed on 10th July 1609 in Munich, Maximilian was its director and Tilly its military commander. After the Cleves-Jülich crisis, the prelates from the Rhineland joined, and the Electors of Cologne, Trier and Mainz signed on 30th July 1610. The battle lines of the disastrous Thirty Years War were drawn up beside these two alliances, with foreign support for both sides completing the picture.

Although the threat of war had been growing for several years, the single flashpoint which actually occasioned hostilities was the so-called 'Defenestration of Prague' in 1618. A large group of Protestant deputies surrounded four Imperial, and therefore Catholic, members of the council of regency for the Kingdom of Bohemia, in the Chancery. The councillors were accused of being enemies of both the liberty and the religion of the kingdom, were asked to explain their part in the ordering of the dissolution of the estates and were threatened with death. As tempers became frayed and voices rose, the windows of the tower were thrown open and two of the councillors, followed by their secretary, were cast out. It is relatively unimportant that the three men fell on to piles of refuse which had accumulated in the castle moat some sixty feet below and that their falls were cushioned allowing them a miraculous escape. What was important was the act of challenging the Emperor so openly. After this 1618 forerunner of Sarajevo, war was not only likely but inescapable.

For a generation, almost the whole of Europe was sucked into what had started as a religious war, but which by the end saw like faiths fighting one another (France against the Hapsburgs) to alter the balance of power in a specific direction, and princes fighting other princes purely for territorial gain. Long after the decisive battles had taken place and victories had been won, the war lumbered on until the eventual long-awaited cessation of hostilities with the Peace of Westphalia in 1648.

By all accounts, and several still exist (including one from a shoemaker near Ulm), it was a horrific conflict which was not to be equalled in either its brutality or loss of life until the Great War. Pointless destruction, rape, and lootings; hordes of dispossessed landowners and lost mercenaries ravaging the countryside and moving in bands from town to town; foreign soldiers to be billeted. Normal life came to a standstill in all but a few lucky places and if the horrors of war were not sufficient, the apparently inevitable reinforcements of pestilence delivered the death-blow to many communities. Although the link between war and plague is not well-defined, statistical evidence points to a more than coincidental relationship. Not only could pestilence take advantage of huge numbers of wandering, displaced people (in former years, local feelings had been directed towards the Jews and gypsies who were singled out, often unfairly, as probable carriers of the plague, being more likely to lead a nomadic existence), but the normal accepted way of life was disrupted: wartime resulted in corpses being left around unburied, sanitation unrepaired, rubbish left in the streets, livestock lying slaughtered in the fields.

The story of how the plague arrived in Oberammergau in 1633 is related in full elsewhere: however there seems little doubt that it entered the surrounding Bavarian countryside at around the same time as (probably in the very ranks of) the Swedish troops of Gustavus Aldolphus. In March 1632 Tilly had attacked and expelled the Swedish garrisons in Bamberg. This provoked retaliation from

195

Gustavus who invaded Bavaria in April and May and put the people and country to the sword. Historians tell us that some 900 settlements were destroyed, most razed to the ground. There was little resistance since peasant vigilantes needed a friendly army nearby to help and fall back on if necessary. In Bavaria there was now no such unit. Tilly, the imperial commander, died during the retreat aged 73, and Maximilian was shattered. He had expected the immediate aid of Wallenstein who instead went straight to Bohemia to defend the military interests of the Emperor. It is indeed ironic that perhaps the only incursion of the Thirty Years War into Oberammergau, apart from the obvious disruption of trade and commerce, was the plague, since it was not directly involved in the fighting and it is claimed that not one single villager took a direct part in the war. The rest of Bavaria was to remain in Swedish hands for several years, despite the occasional retreat and regrouping brought about by defeat suffered at the hands of Wallenstein.

The victory of the anti-Imperialist forces (if indeed it is correct to talk about a "victory" in such a war) was somewhat inevitable. It did not really matter in the long run how many successes fell to the League, since an ally could always be found to shore up a temporary hole in the Union, whereas a single defeat cut deep into the Imperial defences, and at one point it was claimed that one further loss would see Vienna laid open to the enemy, with no army to defend it. Sweden, Spain and finally France were all to turn up at the right moment. In any case, it would appear that the end of the war in 1648 came as a great relief to all, although Mazarin was to rue with hindsight that the struggle had not been prolonged for a while to bring about the complete destruction of the Hapsburgs (at the time of the Peace he was in difficulties himself with the "Frondes"). It was in Maximilian's nature that he would fight on after the rest, and that he would try almost on the eve of the Treaty once more to join up with Imperial forces, only to be routed by the French at Zusmarshausen, near Augsburg, on 17th May 1648, but throughout almost the whole of Germany, indeed Europe, the peace was greeted with tremendous jubilation. Bavarian after all finished the war on a high note with the insistence of France as one of its conditions for peace that Maximilian retain both the Upper Palatine and his title of Elector conferred in 1623. Bavaria was therefore established as second only to the Hapsburg state in importance and had the right to take part in the election of the Emperor of all Germany.

Although there was little chance of instant recovery — Germany had lost almost one third of its population, and the majority of its towns had been put to fire — the end of hostilities brought hope back to the people of Bavaria. Displaced people, soldiers and peasants, were still roaming the countryside in search of employment, a home or even another army for whom to fight, but trade and industry were starting to pick up, albeit slowly, crops and livestock were being raised. For some 50 years peace was the order of the day: Austria and France were at loggerheads and the Bavarians could keep out of the conflict by skilfully playing off one power against the other. Oberammergau could continue to honour its vow every ten years with growing confidence and growing audiences from outside the valley, necessitating a move in venue for the play from the church to the churchyard, ironically overlooking the graves of those who had perished from plague in the troubled 1630's.

Sadly, peace was not to last much longer and the lessons of the Thirty Years War were soon forgotten. The different dukes seemed able to countenance only a short period of peace before the self-destructive urge to pursue foreign ambitions came once again inevitably to the fore. Bavaria was involved in various European dynastic battles like the Wars of Succession (Spanish and Austrian) with the result that the country itself was forfeited, after defeat by the Austrians and English led by the Duke of Marlborough, and returned in a weaker state, only to be invaded and occupied by the Austrians once again some thirty years later.

This pattern of events continued until the end of the 18th century. After the War of Austrian Succession, the councillors of the eight year old Maximilian Josef decided that the only way of preserving Bavaria intact and encouraging prosperity was by renouncing all claims to other European thrones and discontinuing the policy of supporting France against Germany. This was to prove one of the true golden periods of Bavaria's history as country people could concentrate again on their fields and crops, while town dwellers witnessed a revival in the cultural side of life with emphasis on learning and the arts. It was a time of expansive development in the show city of Munich, testified by buildings still standing like the Palace Theatre and sections of the Nymphenburg Palace.

Seemingly unhappy with domestic interests, the next Elector promptly involved Bavaria in another series of wars (this time joining the anti-French powers around the time of the French Revolution, resulting in the country being occupied by its enemies). This rash move decided the foreign policy of his successor, as the prime objective had to be the removal of French troops from the country, with no obvious solution in sight — the commander of the opposing forces was Napoleon. Fortunately, Bavaria at this time was blessed with an able diplomat, Count Montgelas, whose tactical manoeuvring not only prevented the probable absorption of his state into the French Empire, but actually increased its area with territorial gains. Bavaria was allied first to France, and then, when Napoleon was clearly no longer the same power in Europe, after the disastrous 1812 campaign against Russia (in which Bavaria alone lost over 30,000 soldiers), it lined up with most of the continent against the army which had come so tantalisingly close to conquering them all. The Wars of Liberation and the final defeat of the Emperor Napoleon at Waterloo by the forces of Wellington and Blücher confirmed the foresight shown in changing sides.

Oberammergau suffered much interference during these Napoleonic years. The town was bombarded in December 1800, when the Austrians were driven out of the valley by the French. The play was often interrupted by fighting, people were pressed into joining up with one side or the other, the territorial divisions became more and more obscure, high taxes were imposed to pay for the armies, food was scarce and it was dangerous to travel on the highways. Politically, however, the defeat of Napoleon left Bavaria in good shape to enter the second quarter of the 18th century: since 1802 it had almost doubled in size and trebled its population; after Prussia and Austria it was the most important state in German affairs; and with the accession of Ludwig I, there was every prospect of another period of peace and prosperity.

The son of Max Joseph reigned from 1825 to 1848. Ludwig I, grandfather of 'Mad King Ludwig', was a strange mixture of eccentric, artist, liberal yet with a strong reactionary bias when things became difficult. He was responsible for turning Munich into the beautiful city it remains today despite the destruction of the last war. His enlightened patronage attracted architects, sculptors and painters, and enriched Munich with the old and new Pinakotheks, the University, Ludwigstrasse and the enlargement of the Residence. He loved to travel, indulging his artistic tastes in Italy and Greece; nearer to home, he was the first member of royalty to visit the village of Oberammergau in 1831. He presided over a great transformation: the turning of Bavaria from the purely agricultural state of 1806 into a modern industrial power. The first railway of 1835 was followed in 1843 by the first of a network of trams which serviced industrial pockets which had started to appear at the end of the 1830's. By the end of his reign there were some 3,000 factories and workshops employing 40,000 workers out of a total population of $4^1/_2$ million. His success in bringing about this transformation is often forgotten by historians when making an appraisal of Ludwig.

The turning-point of his reign was clearly the outbreak of riots in Munich after the 1830 July Revolution, followed by the necessity of sending the military into the Palatinate to quell disturbances after the festival in Hamburg. The liberal figure who had sent his second son Otto to become King of Greece in his enthusiasm at their liberation, was the same figure who imposed strict censorship on the opposition press. He became despised by the people for the crippling taxes that he imposed on them and by his ministers for his flaunting of public morality. Matters came to a head with his association with Lola Montez, the Spanish dancer, who he elevated to Countess of Landsfeld and whose keep came mainly from the Bavarian treasury, causing yet higher taxes. The people of Bavaria rebelled in 1848, capturing that year's revolutionary mood in Europe, and Ludwig was forced to accept the liberal "March demands" before on 10th March he abdicated in favour of his son Maximilian II, who as Crown Prince had played his own part in the growing fame of Oberammergau and its surrounding region by staying in his castle of Hohenschwangau not far from the village and encouraging dignitaries to come to the region from far and wide, thereby advertising the area throughout Europe.

Both Maximilian II (1848 - 64) and his son, Ludwig II, were much in love with the countryside around Oberammergau. It is no accident that the "Königschlösser" or Royal Castles are to be found here. Hohenschwangau, Neuschwanstein and Linderhof still itself. Maximilian attending the Passion Play for the first time in ative than functional, they remain as a token of the kings' attachment to these parts. Both were often seen in Oberammergau itself, Maximilian attending the Passion Play for the first time in 1840 (no longer staged in the churchyard, but since 1830 in a large meadow just outside the village, due to the numbers attending) and witnessing at least one performance from each cycle for the remaining years of his life. He was a great collector of the local woodcarvings, spent a good deal of time hunting in the nearby woods and to ensure that he could get to the hunting grounds more quickly he had a road built specially. When not involved in leisure pursuits, King Maximilian II was responsible for taking Bavaria into another struggle for power mistakenly backing the Austrians against the Prussians, and resulting in Bavaria being forced to pay a large indemnity to Prussia of some 30 million gulden and to yield part of Southern Franconia. On the home front, Maximilian pursued some of his father's liberal measures, making worthwhile reforms in the social spheres of industry, reducing censorship and freeing the peasants from the land.

Ludwig II, the son of Maximilian and without doubt the most famous king of the Wittelsbach line ("the Mad King"), came to the throne in 1864 at the tender age of 21. With Bismarck trying to unify Germany under Prussia, Ludwig could not have come along at a worst time. He was a lover of the arts and music who had little time for the distractions of government. He spent a great deal of money on impracticable building projects often at the behest of his protégé, Richard Wagner. While Ludwig was in his own dream world, the country was moving inexorably into Bismarck's orbit. The latter's aim was to unify Germany under the great industrial and military power of Prussia. He offered Ludwig the role of leading the south in a 'Little Germany' (i.e. excluding Austria), but this was declined and once again the wrong decision had been reached. Austria and Bavaria were defeated at Maifeldzug and the kingdom along with the other southern lands was forced to join the German Empire in 1871. They were allowed to run their own postal and railway services, to keep any revenue from taxes on beer and spirits and to defend themselves with a smaller standing army. Although Ludwig remained very popular with his subjects, he had become an embarassment to his councillors: an acknowledged homosexual, he became increasingly susceptible to depressions and psychiatric disorders, his country had lost its independence and his extravagant building projects had brought Bavaria to the point of bankruptcy. On 10th June 1864 he was dispossessed of his throne and interned in the castle of Starnberg to the south-west of Munich, and on 13th June he drowned in the lake, although it has never been established without any doubt whether it was a case of murder, suicide or accidental death.

The Wittelsbach dynasty was now drawing to a close. Ludwig's brother also suffered from insanity and the country was effectively ruled by two regents. The second of the regents became Ludwig III, who had little to do but take Bavaria into the First World War. With the end of the war came the end of the Bavarian monarchy.

The years prior to the Great War were years of confidence and prosperity, economically and culturally. Showing all the signs of having moved into the 'Modern Age', Bavaria had become an industrial power with an efficient communications system (every year the railway system was extended) and good support from a revitalised agricultural economy. Despite being a constituent of the German Empire, Bavaria tended to exclude itself from major political affairs, contenting itself with encouragement of the arts and a lack of true absolutism and militarism — some historians have seen this period in Bavaria as "the period of escapism". Inter-

200

est in the theatre and music increased, people could travel more easily and the literacy rate was higher here than anywhere else in Europe. Doubtless these factors contributed to the much greater interest in the Oberammergau Passion Play. Audiences during this period increased greatly and attending a performance of the play became a part of the education of the young gentleman or lady. The first "packaged" holiday to include the Passion Play was organised by Thomas Cook in 1871.

Whatever complacency Oberammergau may have felt at the great success of the play in the immediate past was soon to be dispelled with the advent of war and the political turmoil that defeat would bring to Central Europe. Not only would it prove impossible to stage the 1920 cycle of plays, but the post-war difficulties inGermany made a further series of performances most improbable. Some eight to nine million people died in the war, revolution was in the air, mass unemployment (some 70% of the total workforce were to be without work) and a huge depression was around the corner. The surprising reaction of the villagers of Oberammergau was to indicate their faith in the future and set about preparing for performances of the Passion Play in 1922, against a backdrop of economic collapse and rampant inflation, which would soon render the currency worthless.

The relative calm of today in West Germany is a far cry from the situation at the end of the 1914 - 18 war. Revolution succeeded in removing the Emperor and Ludwig III, King of Bavaria, from their respective positions, but no one was quite sure how they should be replaced. Germany opted for Weimer democracy, which was ultimately unsuccessful, leaving the way open for Hitler's assumption of power in 1933. The Weimar Republic failed for several reasons, amongst which were the large number of tiny parties which would have to be brought together into a coalition for stable government; the reparations demanded by the Allies and the readiness of France, in particular, to exact her 'pound of flesh', occupying the Rhur industrial region as a first, not final resort; the lack of interest in politics of many German people and a sub-conscious desire to look up to an authoritarian leader. In the long run, however, external events were to bring down the Weimar Republic: the inflation of 1922 - 3 (those lucky enough to have a job were being paid twice a day, their salaries were increased hourly, and one U.S. dollar bought a staggering 4,200,000,000,000 marks), its contribution to the high level of unemployment and the final blow of the Wall Street Crash of 1929, which heralded the Great Depression.

In Bavaria, the end of the war saw government by the Bavarian

Socialists (whose leader was assassinated), followed by a coalition with the Majority Socialists, which in turn was toppled by a Bolshevik rising: Bavaria was declared a Communist Soviet Republic on 4th April 1919. The deposed leader of the Majority Socialists returned with the remaining Prussian soldiers to besiege Munich, starve its inhabitants into surrender, exact a terrible revenge on those responsible for the overthrow of the previous government and revert to the conservative, Catholic direction still in evidence today. Separatist feeling in Bavaria was much to the forefront of post-war policy with the Bavarian Nationalist movement being set up and then giving way to Adolf Hitler's own movement along the same lines. The unsuccessful "Bürgerbräukeller" putsch in Munich led to Hitler's arrest and imprisonment, but gradually the economic and political conditions in Germany turned to his advantage and the Nazi party swept to power with the support of large sections of the population.

Hitler's power-base was Bavaria, and many of the towns and cities recall events during the Third Reich: Munich, where Hitler met Chamberlain, the British Prime Minister, and the prospects for continued peace in Europe looked bright despite all the logical indications to the contrary; Nuremberg, where the vast Nazi rallies took place; Berchtesgaden and nearby Obersalzberg, Hitler's "Eyrie", where he could relax close to the highest point in the realm. The "Empire", which was to last a thousand years, actually lasted only twelve years, as Nazi Germany and its allies were defeated with great difficulty and horrendous loss of life, after the realisation by the rest of Europe that policy based on half-baked philosophical theory, racialism, terror and a megalomaniac opportunism was rapidly becoming a monstrous and unacceptable reality. Here was a man who could even twist the message of the Oberammergau Passion Play and see it as an illustration of the Jewish threat:

"Pontius Pilate appears as a Roman so superior racially and intellectually that he stands out as a rock in the midst of the Near Eastern scum and swarm."

The defeat of the Axis powers and devastation and loss of life suffered by large parts of the globe are well recorded elsewhere. The conferences of Yalta and Potsdam split the country of Germany, as it had existed before the start of hostilities, into four zones: British, American, French and Soviet. This was repeated in Berlin. All Germans had to undergo 'denazification' if applying for a position of political or economic importance. The applicant had to sign a form (known as a 'Persilschein') to show that he or she was 'whiter than white'. Since, during Hitler's time, virtually every professional

202

or trade organisation had been compelled to affiliate itself to the Nazi Party, this soon became unworkable. Nevertheless it was enforced in some areas, and even prospective performers of the Passion Play had to be 'denazified'. One wonders how the same performers must have felt when they were representing Jews on stage, as the full truth of the horrific events of the former garden-suburb of Dachau, on the outskirts of Munich, was coming to light.

The partition of Germany into four zones and the growing struggle between the West and the Soviet Union for Central Europe effectively ruled out any possibility of Germany remaining a single entity. In 1949 this fact was confirmed officially by the declaration of two republics: West Germany (or the Federal Republic) and East Germany (or the Democratic Republic). The focus of attention moved to Berlin, the former capital. It was obviously intolerable for the Soviet Union to harbour a free city within the Eastern zone (now Democratic Republic) and various methods were used to try to bring the city into the Communist orbit. The blockade of Berlin, the Allies' airlift which frustrated it and the flow of refugees from east to west served to heighten tensions between the major powers, resulting in the construction of the Berlin Wall by the Soviet Union in 1961 — a concrete division of both the city and the ideologies. Ironically, the definite partition, however inhumane, of both Berlin and Germany has reduced international tensions and the "Ostpolitik" of the early 1970's saw the signature of agreements between West Germany, East Germany and the U.S.S.R.

The days have long since passed when visitors came to Oberammergau purely to witness an actual performance of the Passion Play. Tourism has become an all year round industry. People come to see the theatre, appreciate the woodcarvings and external paintings, and wander in and around the picturesque little village. Great efforts have been made to highlight its attractions during the off-season, which include winter-sports facilities, but it is a different Oberammergau: the animation, hustle and bustle and excitement seen during the days of the Passion Play are missing. As we hope to show in the following pages, the village is also a superb starting point for excursions further afield to places like Ettal, Linderhof, Garmisch, Munich and Innsbruck.

Oberammergau owes its importance to the trade route between Verona and Augsburg which grew out of the old road originally built through the Ammerthal mountains by the Romans. It became a regular stop for travellers and, as the soil was not particularly fertile, many villagers turned their houses into inns, providing much-needed accommodation and sustenance for the wayfarers. This was reinforced by Ludwig's reward to the inhabitants of the valley in exchange for their hard work in the construction of the Benedictine monastery of Ettal: they were granted the sole right to provide the horses necessary to help the merchants' wagons up the steep road to Ettal and as far as Schongau in the north and Partenkirchen in the south. This monopoly made Oberammergau prosperous, and through the many merchants and pilgrims its reputation spread far and wide.

Although the Celts, Romans and different tribes had inhabited the Ammer Valley, it is usual to attribute the founding of Oberammergau to the 9th century AD and the Guelf duke, Ethiko. At this time there was a great power struggle between the Holy Roman Emperor, who was normally a German prince, and the Pope, who claimed the right to rule the Empire in the name of the church. Ethiko, a supporter of the papal party, tired of the intrigues of the Holy Roman Emperor and, saddened by the loss of Guelf independence, sought a quiet haven in the Ammerthal where he and his followers could live free from the struggles of the day. They settled at the site now called Oberammergau, although with the passing of time the village became more accessible and it could no longer remain a 'retreat', except in times of harsh weather.

The village of Oberammergau, 1870

In the 12th century we find the first mention of the village's second great industry, wood-carving, which still thrives today. It was possibly introduced into the area from the Tyrol — though many inhabitants of Oberammergau would argue that the Tyrolean wood-carving owes its origins to Oberammergau! It was certainly already established by the year 1111 as an industry at Rottenbuch, the convent which controlled the religious life of the village, and flourished as a result of natural resources (the dense woods in the surrounding countryside) and the weather (much as in other Alpine regions, the village was cut off during the winter and time hung heavily on the hands of the inhabitants).

At first, the objects carved were simple utensils. Later, children's toys, especially wooden dolls and hobby horses, became part of the Oberammergau range. During periods of affluence the carvings from the region were in great demand in Munich and the larger homes throughout Bavaria. The Reformation and the ferment it caused, culminating in the Thirty Years War, put an end to the prosperity of the village until the relative tranquillity of the 18th century, with excess confined to the grandiose embellishments of the Baroque. This gave a new impetus to the wood-carvers, and pedlars selling the carved statues, religious objects and utensils reached as far as Spain, Russia and Scandinavia. The story of the vow and the Oberammergau Passion Play was scattered with the carvings across the length and breadth of Europe. The carvers began to concentrate on religious objects alone, full of movement and flamboyance. The success of the wood-carving 'profession' (as it had been termed by special ordinance of 1682, thereby raising it above the level of a 'mere' trade) led to an extensive commercial network replacing the itinerant pedlars. The great trading cities of Lübeck, Antwerp, St. Petersburg and Gothenburg set up agencies to satisfy the demand of Europe for wood-carvings from the Passion Play village.

Despite wars, changing fashions and modern innovations the traditional art of wood-carving has remained successful, and, together with the provision of accommodation, is of major commercial importance to the village. There are many shop-windows with examples of wood-carving on show, some of which should be in museums and are not for sale. The quality of the carving is certainly kept at a high level — an obvious result of the influence wielded by the State School of Wood-Carving, set up in the mid-19th century, whose directors throughout its existence have had strong links with the Passion Play (Tobias Flunger who played Christ in 1850, Ludwig Lang who was producer for many years, and Hans Schwaighofer, an assistant-producer of the play). While in Oberam-

207

mergau you should make a point of paying a visit to two permanent displays of the wood-carving art: the Museum, founded in 1906 by Guido Lang and acquired by the community in 1954, which has nine rooms with numerous works in wood and on canvas, taken from the old church, the Monastery at Ettal or donated by private owners; and the beautiful Christmas crib (1780 - 1860) to be found in Number 5 Daisenberger, the house of the famous Georg Lang, whose contributions to the play have already been outlined elsewhere.

The massive Passion Play theatre is well worth a visit, even if you are not lucky enough to attend a performance. Guided tours take place off-season at a small charge, which goes towards the upkeep of the theatre, and feature a fascinating explanation and tour around the whole theatre, especially backstage with its props and costumes. Almost opposite the theatre is the Protestant church, which reminds us that the village is not exclusively Catholic (although the faith is shared by some 85% of the villagers) and that many different faiths and denominations come to see the play. Nearby is the "Kleines Theater", where the off-season 'training plays' are staged.

The more famous church in Oberammergau is the Catholic church of St. Peter and Paul (1736 - 42), which replaced the original Gothic church where the first performances of the Passion Play took place. The latter had decayed badly and was pulled down to make room for the new building. The interior of the church, built by J. Schmuzer, responsible also for contributions to the churches of Ettal and Garmisch, is very ornate in baroque style with impressive paintings by Matthias Ginther and Ignaz Paur, and wood-carvings by Xaver Schmaedl. The crucifix of the Altar of the Cross was originally in the old church. Some of the frescoes are by the famous Oberammergau artist, Johann Zwink, who is responsible for many of the beautiful murals which adorn the exterior of the village houses and give such an airy feeling to a walk through the streets. This style of painting is known, appropriately as, "Lüftlmalerei" (air-painting), and generally features religious scenes, although some of the more modern representations, tastefully retaining the same style, are of fables and fairy stories ("Hansel and Gretel" springs to mind).

There is much scope for a gentle walk within the village and a coffee or something stronger in one of the attractive inns or hotels, but should you desire something a little more strenuous you should go for a swim in the heated open-air "Wellenberg", a complex of three swimming-pools (one for children). The entry price is included in the price of accommodation during the Passion Play season. You might also consider a trip to the top of the Laber Mountain by cable-car, where you can have a marvellous view of the mountains and the Ammer Valley from the restaurant at the height of 5,610 feet.

All in all there is no lack of entertainment in and around Oberammergau whenever you should have the good fortune to visit it!

Oberammergau – "Lüftmalerei"

The small town of Ettal is only a short distance down the road to the south of Oberammergau and is dominated by the huge Benedictine monastery, which has had such a profound influence on the Passion Play and its cast. Since the monastery was founded in 1330 by Emperor Ludwig the Bavarian, it has been the spiritual and religious centre of the region (even visited in the 16th Century by Philip II of Spain and his followers for the Corpus Christi Feast), and its inhabitants have often advised the Oberammergau villagers on the theological aspects of the play (indeed it will be noted that Father Gregor Rümmelein of Ettal was responsible for guiding the present text of the play through the Second Vatican Council). Pilgrims visiting the monastery were almost certainly the communication-links which carried the Passion Play beyond the Ammer Valley.

The first thing that one realises about the monastery is its vastness which is a result of the growth of Benedictine life and the number of pilgrims who still pass this way to venerate the statue of the Virgin, attributed to Giovanni Pisano and carried by the Emperor back from Rome. In exchange for help in his struggles, Ludwig vowed to build a monastery at a place called Amphrang in Bavaria. When his horse fell to its knees three times in front of a fir tree, he took it as a sign that the monastery should be built on that spot. Within two years it could house twelve monks, and such was the aid and enthusiasm shown by the people from the valley in completing the construction, that the towns nearby were granted special rights, including permission to pass on their holdings to their heirs, which were to be the subject of dispute as late as the 1770's.

The present aspect of the monastery of Ettal, although based on gothic, actually dates from the work of Zucalli in 1710 - 26 (the facade and the chancel) and Schmuzer, who was responsible for the cupola, after it had been destroyed by fire in 1744. The great restoration of the monastery was from 1744 - 52. Further restoration became necessary after the monastery was dissolved and most of its artefacts and estates sold off as a result of the Elector's anti-clerical reforms at the turn of the century. Happily one can still admire the magnificent baroque interior.

In front of the church are the grammar school and boarding school. From 1711 - 1744, the latter was a knights' academy where young gentlemen from all over Europe were sent to learn the social graces, attain a high educational standard, and (as the name suggests) receive a military training. It was a boarding-school which had the same status as Eton and Harrow today. These buildings were also gutted by fire in 1744, ignited by a spark from a firework display following military celebrations at the time of the Feast of St. Peter and St. Paul.

The monastery is an absolute must for anyone staying in Oberammergau: before leaving, you should also pop across the road to the stalls selling the famous Ettal herb liqueur which is made from a secret recipe by the monks. You can sample a glass or so (I'd recommend the blackcurrant flavour) at a small cost, purely for medicinal purposes!

People coming to Oberammergau often wish to visit at least one of the famous castles belonging to the tragic "Mad King", Ludwig II of Bavaria. Fortunately you can find within a short driving distance the beautiful castle of Linderhof nestling in another part of the Ammer Valley. Organised tours or the ubiquitous "Postbus" will take you to the car park, from which you follow a winding path through the park and woodland (reserved by the Wittelsbach kings for their private hunting) to the castle itself. In fact it is less of a castle than a palace: the word "Schloss" tends to emphasise the ornamental or decorative aspects of the building, whereas the word "Burg", found most often alongside the River Rhine, points to the defensive function of the construction and is more properly translated as "Fortress".

The visitor has the opportunity to take a guided tour and see the interior of the building, which dates from 1874 - 79, combining the styles of the Baroque and second Italian Renaissance. It is the smallest of Ludwig's castles, and although one could not exactly call it cosy, it does have a certain intimacy, enhanced by our own knowledge of the tragic life of its patron. It is yet another homage to the French 18th century, illustrated most vividly by the hall of mirrors (in the style of Versailles) and portraits and busts of Louis XIV, Louis XV and assorted royal mistresses. It is very impressive, but after a while the extravagance, gleam and glitter can become a little overbearing, and it is then time to move outside and visit the grotto, moorish pavilion and the gardens.

The grotto is in the form of an extravagant cave out of the Arabian Nights. Coloured lights illuminate a boat, shaped like a conch-shell, which floats on a lake. This is inspired by an incident from 'Tannhäuser', the opera composed by Ludwig's protégé and great friend, Richard Wagner. If you follow signs to the "Maurischer Kiosk" you will soon arrive at the Moorish Pavilion, the site of Ludwig's occasional whim of receiving surprised guests dressed and acting as an oriental potentate. It is a reminder of the pavilion in the same style at the 1867 Exhibition in Paris.

However long you have at Linderhof, you should leave sufficient time to idle or wander in the beautiful gardens. The best photographs are to be taken from the end of the ornamental pond with its fountains, the palace forming a picturesque backdrop. The gardens might have belonged to an Italian villa, and are well worth a stroll.

Although it is possible to visit Linderhof during the off-season, you do run the risk of not seeing the gardens at their best and the pond is often drained, but the skiers who take part in the famous Oberammergau-Linderhof "Langlauf" (cross-country race) often argue that the palace looks its best surrounded by snow, as if straight out of a fairytale.

Linderhof

GARMISCH — PARTENKIRCHEN.

Lying to the south of Oberammergau on the road to Innsbruck, Garmisch-Partenkirchen is one of the busiest tourist and holiday towns in the Bavarian Alps. It is popular the whole year round: in the winter it is famous for its World Championship skiing events, while during the summer months it is an attractive health resort with many marvellous walks in the surrounding countryside. It is also the gateway to the magnificent Zugspitze mountain (the highest in Germany at 9,761 feet) which towers above the town.

As the name suggests, Garmisch-Partenkirchen is a combination of two distinct parts, which face each other across the River Loisach. Both were founded in Roman times and reached their zenith with trade in the Middle Ages. They passed to Bavaria in 1803 and regained their former prosperity as people began to realise towards the middle of the 19th century that they would make good holiday centres. The towns of Garmisch and Partenkirchen are very different in character: the former is more modern, more exclusive with the majority of quality shops, a casino and the villa in which Richard Strauss died in 1949; Partenkirchen, on the other hand, is more subdued, more old-fashioned and more typically German than international. There are beautiful churches in both parts, both with rich interiors: the New Parish Church of Garmisch dates from the 1730's and was designed by Joseph Schmuzer, while Partenkirchen's Pilgrim Church of St. Anthony is slightly earlier (1704).

The two parts were joined together in 1935, shortly after they were awarded the 1936 Winter Olympics. Evidence of these Games remains in the town of Garmisch with its "Eisstadion" (an indoor complex of three different ice-rinks and seats for 12,000 spectators) and, not far outside Partenkirchen on the Gudiberg, the ski-stadium with its four impressive jumps (two are for practice), where one of the legs of the famous 'Four Hills' Championship takes place. As befits one of the most exclusive resorts in Europe there are several demanding downhill courses which are as difficult to negotiate as some of the prices in the shops! Garmisch-Partenkirchen, sitting at the base of the Wetterstein mountain range, is at a very low altitude for a winter-sports resort (2,350 ft). However, special climatic conditions obtain here and the annual snowfall arrives during January and February, usually to a depth of some twenty inches. At a height of 4,000 ft (and there are many convenient cable-cars and chair-lifts to take you above this level) the snow is often more than six feet deep.

If you have both the time and weather, a trip to the summit of the Zugspitze is thoroughly recommended. It is without any doubt one of the great European mountain experiences. The easiest way to reach the top is by taking the railway from the centre of Garmisch (Zugspitzbahnhof, near the Ice Stadium) to the Hotel Schnee-fernerhaus, already at a height of over 8600 ft and past several impressive lakes, where you can find a cable-car which will take you to the peak. From the viewing terrace, there are superlative views, mostly of the Austrian Alps, and on the two further peaks you can make out a cross and a radio station belonging to the Bundespost. Once at the sumit, there are places to take photographs of the scenery and to enjoy a snack or a glass of Glühwein (mulled wine). Skiers are much in evidence as this pursuit is possible all year round on the 3 square miles of the Zugspitzplatt. Apart from skiing, there are by three methods of descent (we shall leave out hand-gliding!): the first is by retracing your route, the second is a direct cableway to Eibsee where you can find the road to Garmisch, and the third will take you across the Austrian border in the direction of Lermoos and Ehrwald. A steep glacial tunnel, about half a mile long, starting near the Schneefernerhaus in Bavaria leads you to the Austrian customs post just before the Zugspitzkamm (passports are necessary!). The return journey should cost you about £10 or 40 DM from Garmisch, and you should allow yourself at least half a day, If you are lucky with the weather you will never forget your excursion to the summit of the noble Zugspitze!

INNSBRUCK.

A two-hour drive from Oberammergau, and you have crossed the border and entered Austria. The city of Innsbruck with a population of 120,000 is one of only three alpine cities of any size (the others are Grenoble and Bolzano). It became a city in the 13th century and grew up as the site of one of the few crossings of the River Inn, a fact commemorated in its name, which means "the bridge over the Inn". Nowadays Innsbruck is a gay, carefree city, more Tyrolean in character than Austrian and justly famed as a holiday resort both in the summer and winter.

It is best to start one's sightseeing in Wilten, the oldest borough of Innsbruck, which dates from Roman times. Although it is now a little away from the city centre, it was once the heart of activity and it possesses two of the most beautiful churches of the Tyrol. Both were built in the colourful flamboyant style of the 17th century. The Basilica of Wilten is a resplendent rococo church with a striking yellow facade. If you look above the doorway you will see that it is a Papal church, as it bears the Pope's insignia, and although access is limited inside you should take the trouble to appreciate the work that has gone into the overwhelming ornate interior. It is famous also for the statue of the Virgin Mary, which dates from the 14th century. Looking across the road, one can see the deep red exterior of the Stiftskirche (Collegiate Church) which is in baroque style and whose entrance is guarded by two of Innsbruck's oldest inhabitants. Visitors are welcome to enter the church, but only male sightseers are permitted to set foot in the adjacent monastery grounds.

Continuing in the opposite direction to the city-centre and making sure that you do not miss the turn-off (or you will soon be in Italy!), it is a short ride to Bergisel, which is famous for the battle fought here in 1809 and the monuments to both Andreas Hofer and the "Kaiserjäger", or Imperial Rifles. In that year the Tyrolean forces, led by their indomitable leader Andreas Hofer, defeated the army of Napoleon on this hill. This is the high point of Tyrolean history and is commemorated by numerous monuments throughout the Tyrol. Andreas Hofer holds a place in the people's affections in much the same way as Robin Hood and William Tell in other parts of Europe. Sadly his glory was somewhat short-lived and he was soon forced to flee to Italy, where he was murdered by a Napoleonic agent. Parking near the statue of Hofer and the grand building of the museum, it is a short walk to the top of Bergisel and the Olympic Ski-Jump. Innsbruck has twice hosted the Winter Olympics, in 1964 and 1976, and in different parts of the city and its suburbs you will find the Ice Stadium, Bobsleigh and Luge runs. If the nearest you have been to a ski-jump is a television set, you will find the whole set-up fascinating: the way that the T.V. cameras 'flatten' the gradient of the jump, the disconcertingly small landing-area, the steepness of the braking-slope and its continuation into the cemetery below! Full of admiration for the daring of the jumpers, the more athletic will climb the concrete steps to the top and look out over Innsbruck. The photographer may well find it worth the effort to go the few miles from Bergisel to Igls and take the cable-car up the Patscherkofel (7,370 ft) for the view; in any case I would recommend a walk around the Olympic village of Igls and maybe a refreshing drink or lunch in the central Hotel Bon Alpina.

Innsbruck itself has a compact centre, which owes much of its splendour to the patronage of Maria Theresa in the 18th century. The town grew up as a hunting lodge for the Hapsburgs and was developed by several monarchs into an important and beautiful city. Maria Theresa's contribution was to encourage the brightly-painted exteriors and baroque embellishment. The old centre is small, well-preserved with several pedestrian streets, in which it is a joy to walk. You should keep an eye out for the antique wrought-iron signs hanging outside shops and hotels (to help people who couldn't read), the small courtyards behind the elegant facades and the many fine buildings.

The Triumphal Arch heralds the beginning of the old town and the street named after Maria Theresa. The arch has two faces: one celebrates the marriage of the future Emperor Leopold II, the other solemnly remembers the death of his father, Emperor Franz I, during the festivities. As you look down the street you will see in the middle of the road the Column of St. Anne, which commemorates the successful repelling of the Bavarians during the War of Spanish Succession on St. Anne's Day in 1703, against the backdrop of the Nordkette mountain range. Here the most popular photograph of Innsbruck is to be found. Mariatheresienstrasse is the main street in the city and is lined with impressive houses and churches. If you look closely you will locate the site of the narrowest house in Innsbruck, which is now a souvenir shop. At the end of Friedrichstrasse, which is the pedestrian continuation of the street, the famous Golden Roof of Emperor Maximilian is to be found. Legend has it that it was built by Friedrich the Penniless to disprove rumours that he was a miser; however, in reality it was Maximilian who had a loggia added to the back of the Hofburg Palace in 1500, so that he

222

could witness in comfort the spectacles and celebrations taking place in the street below. Decorated with colourful friezes and interesting designs of his favourite animals and contemporary dancers, his loggia has a roof covered with 2,657 gold-plated tiles. The pedestrian streets around Maximilian's Golden Roof, quiet apart from the occasional permitted delivery van, are among the most delightful in Innsbruck.

Just around the corner is the Hofburg, which was restored by Maria Theresa in her favourite colour yellow, altogether on a grander scale. It has a fine rococo hall, and interesting collection of paintings and tapestries and is open to the public throughout the year. The palace has its own passageway to the Hofkirche (or Court church) but we must use the entrance across the road from the Hofburg. The church is like a miniature Westminster Abbey with the tombs of Andreas Hofer and the other Tyrolean heroes in the battles against Bavaria, the grandiose empty memorial tomb of Maximilian I surrounded by 28 bronze figures, which represent the emperor's actual and legendary ancestors (including King Arthur!), and the 'Silver Chapel' with the tombs of Archduke Ferdinand and his wife. In contrast to the gigantic figures around Maximilian's tomb, the figures on the balcony are tiny and have their backs to those below as they pay homage to the emperor.

Although there is much more to see in Innsbruck, the last sight on our tour is the "Rundgemälde" (round building) which is best approached via the Royal Gardens, illuminated during the long summer evenings. This houses the famous panorama painting of the Battle of Bergisel. A panorama is a circular painting which disorientates you a little at first, because you are in the middle of the action. Very few examples of this form of painting remain in Europe, and this is certainly one of the best.

· While you are sitting perhaps over a Wienerschnitzel or Gulasch, or for the more adventurous a biscuit omelette, you may be considering what to do in the evening. A suggestion is the Tyrolean Folklore Show, which has Schuhplatteln, dancing, singing and yodelling in the time-honoured tradition. The Gundolf Family have put together a marvellous show under the name of the "Tyroler Alpenbühne" which performs most evenings at the Adambräu Bierkeller and the Holiday Inn. It is an enjoyable relaxing, inexpensive and atmospheric evening out.

MUNICH.

There is so much to see and do in Munich, the capital city of Bavaria, that a day-trip can be little more than a sample of the delights that this elegant and vibrant city has to offer, but even if you have the chance just to visit just a handful of the sights or a couple of the many museums, I would suggest that you grasp the opportunity. It will almost certainly help you to commit yourself to a longer stay at a later date!

The name Munich comes from the first recorded occupants of the settlement near the River Isar in the 9th century who were monks ("Munichen" in old German), but it is customary to attribute the founding of the city to Duke Henry the Lion, who in 1158 decided to encourage the salt trade to come across his bridge over the River Isar by destroying that of his rival, the Bishop of Freising. The city flourished due to the increased traffic and tolls. Little remains, however, of those early days, and the majority of the older buildings in Munich today date from the 17th and 19th centuries. (The three great patrons of architectural growth were Ludwig I, Maximilian II and Prince Regent Leopold.) The city was heavily bombed during the war, but fortunately the major buildings either escaped serious damage or were restored along original lines.

Crossing the inner ring road which follows the line of the former fortifications, you soon come to the older parts of the city. Four old gates remain, including the Karlstor with its fountain and modern shopping precinct; the centre, however, is the Marienplatz, where you can sit out and watch the world go by. Attractions around the square include St. Peter's church (the oldest in Munich, called "Old Peter", dating from 1050), the Old Town Hall and the New Town Hall (Neo-Gothic 1867 - 1908). In the middle of the paved expanse is the St. Mary Column which dates from 1638. At 11.00 a.m. every day (in the summer months additionally at 5.00 p.m. and 9.00 p.m.) an expectant crowd assembles below the tower of the New Town Hall to watch the mechanical copper figures perform a Glockenspiel.

Just off the square, the two domes of the Cathedral of Our Lady (Frauenkirche) form one of the most distinctive silhouettes in Munich. Although it was severely damaged during air-raids in 1944, it has been extensively restored and the Late Gothic style church, built by Jörg Ganghofer 1468 - 1488, in dull red brick which houses the tomb of Ludwig the Bavarian (so important in the history of

Oberammergau), is again looking very impressive.

Outside the compact heart of the city there are many varied attractions. You should start by going northwards along Ludwigstrasse, which is named after the Crown Prince, who in 1817 took a seven-month tour of Italy and returned imbued with classical ideas and with thoughts of turning Munich into a new Rome or Athens. The road along which you are travelling is about half a mile long and leads you past the state library, university buildings and Ludwigskirche, all in the same harmonious style, as far as Schwabing, which is the young people's part of the city. At the turn of the century this was the intellectual and artistic centre of Munich — you will still see artists and street performers, but it is now more of a nightclub and bar area. It comes alive mainly in the evening: many people sit at pavement cafés or take the air.

Slightly more to the west is the remarkable Königsplatz (King's Square) where the buildings are in severely Neo-classical style. All were designed by Ludwig's favourite architect, Von Klenze, and date from the first half of the 19th century. The Glyptothek stands opposite the State Collection of Antiquities, with the entrance to the square being formed by a triumphal gateway based on the Propylae from the Parthenon in Athens.

If you were to ask any inhabitant of this city the recipe for good health, he would almost certainly include beer in his list of ingredients. There are many places where you can chat over a litre of beer, sway to the oom-pah-pah band and have a snack of Bratwurst and Sauerkraut (the Bavarian speciality of sausage and boiled cabbage), fried chicken or just a pretzel. The Hofbräuhaus was already in existence as far back as 1589, but the present building dates only from the end of the last century, and is probably everyone's example of a typical Bierkeller. It is even the subject of a famous drinking song! There is a great deal of atmosphere, although it is often very crowded and you must watch out for the inexorable progress of Wagneresque waitresses who sometimes carry ten 'Steine' (litre pots) of beer at one time! Once you penetrate the froth, the beer is very tasty: just lifting the Stein to your lips makes you feel that you deserve another gulp after so much exercise! With over 1600 breweries in Bavaria there are several other well-known beer cellars to choose from, if you find the Hofbräuhaus too crowded: the difference between them being more the degree of authenticity present in the decor than in the beer itself.

Should you wish to enjoy your drink in a more rural setting, there can be few more relaxing experiences than sitting in one of the beer gardens in "Green Lung" of Munich, the English Garden. Set up in

1790, by an American, this park is over 865 acres in size and serves much the same purpose as Hyde Park or Central Park. It has several beer gardens, a lake, a temple, a Chinese tower — a paradise for young couples or improvised track for joggers in the warm summer evenings!

If you are fortunate to be in Munich during the latter part of September, you should not miss the opportunity of joining the many thousands of people at the Oktoberfest. Probably the largest popular annual festival in the world, it is held on the open space of the Theresienwiese to the south-west of the centre. In 1810, Crown Prince Ludwig took Princess Therese for his wife and celebrated this outside the city gates. Crowds of Bavarians came to pay homage and held a horse race, which was so successful that an annual holiday has taken place ever since. Every year the beer "tents" (belonging to the major breweries) are assembled and disassembled, and hundreds and thousands of people crowd into the Theresienwiese to experience the thrills of the fun-fair and enter the "tents". Everything is done on a massive scale: the "tents" resemble small exhibition halls; the fun-fair is like Tivoli; and over a million gallons of beer, 3 dozen spit-roasted oxen, 30,000 grilled fish and 550,000 chickens provide the sustenance. At the far end, the statue of Bavaria (1850) gives the five people, who can stand inside her head, a view of the proceedings from a height of some 100 feet!

Further still to the west are two major sights, which should not be missed. The Nymphenburg Palace is approached by a long road alongside a canal and you come out into an area of gardens and ponds. In front of you is the main building of the palace, the winter residence of the Bavarian Royal Family; behind you are the outbuildings in a semi-circle, one of which is the 1741 home of Nymphenburg Porcelain. The residence is still used for classical concerts and official receptions, and is open to the public for the viewing of Ludwig the First's "Gallery of Beauties" (his collection of portraits) and the magnificent carriages of the Marstall Museum. If you wish you can wander in the palace park, which is over 500 acres, and visit the three miniature palaces: the Amalienburg, Pagodenburg and Badenburg.

It is likely that many of the young visitors first hear about Munich as a result of the Olympics of 1972 and the World Cup of 1974. It is possible to drive or take a guided tour around the sports complex. The facilities are used throughout the year — not only by top-class sportsmen — and the tower-blocks of the Olympic village, where terrorism reared its ugly head in 1972 and left several members of the Israeli team massacred, are now used for community housing.

The tower (over 950 ft high) has become a landmark of Munich with its revolving restaurant near the top. There are three main areas: the Olympic stadium, swimming hall and sports hall (where pop concerts take place). It is fascinating to see from close-up the famous 820,000 sq. ft of what appears to be hard plastic netting which stretches above the stadium.

Unless you are staying more than one day in Munich, it is unlikely that you will be able to spend much time in the museums. There are hundreds of exhibitions every year in this stately, but vibrant city; if you do have time I would recommend the Deutsches Museum, which stands on an island in the River Isar and is the largest science museum in the world, with a planetarium and working models; the Alte Pinakothek, which has priceless paintings, including fine collections of Rubens and Dürer; and the Neue Pinakothek, newiy-opened and situated across the street, with its modern collection, including the paintings of the much underestimated German Romantic, Caspar David Friedrich.

For those who have time over, there are many more museums, elegant shopping streets (especially Maximilianstrasse and around the Marienplatz) and less expensive markets, and the experience (it is certainly no holiday) of a visit to the former garden suburb of Dachau, which you can reach by train. The site of the concentration camp is open to the public as a memorial to the evil side of human nature. The journey is a salutary experience, which helps by contrast to re-emphasize the real meaning of the Passion Play of Oberammergau.

Interior of the church of St. Peter and St. Paul
(Photo from Barnaby's Photo Library)

MASTRO DON-GESUALDO — Giovanni Verga (translated by D. H. Lawrence)

On the face of things, Mastro-Don Gesualdo is a success. Born a peasant but a man 'with an eye for everything going', be becomes one of the richest men in Sicily, marrying an aristocrat with his daughter destined, in time, to wed a duke.

But Gesualdo falls foul of the rigid class structure in mid-19th-century Sicily. His title 'Mastro-Don', 'Worker-Gentlemen', is ironic in itself. Peasants and gentry alike resent his extraordinary success. And when the pattern of society is threatened by revolt, Gesualdo is the rebels' first target. . .

Published in 1888, Verga's classic was first introduced to this country in 1925 by D. H. Lawrence in is own superb translation. Although broad in scope, with a large cast and covering over twenty years, *Mastro-Don Gesualdo* is exact and concentrated: it cuts from set-piece to set-piece — from feast-day to funeral to sun white stubble field — anticipating the narrative techniques of the cinema.

Dedalus European Classics

SHORT SICILIAN NOVELS — Giovanni Verga (translated by.
D. H. Lawrence)

"The Little Novels of Sicily have that sense of the wholeness of life,
the spare exuberance, the endless inflections and overtones, and the
magnificent and thrilling vitality of major literature."
— New York Times

"In these stories the whole Sicily of the eighteen-sixties lives before
us — poor gentry, priests, rich landowners, farmers, peasants,
animals, seasons, and scenery; and whether his subject be the brutal
bloodshed of an abortive revolution or the simple human comedy
that can even attend deep mourning, Verga never loses his complete
artistic mastery of his material. He throws the whole of his pity into
the intensity of his art, and with the simplicity only attainable by
genius lays bear beneath all the sweat and tears and clamour of day-
to-day humanity those mysterious 'mortal things which touch the
minds'.
— Times Literary Supplement.

Also by Giovanni Verga a new translation of I Malavoglia available
from Dedalus in 1985.

DATE DUE